Can love survive a night he can't remember but one she'll never forget?

Anna Barlow is giving herself a fresh start, leaving everything about her old life behind. With a new name, a new career and a new look, everything about her has changed since the night her daughter Becca was conceived. Anna finds out just how different she looks when an emergency farm call brings her face to face with her baby's father…and he has no idea who she is.

Chris Stevenson is on hiatus from the world of competitive show-jumping. He's returned to the family farm to get his life back in order. Nothing's been right for the past year… not since the night that has remained a blank in his memory. When he meets the area's newest veterinarian, Chris feels two things—instant lust and that he's met her somewhere before.

As they struggle to reconcile the night he can't remember, both Chris and Anna must learn to trust each other and the idea of what family really means.

Books by Laura Browning

Winning Heart

The Barlow-Barretts: An American Dynasty
Bittersweet, Book One
Balancing Act, Book Two
Remember Me, Book Three
Broken Heart, Book Four

Published by Kensington Publishing Corporation

Bittersweet

The Barlow-Barretts: An American Dynasty, Book One

Laura Browning

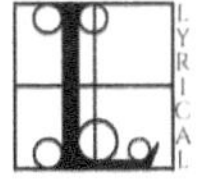

LYRICAL PRESS
Kensington Publishing Corp.
www.kensingtonbooks.com

Lyrical Press books are published by
Kensington Publishing Corp. 119 West 40th Street New York, NY 10018

All Kensington titles, imprints, and distributed lines are available at special quantity discounts for bulk purchases for sales promotion, premiums, fund-raising, and educational or institutional use.

Special book excerpts or customized printings can also be created to fit specific needs. For details, write or phone the office of the Kensington Special Sales Manager:
Kensington Publishing Corp.
119 West 40th Street
New York, NY 10018
Attn. Special Sales Department. Phone: 1-800-221-2647.

First Electronic Edition: December 2011
eISBN-13: 978-1-61650-338-3
eISBN-10: 1-61650-338-6

First Print Edition: December 2011
ISBN-13: 978-1-61650-847-0
ISBN-10: 1-61650-847-7

Printed in the United States of America

To every veterinarian who's had to get up in the middle of the night and work by flashlights or headlights. You all rock!

Chapter 1

The cellphone on Anna's hip buzzed. She had turned off the ring in the hope that Becca, nestled in her carseat in the backseat of the pickup, would stay asleep at least for a short while. Days and nights of colic had drained them both. The programmable swing at home wasn't a luxury but a necessity. Miles of uninterrupted driving making farm calls also seemed to soothe her daughter. Saturday night dinnertime had already come and gone, both hers and Becca's, and Anna felt the pressure to nurse. She had been about to pull over to feed her when the phone had vibrated against her hip. Not now. Just this once.

"Dr. Barlow," she murmured into the phone as she slowed the truck and pulled to one side of the secondary road. The clinic answering service secretary was on the line with an emergency farm call. Anna jotted the address and the directions the operator gave her. Still somewhat new to the area, she was learning her way around, so directions were a must. Getting lost on her way to an emergency was not an option. And at this hour on a Saturday evening, no one called a veterinarian for anything routine, but the nature of the emergency wasn't what made this call different. The owner's name made her stomach jump with nerves.

"Please let Mr. Stevenson know I'll be there in five minutes." Anna hung up, checked there was no traffic and pulled onto the road. She found the first available driveway to turn around and head back the way she had come. She glanced at the address again. Main barn, Fincastle Farm. Of course she had heard of it. Who hadn't? The farm had been the signature of the Stevenson family for several generations.

She had held hope that Fincastle would never appear on her client list. Naive of her to think she wouldn't see him. Some sort of veterinary call had been bound to happen sooner or later. Later would have been much better. Never even more so. Maybe she'd luck out and the Mr. Stevenson in this instance would be father rather than son.

Anna swallowed as she turned down the long driveway bordered on each side by tall, white-paneled fences. In the paddocks left and right, high-dollar horses grazed in the glow of the spring moon. Ahead lay a long, pristine white barn. A darker color trimmed the doors and windows. It would be green, she recalled. Forest green, like the curtains around the Fincastle tack stalls at shows. Light blazed from one barn, which must be her destination. Most barns would already be settled for the night.

Okay. She was headed into the lion's den. Chris Stevenson, the man she so did not want to meet. Anna hoped he wouldn't be there. Sure, she'd known the possibility of meeting existed when she took the job in Redfield. Let him not be there. Not tonight, when she was tired and needed to nurse Becca to the point that her breasts ached. The show season had started, after all, so he should already be on the road at some of the smaller warm-up shows.

She took a deep breath and let it out. It didn't matter. She could do this.

After she parked in front of the barn, Anna shoved two more nursing pads inside her bra and muttered a quick prayer she and Becca could wait a while longer. One glance over her shoulder showed her infant daughter still slumbered in the carseat. She rolled down the windows before she got out and checked on the baby one more time. A gentle tug brought Becca's blanket back to where it belonged. After releasing a soft sigh, Anna straightened away from the truck. She pulled the zipper higher on her cotton coveralls and threw her stethoscope around her neck.

"Dr. Barlow?" someone inquired in a deep, masculine voice.

For an instant, she swayed. That voice. So much for being on the show circuit. Anna stepped around the back of the pickup into the view of the man who had emerged from the lighted doorway of the barn. Even as one part of her brain told her it was him, she shook her head in denial. Not with his reputation, and not on a Saturday night. There must be some horse show groupie somewhere who was willing to jump his bones, and that would take precedence over actual work.

"You're not Dr. Barlow? Where is he?" the silhouetted figure asked. Anna could not see his face, or much else, since the light behind him cast his front in shadow. As much as she might have tried, she would never forget his voice. She didn't need to see his face to know the speaker was Chris Stevenson.

Now, though, irritation kicked in. Where was he? She sighed. In this day and age, women veterinarians were more the norm than the exception. Of course, her height, or lack thereof, also played a role. She had encountered similar questions before, so she shouldn't have been surprised when it came from a man like Stevenson.

"Sorry, my mind was on something else. I am Dr. Barlow. I understand you have a horse in need of stitches." Anna's jaw hardened as she sensed his reluctance as well as his outright hostility. "If it will make you feel better, I would be happy to show you my credentials, Mr...." That was a nice touch. She'd make him think she had no idea who he was.

"Stevenson. Chris Stevenson."

"The man himself." As soon as Anna voiced it, she wanted to kick herself. She hadn't meant to say that aloud. He had half-turned, and in the glow from the barn, she saw his frown at her tone, but she was not going to back down now. Stevenson was nothing to her. Not anymore. Not ever. Once he'd been her hero, the object of teenage fantasies. But that was in the past. There was an injured animal to treat, she had a hungry daughter to feed and a painful need to feed her that only increased as time passed. She'd do her job, get the hell out of there and be done with it.

"May I take a look at the injury, or would you like me to call the answering service to see if someone else is available to take the call?" At the moment, she couldn't care less that Fincastle was one of the clinic's biggest clients. She was tired and wanted to go home, so if he wanted a different vet, that was fine with her.

She braced herself as they walked into the light of the barn. As the fluorescent lights illuminated his lean features and fair hair, she realized he looked different. He was harder, but also healthier. The dissoluteness that had begun to leave its mark last summer was gone.

"You'll do," he grunted in response. "Follow me."

Anna cocked one eyebrow at Stevenson's retreating back. At least he was polite enough not to sigh as he said it. Still, what an arrogant jerk! Thank God she need have nothing to do with him outside of professional calls, and thank God he appeared to draw a total blank when he looked at her.

She supposed she should be used to people questioning her abilities because of her petite size. She had received odd looks through veterinary school, and even had to answer some pretty pointed questions when she talked to people about joining their large animal practices. Just over five feet tall, she was slender to boot, and at the time, she had been very pregnant. At least the vets at Redfield were able to overlook her appearance in favor of the credentials she'd set in front of them.

Her biggest relief was Chris seemed not to recognize her. She shouldn't be surprised. She knew she looked a lot different than when he'd seen her, but part of her hardened with hurt and anger. What was she hoping, that he would remember the night they met? He would fall at her feet like the prince with Cinderella? There was no reason for it to stand out in his memory, not like it forever would in hers. He spent plenty of nights bedding besotted bimbos. She'd been another in a long line.

Stevenson stopped so abruptly in front of the stall midway down the aisle that Anna almost walked into his backside. Quivering at the rear of the stall was one of the biggest Thoroughbreds she had ever seen. The horse snorted and rolled his eyes. On his right hip, she saw a jagged tear about eight inches long, a messy wound that would require careful stitching.

Stevenson turned to look at her, his eyes challenging. "Still ready to take this on?" he asked with a sardonic twist to his lips.

Anna gazed at him without batting an eyelash. "I'll get my supplies. Would you prefer to bring him in the aisle or would you like me to do that when I return, since he seems a bit rattled?" Her tone dripped ice.

Stevenson looked her up and down. "I'll bring him. He's a stud, and I give you fair warning, he's always had more than his share of attitude."

Anna bit back the retort on the tip of her tongue about him having something in common with the horse besides their hind ends and nodded before spinning on her heel. She had dealt with bigger horses' asses than this one, and she wasn't referring to the horse.

She sighed with relief when she reached her truck and saw Becca still slept. "Bless you, sweetheart," Anna whispered to the baby.

She checked to make sure her daughter was still dry and stroked a finger over her soft cheek. With one last sigh, Anna opened the tailgate. She always kept a plastic caddy ready to grab, which she stocked with the supplies most often needed. After picking it up, along with a few other items she'd need, she hurried along the aisle. Chris was snapping crossties on the stallion as she approached. The big horse stomped his front foot before kicking out with his right rear leg as if trying to dislodge whatever it was causing him pain. Anna set her supplies several feet away and slipped the syringe of sedative inside the front pocket of her coveralls.

As she approached the horse, she murmured to him, watching his ears flick backward and forward as she continued talking.

"You can release him, Mr. Stevenson," Anna directed in the same even tone she used with the horse. Once he turned the halter loose, the horse quit stomping and stretched his nose toward her.

Anna stopped in front of him. Her face was scarcely higher than the horse's flared nostrils. He puffed at her and she blew back. The horse's head relaxed and both ears came forward.

"That's it, big man. Why be scared of something as tiny as me?"

Anna touched him on the cheek before stepping to his side and stroking his neck. Before either the horse or the man was aware of it, she slipped the hypodermic with the sedative into the horse's vein and delivered the drug. She continued to talk to the stallion as the horse's eyes drooped.

Anna bent to look at Chris from under the tall Thoroughbred's neck. "Do you have a step stool close by, Mr. Stevenson? If not, I can get the one I carry in the truck."

Stevenson's pale gray eyes had lost their sardonic expression, but not the hostility.

"Sure," he responded in a clipped voice. He stepped away, returning in a couple of minutes with a lightweight mounting block. "Will this work?"

Anna smiled. "Perfect. Thank you."

She sensed Chris's critical gaze on her but dismissed it. He'd have to deal with his own hang-ups without her help. Right now she had a job to do. Anna worked with careful efficiency, first cleaning the wound before checking for any underlying tissue damage. She was relieved to see it was only a tear to the hide and did not involve any muscle.

"How did he do this?" She lifted a brow in inquiry. Even standing on the second step of the mounting block, she stood barely above eye level.

"A fool of a groom who was careless with the gate when he tried to bring him in tonight. Bart caught himself on the latch coming in."

"That explains the tearing more than cutting," Anna mused as she returned to her work. She used small, neat stitches, tying off the sutures as she finished each one. As she was knotting the last one, she heard Becca wail. Oh no! Just what she needed. She hoped she might be able to get away from the farm without Stevenson realizing there was a baby in the truck. A baby she preferred he didn't see.

His head jerked toward the barn doorway. "What the hell?"

Anna felt the tingling in her breasts that signaled her milk letting down and knew she was leaking. Becca's cry was like an instant trigger to nurse, and she was already long overdue. She hunched her shoulders and jumped off the mounting block. There was no way around it. At least he hadn't recognized her, and at the moment, that was a plus she would accept with gratitude.

"My daughter. Your stallion should start to wake in the next fifteen minutes," she explained even as she packed. "He should be fine to go in his stall. I'll check on him in the morning."

Anna shoved everything into the caddy and the buckets she had brought with her and turned to escape. The leaks from her breasts grew heavier as her daughter continued to cry. Her entire focus was on getting away and finding a place to nurse. She was not sure how long the nursing pads would hold.

"Whoa!" Stevenson commanded. Anna stopped, her mouth tightening. "I want you here until this horse recovers from the sedative."

Anna frowned then looked along the aisle to the truck parked on the edge of the light spilling from the end of the barn, and the increasing volume of the hungry wails emanating from it.

Stevenson ran a hand through his sandy hair in obvious frustration. "This is my best stud. I want you here in case there's a problem. Can't you call your husband or boyfriend or someone to take her?"

Anna's eyes narrowed. "No, I can't. She's not a puppy, Mr. Stevenson and she's hungry now." No way was she going to let him know there was no husband, not even a boyfriend.

He expelled his breath. "Go get her and bring her in."

Nowhere had she heard a please, but what had she expected? Anna shifted. Now was not the time to worry about manners. "Fine," she mumbled.

As distasteful as she found him and as tempting as it might be, Anna knew she couldn't afford to anger one of her clinic's biggest clients. The job was too new, she needed it too much, and if she alienated someone like Stevenson, it would leave the vets who owned the clinic little choice but to get rid of her. She might be excused for taking a tone with him after he questioned her identity and credentials, but ignoring his wishes about this was different.

She hurried from the barn. As soon as she picked up her daughter, the baby reached for her, making smacking noises with her lips. Anna laughed and felt everything inside her melt. As she cradled the baby in one arm, she used her other hand to unzip the coverall. She bared her swollen breast and leaned against the pickup with a sigh of relief as Becca latched on and suckled. Her tiny fingers pushed against Anna's breast.

"Is everything okay?"

She almost jumped out of her skin as she heard Chris's impatient voice. She threw the blanket dangling from her hand over her half-bared front.

"She was hungry," she replied in a somewhat shaky voice as she angled herself away from the man coming around the side of the truck.

"You can give her a bottle inside where it's light," Stevenson added as if he were granting her a huge favor.

"I'm nursing her, Mr. Stevenson. She won't take a bottle."

"Oh."

Anna almost laughed as she saw him halt. He was tall enough his face was in the light showing from the barn over the top of the pickup. For the first time since she arrived at Fincastle, Chris appeared at a loss for words, and she felt a small spurt of cynical amusement. Of course he would be unprepared to deal with the normal result of the sex act. The only thing he was interested in was the performance, not any repercussions.

He cleared his throat and coughed, his gaze skittering away from her. He shifted his weight from one booted foot to the other, and if the light were better, Anna would have sworn a blush stained his tan cheeks.

"You may still come inside if you'd prefer. Sit in my office, and I'll keep an eye on Bart."

Anna darted another quick look at the man. Perhaps he was human. As soon as the thought popped into her head, she shook herself. No, not bloody likely. "Thank you."

Stevenson looked anywhere but at her as he led the way to his office. It was spacious and furnished for comfort rather than style, with a large antique desk and a couple easy chairs in addition to the leather chair behind the desk.

"Make yourself comfortable," he murmured with an automatic kind of politeness she was sure had been drummed into him, but the words cut off on a choked cough as Anna sat. The receiving blanket slipped, giving him a clear view of the baby nursing at her breast. She pulled the blanket back in place. Anna had long ago lost any embarrassment about feeding her child, and though she didn't push her breast-feeding on people, she wasn't going to apologize for it.

The door shut with a hasty click. Anna leaned back in the chair and sighed with relief. The pressure eased, at least on one side. Now Stevenson had disappeared, she removed the blanket, burped the baby and switched her to the other breast to get some relief there too. If there was one thing she had learned, her daughter had no problems nursing. The baby was strong and efficient. She had finished burping her again and put her own clothing to rights when he knocked on the door.

"Are you… Is the baby through…uh, nursing? Bart's waking, and none too happy."

The impatience was back in his voice, and it hit her the wrong way. Anna stood. The weariness of the long day was catching up with her, and she lost patience as well. As much as she wished to keep him at a distance, sometimes options ran out. “I can’t juggle him and my daughter. If you’ll hold Becca for a minute, I’ll get him settled and in his stall.”

Chris looked almost as if she had instructed--“here, take this large, poisonous snake and give it mouth to mouth.” To give him credit, he recovered in an instant and held out his arms, uncertainty plain on his face. Anna hesitated a moment before she put the baby on his shoulder, her gut clenching as she gazed at his sun-bronzed forearms and work-toughened hands that rose to cradle the infant. He hadn’t recognized her, so it should be safe to let him hold the baby this once. Beyond that, though, she didn’t want him near her daughter. She settled Becca’s bottom on his muscular forearm and placed his other hand at the back of the baby’s head.

“There you go.” She left him standing in the middle of the office, a nervous, almost frightened look on his face. Serves you right, Anna thought with a small spark of vindictive satisfaction as she walked away. The only thing that would make it better would be for Becca to either spit up or poop, both things she excelled at doing. Imagining such a scenario made Anna smile.

The horse’s ears swiveled forward when he saw her. He quit stomping once again and this time blew at her enough to make a small nicker. Anna’s smile widened. She loved horses—always had, and somehow they knew it. Without hesitation, she walked to the muscular animal, stroked his head before clipping on a lead shank, and unhooked the cross ties. To make sure he was steady on his feet and the stitches weren’t pulling, she walked him the length of the aisle a couple times before leading him to his own stall. The horse followed her and munched the hay in the feeder as soon as she escorted him inside the stall. After unclipping the lead and looping it in her hand, she shut the door and watched him for a couple more minutes. Finally glancing at her wristwatch, she hurried up the aisle to the office.

Chris stood rooted where she’d left him, as if he were afraid any movement might startle the tiny person in his arms. Curiosity had replaced his earlier frightened expression. Becca had her face turned toward him and watched him from her big, blue-gray eyes. Anna swallowed. The baby had a reputation for not liking strangers, so her daughter’s quiet observation of the man made Anna uneasy in a way she did not want to examine. Part of her had hoped Becca would scream bloody murder the moment he touched her, and at least her daughter could have covered him in spit up. Traitor.

"Thank you," she said, reaching for her. "I can take her now."

"I've never held a baby before." Stevenson's deep voice was rough, and he sounded a little embarrassed. He handed her the infant.

His awe made Anna drop her hostility. For just a moment, she felt like she glimpsed the man behind the public persona--and he appealed to her. When she smiled, she saw Stevenson's eyes widen, then narrow with speculation. Her smile turned to a chuckle. "I know."

His gaze swiveled from her to the baby and back. "That obvious?"

Anna pursed her lips. "Yes, but at least you were brave enough to take her." She laughed again before quieting at the curious look he gave her.

Time to go. Right now. Curiosity was not good. The last thing she wanted to do was make Chris curious about her in any way. They had nothing in common, nor should they. She would not take such a risk.

She kept her tone cool. "I'll stop by in the morning to check on your stallion. Good night, Mr. Stevenson."

"Good night, Dr. Barlow."

He turned back to the barn, and she gathered Becca and the rest of her things and headed toward the truck. That was it. He hadn't recognized her. She was relieved. Of course she was relieved. It was the best thing. Her lip trembled and she clamped on it with her teeth until it hurt. He was a despicable human being, which she knew better than most people ever would. The farther she and Becca stayed away from him the better.

Chapter 2

Chris watched as the tiny woman vet reversed the clinic's pickup truck and drove away until her taillights had all but disappeared. Where the hell did he know her from? Had Jim brought her around to introduce her? Maybe that was the case and it had just slipped his mind, but that scenario didn't feel right. He wouldn't have forgotten her, not with her attitude and looks. There was something familiar about her, but he couldn't place what. With a shake of his head, he strode back to check on Bart one more time before closing for the night.

He would have rather had Jim, but on a weekend night, he couldn't afford to be choosy no matter how much business his farm brought the clinic. He was a lot more comfortable with the clinic's senior vet. Hell, he'd known the guy since he was a kid. Jim was almost a surrogate dad. To be fair, though, Barlow had done a good job.

Chris stopped in front of the stallion's stall. He had fired the groom responsible for the stallion's accident. Had it been the first time Rafael had been involved in something, he might have been a bit more understanding, but the man did not pay attention to the horses the way he needed to. Most of the animals in this barn were worth five or six figures, and he couldn't afford carelessness. Staying in town this weekend instead of flying out to watch some of his horses had turned out to be a wise decision. Bart was the best stallion on the place, and Chris had high hopes for what he would contribute to the future of the farm.

The stallion munched hay. At the sound of Chris's approach, the big horse raised his head, pinned his ears and tossed his muzzle as if to say "Back off, I'm not in the mood."

Chris chuckled and turned off the light switch next to the stall. After closing the barn for the night, he walked the quarter mile along the narrow gravel drive to his house. Fincastle Farm had been there for two hundred years, and the large stone house in which he lived was the oldest building on the farm. It contained part of the original log structure, but had been added onto over the generations. His mother had never cared for the house, though, so his father built her a more modern home even deeper on the property. Chris often saw those lights from the veranda of his house.

After grabbing a beer from the refrigerator in his study, he returned to the veranda and settled in one of the rocking chairs there. He lit a cigarette and sighed as he leaned back, studying the glowing ember while he let his thoughts wander. He had needed a break. That's why he was home. After showing all winter in Florida, Chris had decided to spend the spring and summer working with the younger horses on the farm and leave the showing to his assistant trainer and a couple of talented younger riders. On top of that, there was Bess, his favorite mare. After two years, she had finally settled late last breeding season and was due to foal any time.

Those excellent reasons aside, the truth was he was tired of the constant travel. After years of competing, the showgrounds looked alike. Even the people he met blurred in his mind. Now here he sat, thirty years old and alone.

There were always plenty of people on the show circuit to stroke an ego or anything else a person desired, but he'd discovered how shallow such a lifestyle was last year when he caught his girlfriend screwing one of the grooms right in the tack room. He had kicked them both out then gone to a friend's party to get as plastered as possible. He didn't remember much of the night except that he awoke in a spare bedroom the next morning with no clothes on and one hell of a hangover.

Something had had to change. He had quit the hard partying and started watching some of the people on the circuit he had always admired, like Nelson and Wynter Anderson. They seemed so normal. He envied them. The more he thought about it, though, his parents managed a similar relationship. His father had showed years ago, but they maintained a normal life, picking and choosing when they would travel, and doing it as a family. And why the fuck was he thinking about that now? The pretty vet and her baby? He stubbed his cigarette. No, the answer was a whole lot simpler.

His mother was nagging him to start his own family. The thing was, Chris had started to consider it too, until the incident with Sydney last year. He shook his head. He'd come close to asking her to marry him, but not for any of the right reasons. He understood that now.

Since then, he hadn't dated. Hell, he hadn't even been with a woman. His absence and abstinence were no doubt fodder for the show circuit gossips, but he was beyond caring. If and when he got married, he would do it for the right reasons and to the right woman. Let them think he pined after Sydney. If those thoughts kept the groupies out of his hair, so much the better.

A sudden vision of Dr. Barlow popped into his head, her cap of sable curls bent forward as she looked at the baby nursing at her breast. The feeling stabbed him right in the gut. Chris shook his head. Now why did he keep thinking of that irritating little vet? She had a chip on her shoulder where her work was concerned. That was what bothered him about most of the women large animal vets he encountered. They were often militant and irritating.

He finished the beer and headed inside. The phone rang as he stepped from the kitchen into the study--his private line.

"Christopher. It's your mother."

He smiled. As if she needed to announce herself. "Hi, Mom, what can I do for you?"

"Your father is leaving to go on his fishing trip on the Santee-Cooper. I'd like you to attend early Mass with me."

Chris sighed. He wanted to be on the farm when Dr. Barlow came to recheck Bart, but he supposed she wouldn't arrive that soon. "What time do you want me to pick you up?"

"Six-thirty will be fine."

"I'll be there."

"On time?" his mother prompted.

"I'll be there, Mom."

He was a couple of minutes late the next morning. Other than a pointed glance at her watch, his mother had the good grace not to say anything. Chris hid a smile as he held the door for her. He supposed he owed her silence in part to the fact that he had put on a coat and tie. He'd long ago given up the argument that no one dressed for Mass anymore. As far as his mother was concerned, church was a dress-up occasion, period.

They arrived early, as always. His mother was a stickler for punctuality. As Chris pulled his vintage BMW into the parking lot, few other cars occupied spaces. What surprised him was the Redfield Clinic truck parked there.

As they stepped inside the church, Chris found himself glancing around until he spotted the short, dark curls of Dr. Barlow near the front of the church. Without waiting, he guided his mother to a pew a couple of rows behind the vet. Why, he wasn't sure. Curiosity? He had a hard time envisioning the irritating munchkin he'd met last night attending Mass like a good Catholic.

His mother gave him an odd look, but made no remark as she genuflected and sat. The handle of the baby carrier next to Dr. Barlow was just visible over the back of the pew. She must have Becca with her. He wondered where Mr. Dr. Barlow was. His mouth twisted. If there even was a husband. Plenty of women these days were single moms, but the thought disturbed him in some odd way.

The baby fussed. Chris watched as Dr. Barlow's head turned. In profile, long, sooty lashes dropped over blue eyes set below arched brows. A too-straight nose and full lips now cooing to her daughter completed the picture. As the baby continued to fidget, she lifted her from the carrier and rocked her. The girl rested her head on her mama's shoulder and gazed around her with those big blue-gray eyes.

His mother stilled before glancing sidelong at him. "What a beautiful child," she whispered, "like an angel with golden hair and those beautiful eyes."

Chris grunted. No way would he have agreed with his mother, even though he thought the same thing. She was getting bad enough about dropping hints concerning his single, childless status. The last thing she needed was encouragement from him.

The service began. As they stood, he found himself studying Dr. Barlow, not the priest. No figure-concealing coveralls this morning. Instead, some sort of blue-flowered dress hugged her tiny form until it flared below her hips. Beneath the short skirt, a slender length of tanned leg drew his gaze. She continued to sway back and forth as she held Becca. Her hips and derriere mesmerized him. God, did she need to advertise the wares quite so much?

His mother jabbed him in the ribs. "Sing!" she hissed. Her sharp eyes hadn't missed where his gaze was fastened. Damn. He did not need to give her additional fuel for her time-to-settle-down-and-raise-a-family speeches.

He noticed the vet didn't receive communion. Of course, neither did he. It had been ages since he had gone to confession. As the service ended, Dr. Barlow put Becca in the baby carrier and packed everything she'd brought in. She saw him at long last when she stood to leave. As her blue eyes locked with his, he again felt a fleeting sense of deja vu. She nodded, but didn't smile. In fact, she appeared to be doing her best to ignore his existence.

Not an encouraging start. Now where had that come from? He didn't want to start anything, particularly with some hard-nosed, militant woman vet who already had a kid and no daddy in sight. If she was like most women he encountered, she'd have to play "who da daddy be?" anyway. He would at least be polite enough to introduce her to his mother. But in the end, his mother beat him to it.

As Dr. Barlow approached them, his mother spoke. "What a beautiful daughter you have."

The vet smiled, her hesitation obvious. Chris had a fleeting memory of the sounds of a party, and her smile…only softer somehow. What a joke. Anyone less soft than Dr. Barlow he had yet to meet. She oozed independence and capability.

"Thank you." Her tone was polite but not encouraging.

His mother, however, was not taking the hint, and that in itself was unusual. In most cases, she was reserved with newcomers. "Are you new to the area? I don't believe I've seen you at Mass before. My name is Liz Stevenson. This is my son, Chris."

"Anna Barlow," his veterinarian supplied as she held out her hand. "This is my daughter, Rebecca…Becca, for short. I've met your son already."

At his mother's arched brow, Chris stepped in. "This is Dr. Barlow, Mom. She was at Fincastle last night to stitch Bart."

Anna. Now he knew her first name. He followed his mother and Anna, pausing to shake the priest's hand. The two women continued to talk, which surprised Chris. His mother was no snob, but didn't go out of her way to entertain people new to the area, especially when she'd received as little encouragement as she had from Anna Barlow. "Why don't you come join us for breakfast since you were coming to the farm today anyway?" his mother asked, surprising him even more. "I'll be happy to watch Becca while you and Chris take a look at his stud."

"I can't. I'm on call," Anna said, "but thank you for the invitation."

Chris tore his gaze away from the view of the back of her slender neck and shoulders, left bare by the wide neckline of her dress.

"Don't be ridiculous," he heard himself saying. "It will make things much easier if you can recheck the horse without worrying about a baby."

Anna glared at him, and he realized he'd said something wrong. As he tried to work out what had pissed her off, she surprised him.

"All right. Thank you." Her acceptance was reluctant, at best. She followed them to the house. Chris kept an eye on her in the rearview mirror.

"She seems like an enchanting young woman." His mother was studying him like she was cramming for a final, which made him nervous.

"Huh?" Was she crazy? Anna Barlow might be some serious eye candy now he'd seen her in something other than figure-hiding coveralls, but she was irritating and cold. In fact, he considered it a miracle she'd gotten close enough to a man to conceive a child.

"Dr. Barlow, Christopher. Keep your mind in the here and now, please. You've been distracted ever since we walked inside church."

He listened as his mother continued to talk about the veterinarian. She had learned an amazing amount of information just walking along the church aisle. Barlow must have felt as though she was in the middle of the Inquisition, and somehow that made Chris grin with satisfaction. The grilling was no more than she deserved. Yes, she had always been a Catholic. No, she did not have a husband. At least his mother had the tact not to inquire if there had ever been a husband. Yes, Becca was her only child. No, she did not have family close by. Yes, they were settling into the area well.

"I don't see how such a tiny girl deals with a large animal practice," his mother added as she finished relating her tale.

This was something Chris felt he could comment on.

"She did well with Bart last night, Mom." The admission was grudging, but he had to be fair. She had done a great job with the often obstreperous stallion.

When they arrived at his parents' house, Chris helped his mother from the car. He had already called ahead to warn the housekeeper they would have a guest for breakfast. His mother waited on the front steps of the large white antebellum-style home while she sent a reluctant Chris to help Dr. Barlow.

As he approached, she was leaned across the backseat of the truck to unsnap the carseat, leaving him a wonderful view of her backside, from the dress pulled across her buttocks to the length of thigh visible to him. Down boy. The last thing he needed was to go lusting after the irritating doctor, nor did he want to come off as if he was a teenager who had no control over his body's responses, but he was having one hell of a time doing that. He adjusted his half-hard cock before she straightened.

"May I carry the baby for you?" he inquired.

She spun on him with a fierce look. "No!" With obvious effort, she tried to soften her harsh response. "I can get everything. I…uh." She hesitated before she rushed on. "I nurse her around this time. Is there someplace I can do that?"

Chris took in her stiff expression and defensive stance. Damn! All he'd done was try to help. Trying to remember the manners his mother had drilled into him, he smiled, his lips tight. "Follow me."

She needed to nurse. Great! Just what his aching dick needed, something to draw his attention to her bustline. For a small woman, she was generously endowed, and he'd done his best to ignore that part of her since the glimpse last night of one creamy globe. He spun away, afraid she might notice the response he had a hard time quelling, and led the way along the wide front porch to a shady area around the corner. With no windows and rich with honeysuckle vines, the porch offered almost complete privacy. Two rocking chairs stood with a small table between them.

"This is beautiful," Anna said, as if it had been pulled from her. The surprise in her deep blue eyes was evident.

"It's one of my mother's favorite spots."

She set the carseat on the table and lifted Becca. The baby kicked her legs and made smacking noises with her mouth. Did the kid know what was coming? He smiled at the errant vision that entered his head, making him wonder if the same technique would work for him. God, Stevenson, that was wrong on so many levels.

He looked at Anna's dress, swallowed and focused on the baby before he asked, "Do you need anything? A blanket or a towel?"

A faint blush stained her cheeks. "No, we're fine."

He nodded. "Come in the door behind you when you're ready."

Anna glanced at it, and once again her chin jutted. "Thank you, Mr. Stevenson." Her grudging admission made him wonder what he'd done to get on her bad side. They had met only last night.

After telling his mother where their guest was, Chris drove to his own house to change clothes, which was an excuse, and he knew it. What he wanted to do was put some distance between himself and the good doctor. Her dark hair and deep blue eyes were playing havoc with him. And there was that sense of familiarity. He couldn't shake the feeling he knew her from somewhere. But he had sense enough to know he needed to stay away from her.

Militant career woman, single mother. He didn't want to touch the scenario with a ten foot pole. If and when he settled down, he'd prefer to start his family the traditional way, with some careful planning as to when any children would enter the picture.

With relief, he stripped off the coat and tie and exchanged his dress slacks and loafers for jeans and paddock boots to save time later. He wanted to get to the barn without delay to begin working the green jumper prospects he planned to bring along this winter. Twenty minutes later, he returned to his parents' home.

Thinking their guest had already joined his mother in the sitting room, he strode around the corner of the porch and skidded to a halt. She was curled in the rocker, asleep. Becca was nestled in the woman's arms as she continued to suckle, her tiny hand kneading the rounded globe of her mother's breast. The sight blew his hard-won detachment to hell. Chris took the picture in at a glance, also noting the faint shadows beneath the sooty lashes veiling Dr. Anna Barlow's eyes. Her mouth had softened in sleep, and her curly head rested against the back of the rocker.

He recognized the stab of lust tearing through him, but there was another feeling. One he didn't want to put a name to. This was not the irritating, militant "I am woman" vet he had met last night. This woman was vulnerable in a way he hadn't imagined and didn't want to see.

His first instinct was to beat a hasty retreat, but that was impossible. She would already be embarrassed for having fallen asleep, so he couldn't leave her here.

"Dr. Barlow?" he murmured, averting his eyes from the nursing baby.

"Hmm. Chris?"

Chris? She used his name as if she knew him. Her eyes widened in what appeared to be genuine shock.

He turned away and muttered, "I didn't realize you were still here. I'm sorry."

He heard rustling movements as she put her clothing in place.

"It's okay. I'm sorry I fell asleep. I had a colic call in the middle of the night. I guess I'm more tired than I thought."

His smile was strained as he turned to her again. "Not a problem. I understand having horses and losing sleep. It must be even harder for a veterinarian." He bent to retrieve the baby's carrier seat. "Let me give you a hand gettin' this stuff inside. This is worse than packing for the show circuit. You almost need a trailer to lug it around." Jesus. Shut the fuck up, Stevenson.

He was relieved when she smiled and handed him the bulging diaper bag. After helping her carry everything inside, he showed her where to change the baby's diaper before he retreated to the sitting room. His mother was seated in her favorite chair near the fireplace, reading the local paper. He had watched the familiar scene often over the years. Usually his dad was there too, and his parents argued good-naturedly over who got which section first. He smiled.

"Dr. Barlow needed to change the baby. She'll be here in a moment, Mother. Would you like me to let Cook know we're ready to eat?" He wanted to get this over with, get Dr. Anna Barlow to look at his stud, then get her and her baby off Fincastle so he could regain his equilibrium and detachment. They made him nervous.

His mother set the paper in her lap. "Yes, please. The poor girl looks exhausted."

"I'm sure she can take care of herself," he said, trying to shut off the momentary stab of concern he'd felt for her.

His mother's polite inquisition continued through breakfast, making Chris begin to wonder if she had decided to take the job of finding him a wife into her own hands. If that was her thinking, she was way off base with Anna Barlow. Not his type. He preferred his women blond and tall, like Sydney. Bitterness rose like bile.

He studied Anna once more, as she talked with his mother. She wore little makeup, he noticed, if any. Many people found his mother intimidating, but Anna chatted with her as if they'd known each other for years instead of a couple hours. There were two topics, though, about which Anna seemed to reveal nothing: any specific mention of her family, or any real details about her daughter other than the usual baby conversations. Whenever his mother probed too close, a wall of reserve went up at least a mile thick.

"Thank you for inviting me to share breakfast with you," he heard Anna remark. Chris brought his attention to what was said as she turned to look at him. "I should check on your stallion and get on my way."

His mother leaned forward and put her hand on Anna's arm. "Why don't you leave Becca here while the two of you go to the barn," his mother suggested. "I'll be happy to keep an eye on her."

"She can get fussy…" Anna began, her tone hesitant, even cautious. Chris wondered at her reluctance to let the infant out of her sight.

His mother smiled at the younger woman. "I can handle that. This might be the closest I get to having a grandbaby since Chris doesn't seem to be doing much in that area."

He stepped forward when he saw Anna falter as she bent to pick up Becca. She waved him away and stood with the baby's car carrier.

"I've got it," she snapped. She seemed pale, he thought, studying her through narrowed eyes. Was it something his mother said? Or was Anna Barlow teetering on the edge of exhaustion?

Chapter 3

Anna gripped the steering wheel of her truck like a drowning man holding on to a life preserver. Chris lounged in the passenger seat, describing the farm as they drove to the barn. She was thankful he seemed to be unaware of any undercurrents. This had been such a bad idea. She should never have agreed to breakfast. Now his presence was almost overpowering in the confines of the truck.

Last night had been one thing, but everything had shifted when she'd awakened on that porch to find him watching her with those silvery eyes of his. She should have kept their encounters on a business-only footing. What on earth had she been thinking to even take the job here in Redfield? She knew Stevenson lived in the area. She should never have brought Becca here. Too much was at stake, but her other job opportunity had been far too close to where she had grown up.

At the time, being close to her family had seemed to be the greater evil. Now she wasn't sure. She had thought she was immune to him, her hero-worship a thing of the past. And that part of her attraction was, but she couldn't deny the tug she felt every time she looked at him. She'd have to keep any contact with the Stevensons to a bare minimum, invent some excuse so Jim or one of the other vets took any future calls here.

When they reached the barn, Anna jumped from the truck and grabbed her barn clogs from the backseat. She didn't bother with the coveralls since she was just rechecking the stitches and getting away would be much faster if she didn't take time to change.

"Whoa!" Chris ordered from behind her as she rushed down the aisle. "Why the hurry?"

Anna glanced over her shoulder at his lean, tanned face. He had the looks and the body of a god, or perhaps a fallen angel might be more appropriate. And he looked much better than he had a year ago. No matter what her body's response to him, he would never be the man for Anna, but most importantly, she couldn't afford for him to be anything to her. Becca had to come first.

"Sorry," she mumbled, slowing. When she started to enter the stallion's stall, Chris stopped her.

"Better let me bring him, he can be a bit testy."

The stallion flicked his ears and stared at them. Anna scowled, but waited as Chris led the big horse to the crossties and snapped them on each side of his halter.

She should have been used to the overprotective male syndrome. For some reason it seemed to follow diminutive women throughout life, but it hadn't her, at least not until recently. Bart fidgeted, no doubt as irritated for his own reasons as she was. Anna once again approached him from the front and let him smell her. As he lowered his head and relaxed, she stroked along his body and back to the hip she'd stitched.

"Would you bring me the mounting block, so I can get a closer look?"

Chris's hands bracketed her waist and she stiffened with outrage. Part of her reaction stemmed from the instantaneous response she felt at even this simple touch. Her breasts throbbed, and heat coiled through her core. As he lifted her off the floor, outrage turned to genuine anger. All her life, people had treated her like a kid because she was short. This was different than trying to be courteous. She'd had to prove herself over and over again, especially in a family of athletic amazons where misfit didn't even begin to describe how different she was.

"Put. Me. Down," Anna snapped. "I am not a child."

The stallion skittered at her sharp tone.

"Don't get bent out of shape. I was trying to help." He dropped her to her feet. "By all means, let me back off."

Anna glared at him. How dare he look as if he'd been the one wounded? "You would never do such a thing for a male veterinarian."

He arched a brow. "I wouldn't need to. A male veterinarian would be tall enough to do his damn job," Chris retorted.

Anna thought she would burst a blood vessel. "I can do my job fine. Now, are you going to bring the mounting block or do I need to get a stool from my truck?"

Chris's eyes narrowed. So she had roused his anger as well. "That's an interesting tone to take with a client, don't you think, Dr. Barlow?" He spun on his heel and stepped around the corner to the wash stall. After setting the mounting block next to the stallion, he leaned against the wall, arms folded across his broad, muscular chest.

That's right. Keep away. Distance was a good thing.

Anna ignored his slouching form and stepped up to look at the wound. Everything else faded as she entered her world, her element, the place where she felt at ease. The animals and the science possessed her. She pressed on the area around the wound with as much gentleness as she could. The stitches appeared to be holding and there was no sign of heat or swelling.

She climbed down and turned to Stevenson, who still looked at her with narrowed, icy gray eyes. She would not be intimidated, but he was right about one thing--he was one of the clinic's most important clients. Arrogant man! And she'd pissed him off. She would have to deal with the consequences.

"Everything looks fine. If you want to turn him out, that might be better than keeping him hemmed up. Make sure someone checks him twice a day. If there are any problems with the stitches, call the clinic. Otherwise, I'll be back in a week to see if he's ready to have them removed. Do you have any questions?"

"No, ma'am," he drawled in a rich southern accent as dripping in sarcasm as honeyed sweetness.

"I need to be on my way." She paused. "Do you need a ride?"

He studied her in a way designed to make her bristle. "No, I have plenty of riding to do right here."

Anna hurried from the barn and jumped into the truck. She wanted to get Becca and go home. Maybe if she spoke to Jim Douglas, he'd arrange things in such a way she wouldn't have to handle any calls at Fincastle Farm. But as one of their largest equine clients, she knew that idea wouldn't fly. Even so, she would still have to speak with him. There was no telling what Chris might say to him, and she couldn't afford to lose her job.

She had calmed by the time she reached the big white house. After changing out of her barn clogs, she climbed the steps. Liz was seated in a rocking chair in the sitting room, cradling a sleeping Becca in her arms. Anna nibbled on her lower lip as she walked inside the room. Allowing her daughter to spend time with the older woman might not have been the best idea for most of the same reasons she needed to avoid Chris.

"Thank you, Mrs. Stevenson, for breakfast and for watching Becca." Anna refused an invitation to join them for dinner the following weekend, inventing chores as an excuse. As she collected the baby's paraphernalia, Anna smiled at the older woman. "You've been very kind. Thank you."

"It was no trouble, dear." Liz returned her smile. "You're welcome here anytime."

Anna ducked her head. "Thank you."

As she drove past the barn area, she saw someone schooling a horse in the ring off to the side. Chris. She would have recognized his riding style anywhere. The wall of her bedroom had been plastered with photos of him and other riders when she was a teenager. Anna turned her face away. That was a lifetime ago. She had other priorities that put a riding superstar like Chris Stevenson way, way out of her orbit. And it needed to stay that way.

She stopped at the clinic on the way home, glad to get her mind on business as she completed the paperwork on Chris's stud and the colic case from the previous night. Becca grew fussy, and by the time they reached Anna's rented house, the baby had launched into an angry, colicky wail. For a moment, Anna allowed herself the luxury of feeling sorry for herself. There were some times when it would have been nice to have someone around to help, even just to tell her everything would be okay.

Right. Time to suck it up and move on. She'd spent her entire life doing that, so this should be no different.

She had two appointments scheduled Monday with potential daycare providers, but she wasn't sure how that was going to work. Becca had yet to accept a bottle. As the baby slept in the swing, Anna pumped milk. If she hadn't felt like a dairy bar before, she thought, the breast-pumping machine drove the point home with its rhythmic whirring.

Anna tried the bottle again when Becca awoke, but the baby refused to take it, instead turning her head toward Anna's covered breasts and making irritated smacking sounds. Anna slumped her shoulders and gave in. Tears of frustration and fatigue trickled down her cheeks as she leaned her head back in the overstuffed chair. She loved Becca so much, but sometimes the baby left her drained.

The first daycare she visited the following day was out of the question. Toys and books were scattered over the floor, and while some untidiness might be expected with small children around, Anna was not convinced about its cleanliness. The second place she pulled up to was an in-home facility in a quiet area not too far from the clinic. An older woman answered the door and invited her in. Anna liked what she saw. There were only a handful of children and a quiet young woman helped with the toddlers.

The older woman gave her a tour and explained how she structured things and what she provided. She was licensed by the state and had been for ten years. Her credentials sounded good to Anna, and Becca even seemed content to look around.

"There is one problem," Anna admitted toward the end of the interview. "Becca is breastfed, and I have not been able to get her to take a bottle."

The older woman smiled at her. "I've run into that before. Have you tried getting someone else to feed her?"

"That's just it," Anna admitted "There is no one else to help. Every time I try it, she ignores the bottle and turns toward me."

"It's not uncommon. Do you happen to have a bottle with you?"

Anna opened the diaper bag and grabbed one. "Yes, I did bring one."

"Excuse me a minute and I'll warm this."

Anna looked after her with curiosity. In a moment, the woman was back and gave her a reassuring smile. "Why don't you step inside the kitchen for a moment, and I'll call you."

Anna did as requested, her curiosity aroused. She peeked around the corner after about five minutes and looked in to find Becca cradled in the older woman's arms, sucking at the bottle.

"Stand over there where she can't see you, Dr. Barlow," the older woman instructed.

"What did you do?" Anna whispered.

The older woman chuckled. "Nothing. Becca just knows the difference between the bottle and the real thing. Why should she take an artificial nipple when you're right there? Without you present, she can focus on the milk in the bottle rather than the milk in your breasts."

Anna had seen enough. The woman was a godsend. She collected the paperwork needed to enroll Becca and said she would be there the next morning.

Daycare might be a blessing. It would certainly make her life easier, but Anna couldn't help the lump in her throat as she handed her daughter over the following morning.

"If you have any problems, just call me. The clinic's not far away, and I always have my pager on…"

"We'll get along just fine, Dr. Barlow."

Anna nodded, biting her lower lip a little as she returned to her truck. She took a deep breath and glanced at her watch. She would be late if she didn't go. Out of habit, she looked back to check the carseat, but Becca wasn't there.

Anna headed straight for Jim Douglas's office. The clinic's senior veterinarian was seated behind his desk, reading glasses perched on the end of his nose as he studied the charts in front of him.

"Got a minute?" Anna asked.

"Sure, Anna. Come on in. What's on your mind?"

"It's about this weekend."

"Rough one on call?"

She prowled around Jim's office. "Yes and no. I had to go to Fincastle Saturday night to stitch their stallion, Bart."

"Nothing serious, I hope. Chris loves that stud."

"Not too serious. Caught his hip on a gate, and it tore through the dermis. I think it will heal fine."

Jim relaxed in his chair and removed his reading glasses. "What was the problem?"

Anna stopped her prowling and faced her boss. "I had a run-in with Mr. Stevenson. I'll admit, I was rude to him. I'm afraid I might have made him angry."

Jim rocked forward and rested his elbows on his desk. "Would you like to sit and explain what happened?"

After taking the seat across from him, Anna went through both visits, from Stevenson's attitude Saturday night to the altercation on Sunday. She finished by looking at him and offering, "I'll apologize if you want me to."

Jim smiled. "If he complains, we'll deal with the issue. But I don't think you'll need to worry. Let it blow over, Anna. Now, what I will tell you is I won't cut you any breaks in working with our clients. If a call comes in and you're the one available, you'll handle it no matter who the client might be, unless they request otherwise. Understood?"

"Yes, sir." She might not be happy with his answer, but his response was what she had expected to hear. And at least now, she'd brought her concerns in the open.

Her calls that day were routine, and her schedule stayed on time despite one barn where they added in a couple of additional horses for Coggins tests. With the local show season getting underway, there were always owners who decided last minute they wanted to compete.

As she headed back to the clinic at the end of the day, Anna realized she wasn't nearly as exhausted as she had been. Once she'd finished up her paperwork, she grabbed her keys and headed over to pick up Becca.

"So how did things go?" she asked as she came in.

The daycare owner looked up and smiled. "Not a hitch. She took the bottles with no problem whatsoever, but I think she's ready for Mama now."

Becca waved her arms and legs, squirming as she saw Anna.

"Hey, baby!" Anna laughed, feeling her heart turn over at how excited her daughter was to see her. "Did you miss me?"

She cuddled her close and pressed her lips to the baby's cheek. Turning back to the older woman watching them, Anna said, "Thank you. You just can't imagine how wonderful it feels to know she's in such good hands."

The only cloud on her horizon was Chris. The less she encountered him, the better. Still, she had to admit to a small pang when she thought that. And the pang surprised her, but who was she kidding? They'd had one brief encounter. He obviously didn't remember, even if she did… but she couldn't let herself go that road. That was the old Anna. She had more than herself to think about. She had Becca. Doing what was best for her daughter meant keeping Stevenson, and his family, as far away as possible.

So she put him out of her mind. She had a lot of calls that week, most of them routine. On Thursday, she accompanied Dr. Douglas to Pheasant Run to help with routine physical exams and health certificates for their jumper barn. Since the farm was another of the clinic's major clients, Jim wanted her to meet the owners.

They had almost finished pulling Coggins tests when she heard a familiar voice in conversation with a woman behind her.

"Thanks, Wynter. You know you and Nelson are the only ones I would trust to campaign this mare for me."

Chris Stevenson. Anna slid farther back along the horse she was examining. As short as she was, remaining unseen wasn't too difficult. There were some advantages to being petite.

"I still don't understand why you're laying off, Chris," the woman replied—Wynter Anderson, Anna wondered? She'd seen pictures of the tall redhead, wife of Nelson Anderson and an accomplished rider in her own right. They were about the same age, if she remembered what she'd read in The Horse Journal.

"I need a break, Wyn. I'm burned out." The conversation paused as they reached the horse Anna and Jim were examining.

"I understand. Oh hi, Jim. How are you?" Wynter asked. "Thomas is still working with a client in the ring, but he mentioned you'd have your new colleague with you."

Anna cringed. The last thing she wanted right now was to be noticed in any way. She did not want to see Chris in particular. In fact, after another rather awkward discussion with Jim, she had arranged things so he was going to check on Chris's stud tomorrow. Now it looked as if she had no choice. As usual when she spent much time around a barn, she had managed to get dirt smudged all over her, and she knew she was sweating from the heat and the pace they'd set in order to get everything done.

"Anna," Jim called over his shoulder. "Step around here. There's someone I'd like you to meet."

She wiped her hands on her coveralls and stepped around to Wynter Anderson. The woman was even more beautiful in person, Anna thought as she was introduced.

"It's a pleasure to meet you," Wynter smiled. "It's about time Jim joined the twenty-first century and added a woman to the staff," she added in a teasing voice.

Tension knotted in Anna's stomach, but she smiled and tried to ignore the scowl Stevenson shot her way.

Wynter turned to him. "This is Chris Stevenson, Anna."

"We've met," Chris growled at the same time Anna spoke.

"I've met Mr. Stevenson, already."

Wynter glanced between the two of them.

"Tell me about yourself, Anna. Are you married?"

"No," she supplied, embarrassed at answering questions in front of Chris.

"Where's Becca?" Chris interrupted, his silvery eyes cold as ice shards. "Surely not sitting in the truck on a day like today?"

Anna bristled at both his question and his tone but managed to control her temper. "No, Mr. Stevenson, Becca is not in the truck."

"Anna was able to find an excellent daycare provider," Jim Douglas added. "Right, Anna?"

She smiled in relief at her boss. "Yes. Becca loves it there."

"You have a daughter?" Wynter asked.

Anna felt Chris still staring at her, but she ignored him. She was not going to let him intimidate her.

"Yes. Rebecca. She's almost four months old now."

"We'll have to compare baby notes sometime. My youngest is turning one, and the boys are five."

Anna smiled and shifted back and forth. Stevenson still glared at her.

"Come to the ring, Chris," Wynter suggested. "I want you to see the young mare Nelson's working." She turned to Anna. "It was a pleasure to meet you."

"Thanks." Anna's smile felt a bit more natural. Inside, though, she was a mess. She wanted to leave, or at least get away on her own for a minute or two.

Chapter 4

Chris fumed the whole way along the aisle. What was it about Anna that seemed to get under his skin? He had done little but think about her ever since last Sunday. Having her crowd his thoughts was not something he enjoyed. He preferred the women in his life to be in the background until he decided otherwise. Look what had happened with Sydney when he gave her too much freedom to do as she pleased. He couldn't afford to lose control like that with Anna.

What was he thinking? Anna Barlow was not a woman in his life. She was an annoying thorn in his side, and no bigger than a damn horsefly. Maybe he could swat her away and be done with it.

"You can quit scowling, Chris," Wynter remarked in an amused tone. "We're almost to the ring."

They might be almost to the ring, but his thoughts were still stuck on Anna. Why had he asked about Becca? What Anna Barlow did with her kid was no business of his. He had never had anything to do with children or babies, and for all he knew, he didn't even like them. His mind flashed to those big blue-gray eyes staring at him out of her chubby face that first night when he'd held her, and he smiled. She was cute.

Wynter stopped and studied him as if he were a bug on a pin. "What is it with you and Anna Barlow, Chris?"

That snapped him back to the present. He shook his head.

"Nothing. She doesn't mean anything to me. I've just met her, Wyn."

Wynter tilted her head and raised her auburn brows at him. "Whatever you say."

Chris's gaze skittered away as he concentrated on the mare Nelson had under saddle in the ring. She was a steel gray with a mane and tail still pitch black. Coloring like that made a big impact in the show ring, even more if she stayed dark for a while instead of fading like many grays.

"Flashy," he commented as the young horse bent through the back and came onto the bit. Her strides lengthened and floated now at the trot.

"She's for sale," Wynter offered with a grin and propped an arm on the top rail.

"Why?" Chris leaned against the fence. He had difficulty imagining why anyone would want to sell a horse with what appeared to be unlimited potential.

Wynter shrugged. "She belongs to a client. We can't take any more horses on right now, and the owner says she doesn't have the time to work with her or campaign her, so she asked a friend of Thomas's to help sell her."

"Who's the owner?"

"She's from Virginia somewhere," Wynter replied with a wave of her hand. "I don't recall the name, but Thomas knows. Ask him."

"How long have you had her here?"

"A couple of months. She was a bit rusty when she arrived, as if she'd had a lay off, but she's a quick learner and talented. Her mind's right to make it big. Plenty of fire, but doesn't seem to get rattled--at least so far."

Chris wasn't in the market for another horse to campaign, but there was something about this mare he liked. He'd like to get a feel of her to see if she worked with the same smoothness she appeared to with Nelson aboard. He was confident she would. He and Nelson Anderson had competed against each other long enough for Chris to know their styles were similar.

"Can I try her?" He tracked the mare's progress around the ring.

Wynter grinned. "Why do you think I called you to come over, rich boy?"

Chris returned the grin, recalling the insult she used to sling at him with a laugh before she married Nelson Anderson, one of the wealthiest men in the country. Wynter had mucked stalls at Pheasant Run until their trainer, Thomas Sinclair, discovered what a talented rider she was.

"Nelson," Wynter called. "Rich Boy wants to try her."

Nelson's smile flashed beneath the brim of his hard hat and he trotted the mare over on a loose rein.

Chris liked the horse even more once he was on her back. Her canter was powerful and supple, even better than her trot. He sensed the coiled energy in her and called to Nelson and Wynter as he went past, "How is she over fences?"

"Green," Nelson called. "We've been schooling at about three-six right now."

Chris turned the mare toward a vertical and sat deep in the saddle. The horse wiggled approaching the fence, but kept her ears forward before jumping big and bold. Chris nodded to himself and headed for an oxer on the far side of the ring. This, too, she jumped with almost no effort. He continued to work the mare for several more minutes, and then eased her down to a walk. He liked the way she came right back and relaxed.

As he crossed the ring to Wynter and Nelson, he stroked the mare's neck and lifted his eyes to catch Anna Barlow standing in the shade outside the barn. Had she watched the entire time? Even from this distance, tension vibrated in every line of her body. Her hands were shoved deep into the pockets of her coveralls until her shoulders appeared almost hunched, and her blue eyes dominated her heart-shaped face. Their gazes locked for an instant, but in the next moment she hurried away.

Chris frowned. What was with that? She acted as if she'd seen a ghost. He shook his head and jumped to the ground. A groom came to take the mare and untack her. Chris dismissed Anna from his thoughts and turned his attention to Nelson and Wynter.

"How much?"

"Fifty." Wynter priced her, as Nelson stood next to her.

"A little steep for a green, untested mare," Chris observed.

Wynter shrugged. "That's what the owner wants, and Thomas says he's not sure she'll budge. He gets the feeling she's reluctant to sell, even though she knows it's for the best."

As the mare retreated, Chris pursed his lips. "Have the vet check her. I want x-rays and everything. If she passes, I'll buy her."

Wynter grinned and glanced at her husband's profile. "I told Nelson you'd like her."

Chris laughed. "Smart woman. That must be why he married you."

"Oh no," Wynter said, "I'm sure the scads of money I brought into our relationship was the real reason."

They laughed. Wynter had been homeless and trying to gain admission to Duke on scholarships and loans when Nelson met her.

At the other end of the aisle, Anna squatted with a clipboard, putting in information and sketching the horse they were examining before they drew blood to ship off to the lab for a Coggins test.

"She sure is a tiny thing," Wynter remarked as they walked down the aisle. "You say you already met her?"

Chris scowled. "She stitched Bart after that groom let him injure himself."

Anna glanced in their direction before turning her attention to her work. She did look pale. She was working too hard. Between running around in the heat doing barn calls and trying to nurse and care for a baby by herself, she would make herself sick. When would she realize there was no such thing as Superwoman? By the time they drew parallel to Anna, she returned his glare with one of her own, her delicate jaw clenching and letting him know she was raring to fight if he just said the word. Irritating woman!

"Jim," Wynter inquired, apparently choosing to ignore the undercurrents Chris knew she felt swirling around them, "I know you've got a lot on your plate today, but can you fit in a vet check on the gray mare that came in? We need films too."

"Anna? You up for it?" Jim said in a quiet tone, looking over the top of the horse's neck.

Something like pain flashed across her face before she ducked her head. When she lifted her face, her expression was blank.

"Sure, Jim. It's not a problem."

Chris tossed the conversation around in his head as he drove to Fincastle later on. Something was going on with Anna Barlow, and it puzzled him. There was the feeling he kept getting as well, as if he should know her from somewhere and couldn't quite place her. Chris hated mysteries.

Thinking she might have been on some of the show circuits a few years ago, he went through back issues of The Journal. She was small enough and young enough that she might have been showing ponies on the circuit, but everything he checked came up blank. He saw the name Barlow mentioned, but only as a couple references to a Preston Barlow-Barrett at some function or another, but there were never any pictures. Preston Barrett...hadn't he met her somewhere? Of course he'd heard of the family. Who hadn't? They were in the same league as Nelson, only the Barretts' fortune had been built on newspapers not computers. He shook his head at that connection. Beside the difference in the names, he remembered hearing the whole family was built on the mold of Nordic gods: tall, blond, lean and mean. Hardly a description of Anna Barlow. Maybe the mean part.

He would ask her tomorrow. He had scheduled a recheck for his stallion to evaluate how he was healing. The worst she could do was snap his head off, which she'd already done. But he didn't get the chance. When he arrived at the barn, Jim Douglas was exiting the truck.

"Hey, Jim," Chris commented, "I was expecting your new vet, Dr. Barlow."

"She got called to an emergency on the other side of the county. One of the local hog farmers having some problems with a prize boar in this heat."

Chris raised his eyebrows and tried to hide a grin. Somehow he had a hard time picturing tiny Anna Barlow dealing with an overheated boar. The whole idea still had him grinning as he led the way to Bart's stall. The stallion pinned his ears and shook his head at them.

"Pleasant as ever, I see," Jim remarked.

"I'll get him for you."

The stallion continued to misbehave until the veterinarian suggested, "Let me take the edge off him a bit. I'd like him to be still for me to get a good look at the incision to make sure everything's still holding together before we pull those stitches."

Chris nodded, but he thought back to how Anna had calmed the stallion and stood on that damn mounting block in complete faith the horse would behave while she'd pushed and prodded at his wound. The even more amazing thing was the stallion had never put a foot wrong the whole time.

"She is an amazing vet," Jim said as much to himself as to Chris, almost as if he had been privy to his thoughts. "This scar is worthy of a plastic surgeon. A few months, and you won't even be able to tell it's there."

"Mm."

"She was top of her class at Penn State," Jim continued, "and had a great offer at an equine-only practice in Virginia, near DC, but she refused it."

"Really?" Chris kept his tone neutral, but he was so curious to find out more about Anna he would take any tidbits offered.

The vet shrugged. "Their loss, our gain." He checked the area around the wound for any signs of swelling or infection as he added, "Of course, there might have been a lot more offers if she hadn't been pregnant as she was interviewing. There was also one professor who was not high on her, claimed she was a dilettante with a bad work ethic, but she's busted her ass for us."

"I see." It was time to change the subject. As much as he wanted to know more, it somehow felt underhanded, as though he was sneaking around behind her back instead of doing the logical thing by asking her. "How did the mare do on the vet check?" he asked to change gears.

"Passed. Flying colors. I'm sure Wynter will call you."

She did, around lunchtime, so Chris hooked the two-horse trailer to go to Pheasant Run. About halfway, he stopped at a country store to grab a bottle of water. As he came back, Anna, or someone who appeared to be her, was headed inside.

Chris started to say something sarcastic about the dried mud on her until he got close enough to see her face. Underneath the dirt streaks, she looked pale and shaky. She brushed by him as if she didn't even recognize him.

"Anna?" As soon as she glanced his way, he saw she'd been crying. "What's wrong?"

"I had to kill a pig," she muttered as she made to move past him again, but Chris touched her sleeve.

"Come over here in the shade under the tree and sit before you pass out." He knew she was feeling rotten when she made no protest. "Here, take my water. I'll get more."

He returned with some wet towels and two more bottles. He offered her the towel and watched as she scrubbed her face and hands. He tracked her movements as she reached around the back of her neck and rubbed the towel between her breasts. Chris swallowed. She looked wiped out.

"What happened?"

She turned to him with a sigh, and a spark of the Anna he knew burst through. "The boar got stuck in some mud near a farm pond. By the time anyone checked on him, he was already overheated. I couldn't get his temperature down and he started having seizures. I gave his owner the options. Euthanize him or get him to the vet school. He decided to put him down."

She looked away, blinking several times. "I've never had to kill anything before."

"It happens." Chris didn't want to sound callous. He was being realistic. Saving every animal wasn't always possible. Livestock owners simply had to learn to deal with that--apparently veterinarians did too.

She smiled, her face wan. Again, Chris was overcome with a feeling he knew her from somewhere. "Thanks, Mr. Stevenson--for the water, the towels and the ear to bend. I'd better get back."

As she rose, Chris clasped her wrist.

"Have dinner with me tomorrow night."

Her blue eyes widened. "I don't think that's a good idea…"

"Come on," Chris coaxed. "Nothing fancy. Bring Becca and we'll cook at my house, so you don't have to worry about the whole…" He found himself at a loss for words.

"The whole breast-feeding thing?" Anna finished with a sarcastic tone. "No thanks, Mr. Stevenson. It's my personal policy not to socialize with clients of the clinic."

He ignored her tone and smiled at her, not sure why her agreement was so important. "I grill a great steak."

She shook her head again. "I'm hungry enough to eat half a steer right now, but I can't accept your invitation to dinner. Please leave it."

Chris felt... What? Irritation? Surely not disappointment? Trying to keep a check on things, he smiled. "At least let me buy you a sandwich for lunch. I know this place doesn't look like much, but they make a great toasted pimento cheese."

She nodded. "A sandwich would be great, if you think you can stand the mud and pig smell."

"I've smelled worse."

She smiled. The dimple was there. She looked happier, and for once, young and carefree. Chris wanted to kiss her until she begged for more. And he had no idea where that thought came from, since they'd done nothing but rub each other the wrong way since they'd met. Even so, when he turned it over in his head, it didn't seem half bad.

Instead of following the urge, he said, "I have one request."

"What's that?"

"Call me Chris. Mr. Stevenson is my father."

It surprised him when she blushed before she replied, "Okay, Chris."

Chapter 5

Anna wolfed her sandwich while Chris regaled her with stories about the area, keeping what they talked about light, but she was still uneasy. The less time she spent around him, the better. She smiled at him as she finished. From long practice she used one of those impersonal smiles drummed into her since childhood, and did it on purpose.

"Thanks for the water and the sandwich, Chris. I've got to get going." She looked over at his truck and trailer. "Where are you headed?"

He glanced from his rig to her. "Over to Pheasant Run to pick up the mare y'all checked the other day."

Anna tried to keep her expression as blank as possible. Bittersweet. The mare's name fit better now than ever before. It seemed everything in her life had become bittersweet. At least, she thought, if the mare had to be sold, she would be going to a home where her potential could become reality. And now she needed to end this and leave before she bawled.

She stood, and Chris followed suit. He towered over her. Anna tilted her head. "Thanks again."

At his nod, she hurried to the clinic's truck and slid behind the wheel. She put Chris and the mare from her mind. She had to. Thinking about them brought pain. It worked until she was a couple more miles along the road. She turned off onto an old farm road, and sat in the shade, afraid to move a muscle.

As she stared out the windshield, her vision clouded. She did nothing to stop the tears flowing down her cheeks. Bittersweet. Seth had given the mare to her. He'd told her the horse was a gift from him and Brandon, the only people who'd ever cared about her. Now Chris had the mare she loved more than anything. Bittersweet belonged to the man who'd… She was not going there. With an angry swipe of her hand, she wiped her tears and backed the truck onto the highway.

She had several more routine calls during the afternoon and just enough time to shower and change before she picked Becca up from daycare. After nursing her and getting her settled on the floor with some teething toys, Anna ate a supper of a sandwich and a salad. She wasn't hungry, but she had to eat something to maintain her strength and her milk supply. By nine o'clock, she nodded with sleep as she fed Becca one last time before putting the girl to bed for the night. Anna didn't stay up much longer. Like almost every night, she fell asleep from exhaustion.

An insistent beep awoke her in the depths of the night. She fumbled in the dark for her pager as her bleary eyes searched out the alarm clock on her night table. Three AM. Fingers curled around the hard plastic case, she reached with her other hand for the bedside lamp. A couple of punches of the buttons and the glowing green screen flashed the message to call the answering service for an emergency.

Damn! She'd forgotten she was on call. Only by pure luck had she left the pager on instead of turning it off to charge as was her habit. She called the answering service and was given Chris Stevenson's number. She dialed and was not surprised when he answered before the second ring finished.

"Stevenson."

"It's Anna Barlow. What's up?" she asked in the same clipped tone he'd used. Her senses snapped to attention as he described the problem. A first pregnancy in an older mare who had never before settled, she was at the point where the foal should be presenting, but it hadn't happened yet and enough time had passed, Chris was concerned.

He didn't need to add the mare was special to him. Anna heard it in his voice. The man loved this horse. "I'll be there in a few minutes, Chris."

As soon as she disconnected, Anna sprang into action. She might have been groggy before, but she was more than awake now. She threw on her coveralls, slipped her clogs on, grabbed her pager and her phone and headed to Becca's room. She always kept a bag ready to go by the front door. In under five minutes, she'd started the truck and was speeding toward Fincastle. She passed the show barn to stop at a smaller barn at the end of the drive nearer the houses. The lights were on and a stocky figure waited under the circle of light near the entrance.

A bandy-legged older groom met her as she hopped from the truck. "Dr. Barlow?" he inquired in accented English.

"Yes, I'll be right in." Anna checked to make sure Becca still slept before she grabbed supplies from the truck. Chris was coming out of the stall when she arrived. His face was lined with strain, which seemed to ease somewhat when he saw her.

"Anna. I went ahead and gave her 10ccs of Banamine to try to ease the pain and relax her."

She nodded as she pulled out her stethoscope. "Good. We'll see what's going on from the outside first, and I'll see if I can discover if our problem is due to the position of the foal."

She was grateful for Chris's calmness as he held the mare's lead shank and let Anna get about her business. She checked pulse and respiration, then listened to the mare's gut before checking her perineal area. Everything had been cleaned and her tail wrapped, nothing less than Anna would have expected from someone like Chris. She came around to the mare's head. Fatigue and fear widened the horse's eyes.

"It's all right, Mama," she soothed. "Everything will be fine." Anna looked at Chris. "If you'll stay with her, I'm going to wash and get a feel for what's going on in there. The foal is in the birth canal, so it might be a foot out of place or a breech, and we can deal with those."

Anna stepped from the stall and scrubbed both arms before putting on gloves. She instructed the groom to squirt some lubricant on her arms and open the door for her. As Chris would have handed the other man the lead, she shook her head. "If she's a mare you've had for a while, I would prefer you stay at her head. It will help keep her calm."

He nodded, but his frown told her he would rather be at her side.

While the groom held the mare's tail off at an angle, Anna inserted first her fingers, followed by her hand, until she got about elbow-deep. She touched the tip of one small hoof. She rested her head against the mare's hindquarters as she pushed farther in. She was relieved to encounter a knee instead of a hock, but she still didn't feel the other leg. Anna grimaced as the mare's uterus contracted again before she continued her exam to see how the foal was positioned. She glanced over her shoulder at the groom.

"In my kit in the aisle is a large, sealed plastic bag with a nylon strap in it. If you would please bring it in to me?"

"What's up, Anna?" Chris asked.

"Dystocia. The foal has its right front leg and head still curled back. I'm going to break the amniotic sac and work on getting this little one repositioned."

"Is the foal alive?" Chris inquired.

Anna smiled against the mare's rump. "Yes. I felt it move as I attempted to shift its leg. This baby is trying to work its way out. It's just a bit stuck at the moment."

"Do you need any help?"

Anna closed her eyes for a moment. She knew the question was prompted by genuine concern both for her and his horse, not because he doubted her ability. The truth was, though she had dealt with the malpresentation of a foal before, another experienced veterinarian had been at her side. There was no time now to get anyone else over here. She had to put her trust in Chris.

"If you're confident your groom can keep this mare calm, I would appreciate your help here," she admitted. "If you don't mind, wash with the iodine scrub outside and bring me the strap. I'll go ahead and break the amniotic sac while you're getting ready."

The next fifteen minutes passed in a blur. With careful manipulation, she brought the misaligned leg forward to the correct position. Once that was done, it gave the foal room, so with a little extra help from her, the baby brought its nose around front. As she guided the head, Chris used the strap to ease the front feet forward.

"Okay," Anna sighed. "I'm going to slip the straps off and see if Mama here would like to lie down and push this baby."

As they stepped back, the mare groaned and lowered herself on quivering legs to the clean straw. Chris went to her head again to stroke with his capable hands along her sweaty neck.

"That's it, Bess, old girl. You can do this."

The mare groaned with a powerful contraction that pushed the feet through the vaginal opening. Anna squatted to give her help, and soon a small muzzle appeared, followed by a head black as soot, at least right now. Once the baby was clean and dry, the color might be altogether different. With a few more forceful contractions, the entire foal slipped from the mare. Now they had only to wait as mother and baby rested. The birthing process never ceased to thrill her.

Anna stood. "I'm going to clean some while they're resting. Then we'll need to make sure Bess is strong enough to stand."

Chris followed her to the aisle. As she finished stripping the gloves from her arms and tossing them in the trash, she felt a touch on her back. When she turned, she found his overpowering presence far too close for comfort. Without thinking, she stepped back.

His eyes narrowed. "Thanks, Anna. Bess is the first mare I campaigned. We've tried for years to get her to settle. I had all but given up hope when she took this past year. I had visions when I called the answering service of losing her and the foal both."

She ducked her head and nodded. "You called right away. Most people don't do it soon enough." She glanced along the aisle to the truck. "I need to check on Becca to make sure she's still sleeping. I'll be right back." She hurried away, afraid to remain close to him, afraid of the way not only her body, but also her heart responded to this side of him.

* * * *

Chris watched Anna as she walked away from him toward the truck parked outside the barn. Her mop of curly black hair glinted with blue highlights every time she crossed beneath one of the lights in the aisle. She might be petite, but he was beginning to see now why Redfield hired her. She was a brilliant veterinarian. More than that, despite the fatigue nagging at him, he realized he wanted her.

Forget tall and blonde. She was the woman he'd waited for, but he'd already read the signs loud and clear. She not only was not looking for a relationship, she did not appear to want one with him in particular, and that puzzled him more than anything else. He was washing his hands and forearms when he heard her footfalls returning. Becca nestled against her, one sleepy fist curled against her mother's chest. Anna grimaced as she reached him.

"I'm sorry, I had to bring her in. It felt warm in the truck to me, so I was afraid to leave her."

Chris stared at the pale, golden curls on the baby's head. "It's okay. I'm sure between the two of us we can handle her and a mare and foal." Anna smiled and recognition once again nagged at the edge of his consciousness. He started to ask her when Sergio called to them.

"Hey, boss! Bess is cleaning the potro. It's a boy!"

He let Anna precede him to the foaling stall where Bess indeed licked the foal dry. Finished, the mare struggled to her feet, and the umbilical cord snapped. Once standing, the bay mare nuzzled the baby, which still looked as black as midnight. She whickered to her colt and received a high-pitched whinny in answer. The foal stuck both front feet in front of itself and attempted to rise on its long, shaky legs. Chris smiled as the baby made a couple of false starts before standing on quivering, gangly legs. It fell two more times before it stood and searched for food. After not finding any in front, the foal shoved its muzzle against Bess's udder and suckled.

Anna laughed. "I'm glad Becca has better manners."

Chris smiled as he saw Anna clap one hand over her mouth. What a delight she was. One minute she was as prickly as a pinecone and the next as unguarded as if she'd known him for years.

"Well, Doc," he said, ignoring her blush, "I'd say this has turned out fine."

Anna nodded. "We need to wait for the placenta. I'll check to make sure she's delivered it all." She ended with a yawn and looked at her watch.

Chris looked at his groom. "Why don't you head to bed, Sergio. I think Dr. Barlow and I can handle things from here."

The older man nodded. "Gracias, Mr. Stevenson. I will see you manana."

After the groom ambled away, Chris turned to Anna. The barn had a quiet, intimate air at this hour. "Here, let me take Becca while you finish with Bess and her baby."

If Anna was surprised by his offer, she didn't show it, and for once she didn't seem even reluctant to let him touch Becca. As he held the sleeping infant in the crook of his arm, he looked at the soft, rosy cheeks and the thick sooty lashes resting against them. He marveled at the baby's golden curls, wondering where they might have come from since Anna's hair was as black as a raven's wing. With one finger, he caressed Becca's cheek then snuggled her against his chest. He had never given much thought to babies, so his mother's none too subtle hints over the past year had had little effect until now. Seeing Anna's baby up close made him wonder…

He looked in time to see Anna at Bess's hindquarters as the mare passed the placenta. She caught it in a bucket, her arm sagging as the full weight fell.

"Need some help?" he asked, but Anna shook her head.

"I've got it."

Another half hour passed before she seemed satisfied all was well. Chris watched as she yawned yet again, her blue eyes red-rimmed from lack of sleep. He carried Becca to her carseat and helped Anna pack her supplies in the truck. He noticed with alarm the lethargy to her movements. When she opened the driver's door, he put his hand on her forearm, ignoring the way she cringed away from his touch.

"I have a guest bed and my house is a few yards more up the road. Why don't you stay here and get some sleep?" She began to protest, but he shook his head. "I won't accept a no, Anna. It's going on five in the morning. You're wiped and so am I. You're too tired to drive home, and I'm too tired to drive you. If you won't think of yourself, think of Becca."

He didn't realize how tensely he was waiting for her answer until he saw her shoulders sag and she nodded. He relaxed.

"Get in the other side. I'll turn off the lights in the barn. I'll drive since I know where we're going."

That she made no protest, but did what he suggested, was a measure of her exhaustion. In a few minutes, he carried Becca's infant carrier inside the house while Anna followed with the diaper bag. He took her up the narrow stairs in the front hall to a loft converted into a couple of bedrooms and a bath. He opened the door on the left and flipped on the light switch. Instead of an overhead fixture, a small bedside lamp glowed, revealing a plump-looking double bed.

Glancing at Becca, he observed, "I don't have anything like a crib. Can she sleep in the bed with you?"

Anna nodded. "If you have a couple of extra pillows, I can arrange those so she won't fall off." She hesitated a moment before adding, "I need something to sleep in. I only have my coveralls."

There was a blush again, and that baffled him. For a young mother, which meant she must have been intimate with someone, she seemed as unsure of herself as a girl before her first date.

"I'll get you a shirt to put on. Would you like something to drink? I've got some tea downstairs."

Anna shook her head. "Water would be fine."

Chris turned on his heel and went to the kitchen to get the water. On his way back, he stopped by his room and grabbed a silky, cotton dress shirt off a hanger in his closet. As he climbed the steps, he heard Anna crooning to the baby.

"Hey, sweet girl. I know you're hungry, and I'll feed you in a minute."

She was changing the baby's diaper when he walked in, her movements quick and deft. Becca's face scrunched as she kicked her legs.

"Temper, temper." Chris chuckled.

Anna smiled at him over her shoulder, looking exhausted. "I'm surprised she waited this long to demand food."

"Can I get you anything else?"

Anna glanced around the room. "No, I should be fine. I can sit in the corner chair to nurse, and we'll be ready for bed."

Chris nodded. "I'll say good night."

He closed the door. For a moment, he rested his palm against the thick wood before descending the stairs. He couldn't remember the last time a beautiful woman spent the night in his home and he'd shown her to a guest bedroom…if they'd ever made it to a bedroom.

Chapter 6

As Anna sat curled in the overstuffed chair in the corner of the room nursing Becca, she heard Chris move around downstairs. She pictured his movements based on the sounds and found her mind wandering, wondering what it would be like if this were their home and he was preparing to come to their bed.

Her mind shied away from that thought. It was a teenager's dream. A dream gone up in flames a year ago, a girl's fantasy forced to give way to the reality of life. And the reality even now suckled, her tiny fingers kneading and pushing against the mound of Anna's breast.

Anna let her head drop back against the chair. In addition to the fresh, laundered scent of the shirt he'd given her, her sensitive nose picked up Chris's unique fragrance. The aroma intoxicated and reassured her. And it made her very, very nervous. Distance, she reminded herself. She had to keep her distance.

She might tell herself whatever she wanted, but her body had other ideas. As she settled Becca, Anna was conscious of the ache between her legs. She knew if she slid her fingers over her sex what she would find. She was wet and ready for Chris, so ready just thinking about it made her breathing quicken. She pressed her legs together, trying to tamp those wayward feelings. They would sleep, and when she awoke in the morning, she would thank him for his hospitality and do her best to stay out of his way.

When he helped her downstairs with Becca the next morning, he repeated his invitation to dinner. Anna refused, but she saw by the look on his face he would not take no for an answer.

"Look at it as a thanks, Anna, for saving not only my mare but also her foal. Though I can handle some problems, I don't think I could have manipulated the foal with the same ease you did."

Anna shook her head. "I don't think it's a good idea."

He stared at her with curious and determined silver eyes. "Why?"

"I told you before…"

"If you're going to start back with that not socializing with clients bullshit," Chris said, "I don't buy it. I won't buy it. I've met Jim Douglas at plenty of functions around here, including pig pickings at Pheasant Run, your clinic's biggest client. Let me cook you dinner. It's the least I can do. I told you before, I grill a mean steak."

Anna stared at him, half angry and half exasperated. She was trying her damnedest to stay away from this man, yet it seemed everywhere she turned, he was there. And it would be just a matter of time before she had to scratch the itch looking at him caused.

"Oh all right."

Chris grinned. "I'll pick you and Becca up at six."

* * * *

When she saw his BMW arrive that evening, Anna thought she should never have agreed to the invitation. Spending any more time around him was a mistake, and in the long run would do neither her nor Becca any good. In fact, it might create problems she did not want to think about. The less contact he had with her daughter, the better.

If they weren't around him, he couldn't begin to question, and neither could his family. Part of her, though, kept hoping. That hidden, sheltered part of her she seldom showed anyone, least of all her own family, hoped he would look at her, tell her he remembered.

Anna watched him exit the car. The faded jeans and polo shirt molded to his frame, showing off his lean strength, a characteristic of many top-level riders. This was the man she'd hero-worshipped as a teenager when he was still the newest and brightest star on the show-jumping circuit, and not much older than her. Every horse magazine in the country counted it a coup if they put him on their cover, and those pictures ended up tacked and taped to the walls and bulletin boards around her boarding school, and around her room. There were plenty of nights she'd done more than dream while she stared at those pictures.

Now, she looked away and continued to pack Becca's diaper bag. She started when he knocked at the door. Her life had changed. She was no longer that teenager with a crush. She knew better than most this hero was all too human. So why even put herself where she would risk getting hurt again?

"Ready?" Chris asked when she answered the door.

Anna didn't quite meet his eyes. "Just about. Come in while I finish here."

Hoping to avoid having to excuse herself to nurse, she had pumped a couple of bottles of milk earlier in the day. With them packed in an insulated case, she added extra diapers and a change of clothes. She already had a blanket and some toys, and the car carrier was ready to go, with a sleeping Becca nestled inside.

"Nice house," Chris commented as his silvery eyes took everything in at a glance. "You know, this is nearly as old as mine. Did you rent or buy?"

"I'm renting, right now," Anna replied. "Although I should have enough money soon for a down payment."

"Do you plan to stay in the area?" Chris asked. At her nod, he smiled and stared at the baby paraphernalia. "What can I help you carry?"

"Get Becca. I'll carry the rest of her things and help you get the carseat belted in."

Anna walked behind them, admiring Chris's broad shoulders and the way they tapered to lean hips and long legs. He looked thinner than last year. Anna stopped herself short. That was dangerous ground, better not to go there. He was already far too sexy, and she was far too turned on.

The drive to Fincastle was short. Chris waved at Sergio. The groom was closing the main barn for the night as they drove past to the stone house nestled in the midst of a grove of oak trees. It looked different in the daylight. Anna remembered him saying his home was the oldest building on the farm, and she was anxious to see more of the house. This morning she had seen hardly more than the guest bed and bath since she refused his offer of breakfast.

Somewhere in the back of her mind, from one of the many rider profile articles she'd read as a teenager, she recalled the farm had been in his family for around two hundred years. This house looked as if it had stood the test of time. In fact, up close, she saw some of the original log structure at one end of the house.

Chris carried Becca inside and took her through the spacious entryway, past the narrow stairway and the center hallway to a cozy, paneled room at the rear of the house. Its low ceiling and thick overhead beams gave away the fact that this was the oldest, log portion. Anna followed, taking in the antiques visible in the dining room and along the hall. They weren't the don't-touch showpiece type that adorned her parents' home. These antiques were pieces of furniture used on a daily basis. The room Chris brought them to was obviously one he enjoyed spending time in. In addition to the large-screen TV, there was a wide stone fireplace with a thick, Berber rug in front of it. Oversized chocolate leather chairs and a couch were arranged so both the fire and the television were focal points. Anna smiled. Chris lived in his home. She liked that it looked nothing like some playboy showplace, which was what she had half feared.

"You're surprised?" Chris asked as he set Becca's carseat in one of the armchairs.

"A little," she admitted. "It's so comfortable-looking."

Chris laughed. "I know, even after the guest bedroom last night, you still expected a lot of chrome and black lacquer?"

Anna knew she was blushing. Chris laughed again.

"Is it okay to leave Becca here?"

Anna nodded. "She'll be fine. Can I help you with anything?"

"It's ready to go except the steaks," he reassured her. "Would you care for something to drink? A beer or a glass of wine?"

Anna shook her head. "No alcohol. Not while I'm breast-feeding. Tea would be great, though."

Chris disappeared out the door, giving Anna an opportunity to look around. Hanging on the wall behind the large, weathered oak desk in the corner were more than a dozen framed photographs. Though there were a few recent ones of Chris at some show or another, many were from his childhood, or even older photos of his father in his days on the international eventing circuit. She had decided to take a closer look just as Chris returned. He handed Anna a glass of tea and hung on to the bottle of beer in his other hand. His gaze slid to Becca, who still snoozed.

"Would you like to leave her in here while we sit on the patio?" he asked. "I can leave the doors open so you can hear her if she wakes."

Anna nodded. She hadn't expected his thoughtfulness, given the reputation he had on the show circuits as a rider who played a whole lot harder than he worked. She wondered now if that description was fair. Riders didn't get to the top echelons of show jumping without putting in some hard work along the way, even with a famous father.

The patio was cobbled brick, worn smooth with age. Set at the back of the house, it received some of the evening sun, but was still shaded enough by the large trees surrounding the house that the heat would not be overpowering. Anna was already getting a feel for the North Carolina heat, which was more than she was accustomed to from growing up in northern Virginia. In the summers, her family had headed for the ocean, much to her dismay. She preferred the rolling hills and the sleek hunters and show horses to the sand and the salt, but that was just part of what always made her different from the rest of her family.

Chris waved her to a seat and Anna sank with a contented sigh. She seldom had the chance to kick back and relax for a while. As he grilled the steaks, they talked about his life at Fincastle and riding under his dad's tutelage. Anna was more than happy to keep the conversation centered on him, not her. She knew she looked so different from the young woman he had met last year the chances of him recognizing her were next to nothing, but her family was something else, and the less said about them, the better.

Becca had begun to stir as Chris pulled the steaks off the grill. He smiled at Anna. "I'll get everything set on the table here while you tend to Becca."

Anna picked up the baby. She wasn't hungry yet. After a change of diaper, she was ready to play. Gathering the thick blanket and some of her toys, Anna carried her to the patio.

"That was quick."

Anna grinned. "She woke up and wants to play. Here." She offered the baby to Chris, who took her with a trace of awkwardness, but a grin. Anna smiled as she heard Chris talk nonsense to her daughter while she laid the blanket on the ground and put the baby's toys on it.

As she turned to take Becca from Chris, he stood. "I'll do it. Should I put her on her back or her stomach?"

"Either way. She can roll over, so it doesn't matter."

She watched as Chris placed the baby on the blanket, his lean, long-fingered hands supporting her. The grin that lit his face as he glanced at her over his shoulder before straightening to his full height almost took her breath away.

"Ready to eat?" There was a gruffness to his voice as he asked the question.

Anna laughed. "Hungry as a horse."

Chris chuckled. "Horses, I know how to deal with. It's babies that are new for me."

Becca grasped first one toy then another, bringing them to her mouth, as Anna and Chris ate the meal he'd prepared. Nothing complicated, the meal was one of the best Anna had tasted in quite some time, maybe because she hadn't needed to lift a finger to fix it. She was about halfway through when Chris turned the conversation to her family.

"Jim Douglas mentioned you attended Penn State. Are you from Pennsylvania?"

Anna didn't look his way as she continued cutting her steak. "No." She would have liked to stop there, but knew she had to say something. "I'm from Virginia."

Chris seemed to want to ask where, but instead asked, "Do you have brothers and sisters?"

Anna set her knife and fork on her plate and looked across the table at Chris. If she shared anything about her family, he would soon figure out who they were. "I'm sorry, but can we not talk about my relatives? We don't get along, and it makes me uncomfortable."

Chris's gray gaze narrowed. "I'm sorry. Of course we can talk about something else. You choose."

Anna smiled in relief, not only at the change in topic, but that it didn't seem to bother him. "Thank you. Tell me more about this house. Parts of it look much older than other portions."

As he warmed to a topic that appeared to be near and dear to his heart, Anna relaxed. As she listened to him, she marveled at the depth of character he showed compared to the man she had encountered on the show circuit. There, he had a reputation for being a playboy who never got serious about anything or anyone. Had he changed that much, or had this side of him always been there? It made her begin to question the image she'd constructed of him.

"You must really love the house and farm," she observed as he paused.

"Land won't ever betray your trust," he murmured almost more to himself than her.

His cynicism startled her. She was about to respond when Becca threw the toys, stuck a fist in her mouth and wailed.

"What's wrong?" Chris half rose from his chair in alarm.

Anna laughed. "Now she's hungry."

She pulled a bottle from the diaper bag where it had been sitting in a warmer, but when she tried to give it to Becca, the little girl turned her face away, angling it at Anna's breast. She sighed in frustration. She didn't feel full and was afraid she wouldn't have enough milk yet to satisfy her daughter.

"May I try?"

She glanced his way and surprised an almost wistful expression on Chris's face. As dangerous as she knew it might be, his look was hard to resist.

"Sure."

He scooted back from the table, and Anna placed the baby in the crook of his arm. Becca quieted as she gazed at this new face. Anna handed

Chris the bottle and showed him how to position it, then stepped away. She watched in amazement as the baby continued to stare at his face even as she latched on to the bottle.

Chris looked at Anna and grinned before dropping his eyes once again to the baby nestled close to him. His lean fingers supported the bottle while his muscular forearm, with its dusting of golden hair, cradled her next to his heart. Anna swallowed around the sudden lump in her throat and glanced away.

"She sure is greedy for such a tiny thing! Is this formula?" His gaze went from the contents of the bottle to Anna's face.

"No, it's breastmilk." She flushed as she saw his gaze drop to her chest. "I...I pump it so she has milk to drink while she's at daycare."

"Pump it?" he asked with an edge of incredulity in his voice.

Anna scowled at him. "Yes. Like the dairy cows. Now will you stop staring at me like that?"

Chris shook his sandy head, flushing as he redirected his gaze away from her breasts. "I'm sorry. I never thought about the practicalities involved in having a baby around."

"I hadn't either," Anna admitted before she could stop herself.

"You didn't plan on getting pregnant?"

Anna frowned. "Not hardly. I think I might have preferred a husband before getting pregnant. Look, can we talk about something else?"

"You could have had an abortion," he observed. "Most of the women I've known would have."

Anna was horrified. "Not me. It's a baby, not a disease." Her lips quivered. "For God's sake, Chris, I'm Catholic. You're Catholic. You know I could never do that."

The baby stared at him without blinking as he continued to feed her. "I'm beginning to understand. I meant there are a lot of women who would have made a different decision in your shoes--unmarried, trying to finish veterinary school. It must have been a lot of stress on you. Did the father help?"

This was dangerous ground. Anna didn't want to have this conversation. "No. I--it wasn't that kind of relationship." She didn't care if he thought she was some sort of slut, she told herself.

"I see."

Anna expected to see censure. Instead, his eyes held a gleam of admiration. Sudden tears started to fill hers. Few people had looked at her that way in the past year. Few people had ever looked at her as if they admired her for something she'd done. A wave of bitterness threatened.

"Excuse me," she muttered and hurried inside the house, wiping her eyes as she went.

"Anna!" Chris called from behind her. "Anna, wait."

She was going through the French doors into the den when she heard his chair scrape and a muffled. "Shit!"

She stopped and turned. He was crossing the patio, Becca still cradled in his arms and suckling away on her bottle, unaware of what was going on between the adults around her. He stopped on the step below Anna so they were almost eye level.

"Anna," he murmured again. "I'm not criticizing. I admire you."

She wiped her eyes.

"I know," she whispered. But he wouldn't if he knew the whole story. No, he wouldn't. He'd be furious. "It's been hard the past year," she added. "There haven't been many people who've been either supportive or understanding."

"Like the professor Jim mentioned?"

Anna snorted. "Pompous prick!"

Chris laughed. "On to another subject here, sweetheart. Your daughter seems to have finished. What do I do now?"

"Burp her."

"How?"

Anna explained, giggling as Chris attempted to follow her directions. Becca was more interested in sleep, but Chris was persistent. When he got a resounding burp, he chuckled. "Wow. Don't let that girl drink beer when she gets older."

Anna laughed and took the drowsy baby from his arms. "Here, let me put her in her carrier so she can sleep."

As she settled her daughter, Anna was conscious of Chris standing over her and found herself all but in his arms when she turned. Anna couldn't quite meet his eyes.

He lingered for an instant, as if he wanted to pull her even closer, but then stepped back. "Would you like coffee, or is that a no-no too?"

"A cup would be okay, with cream and sugar."

"Make yourself comfortable. I'll be right back."

Anna curled on a corner of the couch. The leather was buttery smooth and the cushions deep and comfortable. She smiled at Becca's sleeping face. She remembered how she'd felt when she discovered she was pregnant. Stunned and even frightened, but never once had it occurred to her to seek an abortion. Her decision to not only have the baby but also keep it had angered her parents. She had always thought they were the staunchest of Catholics, but when the threat of an unwed pregnancy became reality, she discovered in no uncertain terms they preferred the sin to the embarrassment. Anna gazed off into the distance, her mouth tight.

Of course, angering her parents was nothing new, it seemed she'd been doing that her entire life. They sailed. She got seasick. They rowed, she read. In a family of athletes and socialites, she was a scholar and a loner. She sometimes felt her mother looking at her as if she wondered how she'd ever given birth to someone who obviously didn't fit the family mold.

Anna had her own family now. She had Becca.

Chris returned at that moment with a tray with two cups on it, a small creamer and a bowl of sugar cubes. Anna had to smile at the last. Leave it to the horseman to have sugar cubes on hand. As she made a move to uncurl her legs, Chris stopped her.

"I'll fix it. Stay there. Just tell me when to stop."

He handed her the cup before picking up his own mug of steaming black coffee.

Anna decided to try a safer topic of conversation. "Tell me about some of the horses you're working."

She enjoyed listening to him when he warmed to a topic about which he was both knowledgeable and enthusiastic. He talked about his horses the same way he spoke about the farm, and his tone revealed so much about his true depth, as well as how much of a mask he wore on the show circuit. This man was infinitely more appealing.

"How is the new mare?" Anna inquired, as casually as possible.

"I'm working her tomorrow morning. Would you like to watch?"

Anna sipped her coffee. She would like nothing better, but it might be going too far in more ways than one.

"I don't know if that's a good idea," she replied.

"Why?" Chris asked. "What can watching me work a horse matter? Are you still concerned because Fincastle is a client of your clinic? I can assure you Jim won't care."

"Don't push, Chris," she whispered.

"Don't say no, Anna. Will you be at Mass in the morning?"

"Of course."

"Come to breakfast again. You know Mother would love to have you."

* * * *

Anna smoothed the material of her skirt over her bare toes. The gesture was so sexy without her even being aware of the effect, that it made his cock twitch. Lord, he'd be tenting his pants here in a minute. She had no idea how appealing she was as she raised her deep blue eyes to stare into his.

"Chris, you make everything seem easy. I want to say yes."

"Then say it," he urged. "It's easy. I'm not trying to push. I just want to spend time with you." He leaned forward and took the coffee mug from her, setting it on the tray next to his own. "Is that wrong?"

Anna only stared at him. Chris held her gaze as he trailed his knuckles along her cheek and rubbed her trembling lower lip with the pad of his thumb. He watched heat build in her eyes.

"Is that wrong, Anna?" His voice grew husky. He caressed the back of her neck, steadying her head as he leaned closer. There was a whole lot more to Anna Barlow than the brilliant veterinarian. She was a strong woman who put her daughter before everything and everyone else. What was wrong with that?

* * * *

Was it wrong? Anna asked herself that same question. Was it wrong to want something that had turned out so awful before? Was it wrong to want to know if it would be different now?

She did nothing to stop the kiss. She feared what it might lead to, but she longed to feel his lips on hers again, the coil of heat building between her thighs before it exploded into full-fledged flame as his firm mouth covered hers. It didn't feel wrong. In fact it felt much better than before. She wasn't scared and drunk, with a self-image that was lower than low.

"Anna," he whispered against her lips. His strong arms cradled her and pulled her onto his lap, where he plundered her mouth at will. She opened to the stroking of his tongue and twined her arms over his broad shoulders. She felt the lean play of muscles in his back, the tautness of his thighs and the thrust of his erection. He groaned against her and tangled his hand in her thick, short curls.

Anna felt a tingling in her breasts that matched the ache in her belly. She moaned. She wanted him. Even more than that night, because she now knew what she was missing. It would be much better now. There had been pleasure as well as pain, even then. Now it would be so much better.

But he would know, and oh what a mess that would bring.

"Stop, Chris." She tore her mouth away from his and pressed her face against his chest, her whole body shaking with need.

"Jesus, Anna." Chris's voice broke and he buried his face in her curls. Breaths rasped from both of them. As his calmed, he tilted her chin and gazed into her eyes, his expression still hot with desire, but also mixed with confused irritation, at her or himself, she wasn't sure. "I'm sorry. I didn't mean to let things go this far."

Becca chose that moment to awaken, her hungry cry splitting the air. Anna slid from Chris's lap. The telltale tingle in her breasts was a sure sign her milk had let down.

"I--I need to nurse her this time," she mumbled.

"Do you want me to leave?"

Anna glanced back at him and shook her head. "No, it's all right. It's not as if you haven't already seen it." She blushed. The real fact was she wanted him there, wanted him to see, needed that closeness.

She sensed more than curiosity from him as she settled Becca, then unbuttoned the top few buttons on her blouse and shrugged it off one shoulder. As soon as she offered her nipple, the baby latched on. Becca stared at her mother, pushing and kneading as she nursed.

"Does it hurt?"

Anna turned her head to find that Chris had slid over next to her, one long arm along the couch behind her. He studied Becca.

"It did some at first," she admitted, "when she would latch on wrong, or I wouldn't switch her soon enough. But now that we both know more about what we're doing, no, it doesn't hurt."

"It's beautiful," he said, his voice gruff. "Your breasts, the way you feed her…beautiful and sexy."

She looked into his dark, questioning gaze, then dropped hers first. When she switched Becca to her other breast, she heard his hiss of indrawn breath. The tip of his tongue touched the edge of his lips, and he stared at the nipple Becca had let go. He shifted next to her, drawing her glance to the bulge tenting his slacks.

"Do you have any idea how much I want my mouth on you right now?" His guttural tone was almost a growl. Wet heat flooded between her legs. "Can I touch you?"

Anna swallowed. "Becca. She has to finish. Burp."

Anna found it difficult to breathe. When her lips parted, Chris swooped to cover her mouth with his. Hot. Hungry. Heaven. And the caution she'd worked so hard to build, crumbled.

Becca's sucking slowed and Anna tore her mouth away from Chris's to look at her daughter. The baby had fallen asleep.

"I'll burp her," Chris murmured and took the baby from her. When she started to cover herself, he touched her hand with one of his. "Don't. Please, baby."

Anna swallowed and shifted so her back was in the corner of the couch. Chris's eyes devoured her while he burped Becca and strapped her in her baby seat, setting it backward in the chair. When Anna gazed questioningly at him, his smile was rueful. "I don't want an audience."

Anna couldn't help it. She giggled. Chris knelt next to the couch, his eyes going once again to her bare breasts. The heat in his gaze was sending her up in flames and he hadn't even touched her yet.

After bracing his hands on either side of her head, he lowered his face to kiss her. Their lips and tongues tangled and played, licking and sucking. When his fingers touched her bare breast, Anna whimpered and arched against him. She hadn't thought about how sensitive she would be to a man's touch. They separated for an instant and he added his other hand so he played with both of her breasts. Anna watched the gentle caress and flick of his fingers over her darkened nipples. She felt the press of his erection against her thigh and looked into his eyes again.

"Let me kiss you here." His thumbs brushed her nipples.

"Yes."

* * * *

He had never seen anything as beautiful as this woman reclining against the corner of his couch, her breasts bared to him, her mouth trembling a bit as if she wasn't quite sure what to expect. She was much more than he had expected, and surprising in the way she mixed boldness and uncertainty together. Feeling as though he had to move with the utmost care, he covered her breast with his mouth, sucked her nipple between his teeth and tugged. Anna cried out and he froze. "You okay?"

She nodded, so he lowered his head to suckle and caress her again. Her response was instantaneous. Her torso arched against him, her moans almost wild.

"Anna." Chris raised his head to look at her, and the sight of her flushed face made his balls tighten. As he brushed his thumbs back and forth across her nipples, she whimpered. He repeated the caress, and she stiffened, her entire body shook, and she went limp against him.

"Jesus, Anna." She'd climaxed. Chris blinked several times in quick succession as a mixture of wonder and uncertainty flowed through him. She buried her face against him, her breathing ragged and uneven. He let his hand hover for an instant before he stroked the curls on the back of her head.

"I'm sorry," she said on a half sob.

He cradled her while he tried to regain control over his own emotions. Never had any woman responded to him with such passion. "It's all right," he comforted her, realizing she was embarrassed by her reaction. "It's okay."

"But you..." she protested.

"I'm fine," he lied. As much as he wanted to bury himself inside her, now was neither the time nor the place. He sensed she had never meant for things to get serious so fast. A few kisses were all she'd intended, nothing more. Neither of them had been prepared for each other's response. He would wait. Her eyes were downcast and her cheeks were pink, whether from passion, embarrassment, or both, he was unsure, but rushing her was not his plan.

"Look at me."

She raised her eyes to his. He smiled and touched his lips to her forehead. "Am I pushing?" he murmured.

She nodded.

Chris unfolded his length from the couch and picked up the coffee tray. "I'll get things straightened while you get Becca ready. I'll run you home. Okay?"

After leaving the room, Chris leaned against the wall in the hallway and let his head drop against the rough plaster. He knew the right thing to do was let her go, take her home, but it felt wrong. He wanted her to stay, here in this house. With a moan of disgust, Chris adjusted himself inside his jeans to ease some of his discomfort. He had to go slow. She wasn't a one night stand. He wouldn't do to her what had already been done to her, by all appearances. If they were going to be together, it had to be a relationship, not a game.

Chapter 7

Chris couldn't help the relief that swept through him the following morning when he accompanied his parents to Mass and saw she was sitting on a pew near the front . He'd kicked himself last night for rushing her. She was gun-shy about any kind of relationship, and he wondered about the man who'd left her to bear his child on her own.

He walked right to the pew where she was seated. Propriety be damned, he was going to sit next to her rather than in the pew his family occupied most Sundays, and let the whole community digest that one. The first glance he got was from his mother, who raised one perfectly plucked brow at him, then ruined it by smiling. When Becca got fussy during the sermon, Chris took her from Anna and bounced the baby on his knee. That drew another glance, this time from his father, who looked as if he would faint from shock.

The one awkward moment came at the end of the service, when the priest questioned Anna about getting the baby christened. Her cheeks went red with embarrassment. "I hadn't thought about it yet, Father."

"You need to do it soon, my child, even without the child's father," he admonished her.

Anna flushed, glancing at Becca before looking at the priest. "I'll think about it, okay?"

Chris saw the stiff set of her shoulders as she marched down the steps and across the parking lot to the small SUV he had noticed yesterday in her driveway.

"Anna, wait!" When she turned, her mouth was set in an angry, mutinous line, but below that lay a hurt she couldn't quite hide. "I would stand up with you."

"No!" she retorted with such speed it seemed to shock even her.

Chris felt as if she'd slapped him. She'd sounded panicked at the idea of having him be a part of Becca's christening, and what was up with that?

Anger boiled. She was back to being the same irritating and independent person he'd first met. He'd thought they'd progressed beyond that.

"I didn't mean that the way it sounded," she stammered in apology. "I just don't want to think about it right now."

"Mother and Dad would like you to come for breakfast," he offered in a cool tone, wary of opening himself again. Perhaps they were rushing things a bit, but he blamed the feeling he already knew her from somewhere for that. Even though logic told him his imagination was to blame, the notion persisted, making him want to hurry through the initial back and forth of a new relationship to something deeper.

"And what about you, do you want me to accept?"

"Yes," he responded without hesitation. So much for being wary of this woman. "I also still want you to come to the barn with me. Did you bring a change of clothes?" He didn't realize how tense he was until she nodded, and he felt the instant relaxation.

Breakfast was more casual this time with Chris's dad around. David Stevenson was as informal as his wife seemed to be a stickler for appearances. Anna retreated to the corner of the porch to nurse. Chris would have liked to watch but decided it would give his parents too much fuel for a fire he doubted Anna was ready to start or even wanted at all. Every time he tried to get near, she backed away and froze.

He watched her go around the corner of the porch. Because he still was unable to shake the feeling he knew her, he had continued to check through old magazines and newspaper clippings, but kept drawing a blank. Other than the odd flash of recognition--her smile, her laughter, the sound of a party, her blue eyes dark with passion--he couldn't tie anything together. The latter disturbed him most. How clearly he envisioned her expression glazed with passion. The rest was wishful thinking, fantasies born of having gone too long without sex. And last night hadn't helped that.

Chris broached the idea of his mother looking after Becca while Anna was still outside with the baby. Her instant acquiesence to the idea of watching Becca while he showed Anna the new horse surprised him. Anna changed clothes in a spare bedroom and reappeared in form-fitting jeans, paddock boots, and a sleeveless t-shirt. She looked as attractive as if she were in a slinky dress--or nothing at all.

Anna left instructions for his mother and showed her how to work the baby bottle warmer.

"I can't get over all of the conveniences available for mothers nowadays. And I thought disposable diapers were such an innovation," his mother said.

Anna laughed. "Wait until you see the baby wipe warmer."

Chris held the door on the BMW for her before going around to the driver's side. Anna was quiet on the way there, but he had begun to realize she was unlike most of the women he knew. She didn't feel the need to chatter all the time. He liked that, but her silence also made gauging her mood more difficult.

His first surprise came as they entered the barn. The groom already had the big gray mare brushed and tacked. He'd seen the way his stallion reacted to Anna, but it paled in comparison to the mare. She nickered as soon as Anna entered the barn. The mare even took a step toward her. Anna's eyes welled with tears. What the hell?

"I can't do this, Chris," she whispered as she touched a trembling hand to the horse's muzzle. The mare blew in recognition. "I thought I could, but I can't."

Chris looked from the woman to the horse and back again.

"You were the owner." He had suspected it, even the day he rode the mare at Pheasant Run. At her nod, he asked, "Why did you sell her if you feel this way about her?"

Anna's expression clouded and her gaze slid away from his. "I can't give her what she deserves. Look at her. She deserves to make it. I can't do that. Who wants to see someone like me on a mare like her?"

Chris tilted his head and stared at her in genuine puzzlement. What an odd remark. They would look fantastic together.

"Would you care to ride her?" he offered.

The answer was in Anna's eyes even as she shook her head no. Chris pressed his lips together in exasperation.

"Get me a helmet and some chaps for Dr. Barlow," Chris directed the groom.

"Chris, I haven't ridden in almost a year."

"Ever since you learned you were pregnant?"

Her eyes widened. At her nod, he scowled. This woman seemed to have given everything for the sake of a pregnancy many women in his crowd would have ended with no more thought than they gave to getting a facial or a haircut.

Even though she protested, Chris strapped the helmet on and adjusted the strap. He put the chaps on her and tightened them some at the waist, while she still told him no. Her protests died when he tossed her in the saddle. He smiled in satisfaction. They looked superb together, just as he had thought.

"Ride her, Anna," he urged. "Show me what she can do. You must be the one who trained her."

As long as he had been around horses and show rings, he was still astonished when he saw a horse and rider who meshed and became a team. That was the case here. Anna took about five minutes to get comfortable again before she worked the mare on the flat. Bending, leg yields, changes of tempo at the walk, trot and canter, and as he watched, the mare performed tempi changes along the outside line of his jumper ring, so it looked almost as if she danced.

"What the hell?" he exclaimed even as he heard his father step to the rail next to him.

"Who is that?" David asked.

"Anna," he ground out in amazement. "Full of secrets and surprises Anna."

They watched as she let the mare relax on a long rein. The big gray stretched her nose almost to the ground. Anna collected her again.

"She's going to jump her," his dad observed.

Chris found himself holding his breath as tiny Anna turned the big mare toward a complicated line of combinations. They sailed over them, hitting each spot perfectly.

Bittersweet. He wondered how significant the mare's name was as he watched Anna slide out of the saddle on the far side of the arena and rest her forehead against the gray's damp neck. Her arms stretched around the horse's neck for a moment before she turned and walked her toward him.

Bittersweet. There was significance to the name.

"Where did you learn to ride like that?" David asked as Anna drew near them.

Anna's laugh held scant humor. "I had the best trainers boarding school provided."

"You showed?" Chris asked, thinking perhaps he was getting somewhere in figuring out where he knew her from.

Once again, that humorless laugh. "Oh, no, not me. My parents would never allow that. I watched my classmates show while I either stayed at school or helped fetch for them."

"Let me give you a leg up. The groom's bringing my gelding. We can go for a trail ride, okay?"

He saw the longing in her face. In that moment, Chris thought, he would have done almost anything for her. Anna Barlow seemed to have more than her share of secrets, and few of them happy ones. She obviously loved this mare almost as much as she loved her own daughter, yet she'd sold her.

"What about Becca?" Anna hesitated.

"She's fine. Mom will take good care of her, and you left a bottle with her. Relax, Anna. Do something for yourself for a change."

He saw the longing on her face, so without giving her another chance to find a reason why they shouldn't go for a ride, he vaulted over the railing of the ring and boosted her into the saddle. She was such a tiny thing, he had to be careful not to throw her over the mare. He smiled to himself as he straightened the stirrup on her foot. The chaps she had on belonged to one of the kids showing ponies this summer.

"Meet me at the front of the barn. I need to grab my helmet."

She looked unsure, he thought, as he rode on his bay gelding. Her uncertainty wasn't due to a lack of confidence in herself as a rider, but because she doubted it was okay to simply ride for fun. Chris smiled to reassure her and led the way along the pasture fence to a wide trail through the woods. The ride was an easy one that would take less than an hour. Chris decided to let her set the pace.

He grinned about five minutes later when she asked, "Can we gallop anywhere through here? That is, if you don't mind. She is your horse now."

Chris frowned. He might be Bittersweet's owner of record, but he had a feeling that would only ever be on paper. Anna and the horse seemed to have a permanent bond.

"After you," Chris challenged with a smile. Anna leaned forward and gave Bittersweet a kick and a cluck. The mare, like a coiled spring anyway, needed no other invitation. Chris urged his gelding on, smiling as he watched Anna and the horse fly the trail a couple of strides in front of them. They sailed over a log lying over part of the path. He heard Anna's laughter wafting to him on the wind.

She slowed as they reached a fork in the trail and stopped there, still laughing as the mare jigged underneath her a couple times before standing still.

"Oh, Chris, that was fun. Thank you."

He pulled up next to her. Her eyes were alight with excitement, her cheeks rosy and lips parted in a wide smile. Before he thought better of it, he brought his gelding alongside, leaned over and kissed her soundly on the lips.

"I'm glad you enjoyed it, sweetheart. The left fork is about a two-hour trail ride. The right will bring us to the barn in about an hour."

She studied the path to the left for a moment then shook her head. "I don't want to be gone that long. Let's take the right fork today."

Chris nodded. Today. He liked that. It implied he might be able to get her to come riding again. They rode side by side at a walk, chatting. He told her about his childhood and how he got started riding, but he noticed she almost never mentioned her family. She talked a lot about school, but never mentioned names.

"What boarding school did you attend?" he at last asked point-blank.

She was silent for such a long time, he wasn't sure she was going to answer. When she revealed the name, Chris whistled. She'd attended one of the most exclusive and expensive schools on the East Coast. They often arrived with a vanload of students at the "A" Shows in the DC area. Their alumni included Maclay Medalists, diplomats' daughters and children from some of the wealthiest families in the country.

"Who are you, Anna?" Chris asked in a gruff tone. Maybe he would get an answer, as he had with her school, but she shook her head.

"Nobody, Chris. Nobody at all." She pushed Bittersweet into a gallop once again, but this time he didn't sense she got any enjoyment from it. She rode as if she were riding to get away from something. When she slowed the mare the next time, she kept her face averted. He saw the stiff set of her shoulders and was sorry he had tried to press her, but damn it, he wanted to know more about her. He had to figure out where he had met her before.

"Anna. I'm sorry I pushed. Please don't let it ruin the day."

She looked over at him with shadowed blue eyes. "I'm sorry too. I didn't have a happy childhood, Chris. I was the middle child of six kids and not at all like my brothers and sisters. I used to wonder if there had been a mix-up at the hospital." Her laugh held an edge of bitterness. "I sometimes think my parents wondered the same thing."

Anna shifted in the saddle and patted the mare on the neck before she looked at Chris. "They shipped me off to boarding school as soon as the school would take me. None of my brothers and sisters ever went to boarding school until high school. Brandon was away a lot because of his skiing, but during the summers, everyone was home except me. I was shuttled from one camp to another.

"It didn't even make them happy when I got accepted at vet school. My father couldn't understand why I wanted to muck about with a bunch of farm animals, and my mother was furious that I wouldn't attend the round of parties, like my sisters were doing, before making a wonderful marriage and settling down."

Anna looked at Chris and made a face. "To top everything off, I also wound up pregnant and unmarried."

"And was that the final straw?" Chris asked.

"Oh, yes. I have been persona non grata ever since. My parents didn't even attend my graduation from veterinary school. I think my mother might have been afraid I would ask her to hold my bastard."

Chris tightened his fingers on the reins, and the big gelding jigged beneath him. His jaw clenched in helpless anger at the way Anna's family had treated her.

"Seth came, though," she continued. "He's as big a son of a bitch as my father in his own way. That may be why. He held Becca for me. Brandon was crewing on some international sailing race, but even he called on a satellite phone…from the middle of the Pacific Ocean." She shook her head and smiled. "They both pitched in to buy Bittersweet as an early college graduation gift."

"Who are Seth and Brandon?" Chris asked, feeling a stab of something like jealousy.

"My big brothers."

He was amazed at the relief he felt when he heard her answer. Her brothers. Seth and Brandon. More clues.

"Let's take this side trail," he suggested. "It's a shortcut to the barn. We'll grab a cold drink at my house before we head to my parents' for Becca. Expect lunch when we arrive."

"I don't want to keep imposing, Chris," Anna murmured.

"It's no imposition."

As they headed to his house later, Anna was once again silent. He wondered if she regretted revealing what she had. He knew if he was determined, he could discover who she was based on what she'd already revealed, but that wasn't his aim. His real aim was to understand why he wouldn't have remembered someone so striking. True, she wasn't what he would have considered his type, but she was stunning in her own way.

Chris held the front door open for her and Anna walked past him into the hall.

"Straight back to the kitchen. Would you like tea or something else?"

"Tea sounds perfect. Is there a bathroom where I can wash?"

"Last door on the right. Come on in the kitchen when you're ready."

Chris poured two glasses and set them on the counter of the breakfast bar. As he waited, he perched on the edge of one of the stools. Anna walked in and pulled another stool out. He leaned forward, put a hand on either side of her waist, and lifted her. For a second, she was inches from him, and he smelled a tantalizing mixture of aromas: the salty tang of sweat, baby powder, horse and a scent that was Anna's alone. As always when he touched her, his cock swelled.

Her eyes met his over the rim of her glass as she took a long sip. Chris's gaze dropped to the slender column of her throat and the V of her t-shirt. He slid off the stool and stepped closer to her. Seated as she was, it brought her almost to eye level. He took the glass from her and set it aside.

"Anna?" he murmured as he slid his hands up her arms to cup her face. "I keep thinking about last night. How pretty you looked."

Her generous lips parted. Even as he watched in fascination, her breathing became shallower and faster. He eased his head closer, giving her time to tell him no, but the word never came, and he pressed his mouth to hers, probing with his tongue then tangling it with hers. The slow heat building during their ride exploded into a ball of urgent need. He pressed forward, pushing his hips between her legs so she felt his reaction. She moaned against him. They kissed again and again, parting to look at each other before coming together once more, mouths meeting and melding. It seemed to go on forever.

He caressed her breast, and her instantaneous response made him smile. "I loved watching you last night," he murmured.

She shivered against him. "I thought about you all night," she admitted, "feeling you press against me."

He smiled at her. "Then feel it now."

Her fingers shook as she unzipped his fly and pulled him free of his jeans. Chris groaned. With one swift movement, he pulled her t-shirt and sports bra over her head, dropping them on the chair behind him before he bent his head and suckled her. He licked her, loving the way she moaned as she slid her fingers through his hair to hold him closer. Chris released her from his mouth and removed her boots before he moved his fingers to the waistband of her jeans.

"I want to taste you, Anna." He set her on the floor to strip her jeans and panties from her, and then lifted her onto the counter. He pulled her hips forward. "Open your thighs for me. Let me taste you."

As she leaned on her elbows and spread her thighs for him, Chris groaned. He kissed along their creamy length and touched her moistness. God, she smelled and tasted wonderful, and he ached. When she whimpered, Chris probed with his fingers, surprised at how tight she was.

“Please,” Anna gasped. “I want you inside me.”

Chris stripped his shirt off and pushed his jeans down. His cock bobbed, swollen and rock-hard. “Yes, baby. I need to be there.”

“You have a condom?”

“In the bathroom.”

He picked her up and took her with him, barely giving her a chance to look around his room before he had her in the door and was turning her around to bend her over. He tore the package open with shaking fingers. When he’d covered himself, Chris stepped in behind her. Anna moaned, the sound driving him over the edge. He grabbed her hips and shoved forward, pounding into her in short, sharp thrusts that had her gasping and coming all over again.

After peeling the condom off and tossing it, he carried her to the bed. He wanted to keep her there, make love to her the way it should be. She should be cherished, not rushed as though she didn’t mean something. But when he looked at her to tell her, he paused. Her blue eyes were worried, and he saw wariness creeping in. Shit. He’d rushed it. When he’d sworn he wouldn’t.

“We should get back.” Her tone was stilted.

He leaned over her and kissed her. For a second he closed his eyes, knowing he would drive a wedge between them, but he’d rather have her pissed than awkward about what had happened. He stroked her curls. “We will, baby. In a minute. Thank you.”

“Thank you?” She looked at him in confusion.

“You’ve done wonders for my ego.” This time he wiggled his brows.

Anna scowled at him and pushed him away.

“Take me to my daughter.”

Chris’s shoulders sagged behind her back as she stomped away from him to get her clothes. He followed at a slower pace. He preferred her mad than in the melancholy mood that seemed to have overtaken her for much of the day. As she slammed the door behind her, his mouth twisted. Damn it, no matter what he did, he was doomed to be the bad boy.

Chapter 8

Anna was mortified and mad. She hadn't realized how starved for sex she was. How embarrassing. Gratifying to his ego, indeed. Arrogant, insufferable man. She stood next to the BMW, her jaw stiff, waiting on him to come outside. As soon as Chris walked out the door, Anna opened the car door and slid onto the seat.

He did nothing to make her feel better. In fact, the smug expression on his lean face made things worse. All she wanted to do was take Becca and go home, but as Chris had predicted, his parents invited her to stay for lunch.

Refusing would have been rude, so Anna found herself at the table on the screened in porch making small talk over sandwiches and more iced tea. She ignored Chris, but that seemed to goad him to even more outrageous behavior.

"You know, son," David remarked, "I was thinking about driving to Upperville next week to see how our horses are doing. We could make a road trip of it."

"You should come too," Liz said to Anna. "You would love the area around Upperville. Have you ever been there?"

Too many times. The area had been the scene of many disappointments and embarrassments over the years, from last-minute reneging on promises from her parents that she would get to show to the greatest embarrassment of all. She remembered Upperville very well. She had a daily reminder of her final visit.

She smiled. "Yes, I have. It is a lovely area."

Chris looked at her. "There is a lot to see. Would you like to go?"

Anna's stomach twisted. "I can't, I'm on call next weekend." She dabbed her mouth with her napkin and set it next to her plate. "I-I should be going. Thank you for a lovely day."

Inside, Anna cringed. What she was mouthing sounded like the artificial, polite conversation she had grown up with and her parents had tried to have drummed into her between boarding school and summer camp. Liz and David smiled as if they sensed nothing out of the ordinary, but Chris was not fooled.

"I'll help you with your things."

He waited until they reached her car to pounce.

"What's the problem with going to Upperville?" he asked, his tone dripping with cynicism. "The boarding school voice doesn't wash with me. You know one of the other vets would trade on-call weekends with you."

"I don't think I'm ready to take a trip with you and your family, Chris. Isn't that kind of rushing from a quick fuck to a relationship that's non-existent?" She knew the words were more than crude. She was being cruel, but he was getting too close for comfort. She had to find some separation for herself--and for Becca. No matter how appealing she found the man she'd come to see the last few weeks, there were so many reasons a relationship between them simply couldn't be. Falling into this, allowing things to happen--when they never should have happened in the first place—would be too easy.

"Funny," Chris bit back, "I thought things got off to a fast start today."

Anna felt herself pale. "That's unfair!"

"Oh, and what you're spouting is fair?" Chris scowled at her. He opened the rear door and replaced Becca's infant carrier, glaring at her across the roof of the car. Despite the fury she saw in his face, he shut the door so as not to wake the baby. "Afraid someone might recognize you?"

He was so close to the mark, but Anna doubted many people would recognize her as the same young woman who had been in Upperville last year. She had changed beyond belief. Her mouth twisted. Chris hadn't even recognized her despite getting to fuck her…again.

Anna leveled him with a stare she hoped would make him back off. "No. I can say for a fact that I don't think anyone would recognize me. In fact, I doubt many members of my family would even recognize me as the same person they last saw."

She slipped behind the wheel and had the satisfaction of seeing Chris frowning at her in a puzzled way as she reversed and turned the SUV around and drove home.

The week that followed was exhausting. Becca began teething, and her crying and fussing kept Anna from getting much sleep. When she dropped the baby off at daycare in the morning, she felt guilty for the relief she experienced. By Thursday night, Becca had two front teeth poking through her lower gums, and Anna had dark circles under her eyes.

Chris hadn't called her. What did she expect? Some things didn't change.

She put Becca in her crib. After the baby settled, Anna opened the filing cabinet next to her desk. Inside was a photo album. She seldom looked at it. Unlike the family albums most people kept, this one did not bring with it a rush of pleasant memories, but tonight Anna felt as if she had to look at it. Perhaps she was punishing herself for even taking the job in Redfield. She had only been kidding herself when she'd thought she wouldn't run into Chris Stevenson. How could she not? Working as a vet for the biggest large animal practice in the area? And she'd kidded herself thinking she could stay away from him. He was a drug. She was the addict. She had been as a teenager, and it was even worse now because she no longer looked at him as a hero to worship, she saw him as a man she could…love.

She forced herself to look at the photo album in her lap. The pictures went back to when she was about six years old. There was a picture of the whole family, all tall, slender, and blond with one notable exception. Clinging to the leg of a rebellious-looking teenage boy was a chubby dark-haired girl. Even then, Anna looked at Seth as her guardian angel, the brother who had run interference for her the most. She touched her finger to Brandon. Her brother had always been able to charm their father, but Brandon had been gone so much. A prodigy on the ski slopes, he'd already been competing among the top skiers. She glanced at a picture from Thanksgiving two years later. Seth was even taller, and she was even chubbier. But now she sported a school uniform.

Anna remembered that Thanksgiving. Brandon had been in Colorado. That seemed to be the story of his life, somehow always slipping through the grasp of Alexander Barlow-Barrett's iron-fisted rule. She wasn't that lucky. She had begged her parents not to make her return to school, but they hadn't listened. She had even tried hiding in Seth's room when the day arrived for her to go. Seth had known she was there, but didn't tell on her. They'd both gotten spanked, even as old as Seth was, and the next thing Anna knew, he'd been packed off to military school. She'd felt crushed by guilt, but her brother had never blamed her.

The pictures from summer camp were even worse. Her parents were determined to turn her into a slender Barlow-Barrett even if she would never be tall. After three summers of near starvation diets at expensive "fat camps", they gave up on that idea and simply sent her away to keep her out of sight.

Of course, there were a lot of memories that couldn't be captured in photographs. Years of being the fat geek at boarding school, the brunt of every practical joke. The only memories that brought her pleasure were of the hours she'd spent at the school's stables. One gift she did have was an ability to ride even if she was overweight, but her father refused to let her show until she "slimmed down." Since that hadn't happened, she had never shown.

Anna reached the last page of the photo album. A Polaroid snapped at a party fell to her lap. She stared at it with something akin to revulsion. There she stood, short, fat, with long, bleached-blond hair and too much makeup, and next to her was Chris, a polite and inebriated smile on his face.

Yes, Anna remembered Upperville, but she was pretty sure no one would recognize Anna Barlow as Preston Barlow-Barrett. After all, the man who'd bungled her sexual initiation that night didn't even recognize her.

Chapter 9

Chris refused to call Anna. He half hoped she would phone him, or he might see her. But when that didn't happen, he spent the week working everyone, including himself, to the limit. It kept thoughts of Anna at bay during the day, but nighttime was a different matter. He was haunted by the most erotic dreams of her, yet it wasn't her. Several times during the week, he awoke aroused and wanting her with a desperation new to him.

This was one of those nights. They were leaving in the morning for Upperville. He would have liked to convince Anna to change her mind, but he was too stubborn to call her, and she still hadn't called either. He sat on the veranda, smoking a cigarette. He still felt and saw the way she responded to him. Thinking about it now made his cock twitch. He could give himself some relief, but it didn't replace the feel of her wrapped around him. He swore in frustration.

He'd considered Becca too. He would have no problem raising her as his own. His parents adored both the baby and her mother. He took a long draw on his cigarette. Anna would make the perfect wife. She was attractive, smart and knew her way around not only the horse world, but also society--even if she didn't enjoy it. He could do a lot worse--and almost had, he reminded himself. He had been on the point of asking Sydney to marry him when he'd caught her screwing the groom.

He didn't think that would ever be a concern with Anna. She might be hot, but she obviously held some strict ideas when it came to relationships, so Becca's presence became even more of a puzzle. Ending up pregnant, unmarried, and by her own admission, pregnant as a result of casual sex seemed out of character.

She fucked you.

Totally different. There was nothing casual about what was going on between them. Chris stubbed his cigarette and yawned. Morning would arrive soon enough without him sitting up all night worrying over a woman who seemed to not even want him.

They arrived in Upperville around mid-morning. The horse show was as big and chaotic as he remembered. He and his dad spent most of the morning watching the schooling jumpers for any potential prospects they might find for sale. He waved to Wynter and Nelson, who had both chosen to show. Of course, it might also have been an excuse for the two of them to get away together. Even after three kids, they still looked at each other gooey-eyed. Though he teased them on the surface, deep inside Chris envied their close relationship.

His mother dropped Chris and his dad off at the showgrounds that morning with an airy wave and said she was going shopping. Almost everyone recognized Chris and David Stevenson. Both men signed autographs in between chatting with friends they hadn't seen in a while.

Though he knew it was inevitable, Chris didn't see his former fiancee, Sydney, until after lunch. She was on the arm of an older man with the starched-casual, tanned and groomed look that marked him as new money, still uncomfortable in a world he hadn't grown up in. While he looked at Sydney with adoration, her expression was already twisted with boredom. Chris found himself comparing her blond hair, heavy makeup and perfect boob-job to Anna's clear, pale complexion, her raven's wing curls and breasts made large only because of the milk she carried for her baby. He was overcome with a sudden longing to speak to her. Just looking at Sydney made him feel dirty compared to Anna's clean, natural earthiness.

He had pulled his cellphone off his belt when he heard a woman's voice behind him purr, "Chrisss! Darling! We've missed you on the circuit this summer."

He sighed and clipped the phone on his belt before turning to greet the woman behind him. "Thea," he said coolly. "How could I skip Upperville and the wonderful parties you always throw?"

Thea DuQuesne laughed, an artificial and irritating sound that matched her appearance. Perhaps knowing she could never compete with the bleached-blond Sydneys of the world, Thea had gone to the other extreme. She was gaunt to the point of being anorexic, with dyed-black hair, which she pulled straight back from her forehead. That only served to emphasize her overlarge nose and thin-lipped mouth. The dye job and hairstyle were meant to be distinctive, instead she looked weird.

"You seemed to enjoy last year's get together."

Chris cringed. He remembered that party, or rather he didn't remember, part of the reason he had decided his lifestyle needed to change. He hadn't left the DuQuesne mansion until the following morning, and with a hell of a hangover and a vague feeling of guilt he'd never been able to pin on anything specific.

Thea continued as if he agreed with her. "It was too bad of that group of Sydney's from Loudon to keep throwing fat little Preston Barlow-Barrett at you."

"Who?" Chris asked, disguising his sudden interest with a bland blankness he was far from feeling. He remembered the name. He'd encountered the Barlow-Barrett name a few times in trying to discover how he knew Anna. Of course there was the shared Barlow in there. A coincidence, no doubt.

"Preston Barrett, darling. You know, the newspaper family, although poor Preston has always been a misfit in that bunch!"

Vague wisps of memory teased him. Tear-soaked blue eyes, a lush, curvy body.

"A misfit?"

"Oh yes," Thea continued in a confidential tone which did nothing to conceal the maliciousness. "They're tall, blond and gorgeous, and poor Preston was always short and dumpy, although she did try the blond part during college with the most hideous bleach jobs."

"Really?"

"Yes. I'm surprised you can't recall her, dear, as much time as you spent with her at the party. Although," she touched his arm as if they shared some great joke, "you were so shit-faced after dumping poor Sydney, it amazed me you stayed upright as long as you did. You managed to outlast poor Preston. I saw someone carry her upstairs like a sack of potatoes. You stumbled after in a few minutes."

"Fascinating," Chris drawled. "As you can see, Thea. I am here and in one piece. I assume you're having another soiree tonight?"

"Oh yes, and you must come, Chris darling. It wouldn't be the same without you. You are such a stud!"

Chris smiled again, but he felt frozen inside. "I wouldn't miss it for the world, Thea dear."

He felt an almost overpowering need to shower, vomit, or both. But another concern grew more urgent. He needed to know what had happened at that party last year, and needed to find out from some other crowd than Thea's. The awful conviction something monumental happened that night prodded him like a sore toe.

He looked around the showground as he tried to remember who else might have been there. The problem was most of the crowd he associated with now were not the types who would have gone to the DuQuesnes. Sure, the family had plenty of money, but they also had a reputation for pretty wild parties. Rumors floated around about drugs of all kinds, and sex stories that he never gave any credit. Now he wondered.

He saw his dad standing near the fence beside the main ring and walked over to join him. David knew everyone, and if anyone was capable of steering him in the right direction, it would be him.

"Hey, Dad," Chris greeted him and leaned on the rail. "Seen anything you like?"

His father pursed his lips. "Nothing that would beat what we've already got in the pipeline, especially that gray."

"I'm thinking about giving her to Anna."

David turned his head to search his son's face. "Kind of an expensive gift, son. Any reason?"

Chris studied his clasped hands. "I'm hoping it will be an engagement gift."

"That serious?" His dad regarded him with the same silvery eyes as his own, just with a few more crinkles at the corners from a lifetime spent outdoors.

"Yeah. Anna will make a wonderful wife."

David frowned as he looked at Wynter Anderson, now on course aboard a young horse. "I don't disagree with you on that score, but do you love her?"

Chris hesitated. "I'm not sure I know what that is. Anna and I are well-suited. I can make Becca a good dad."

David shook his head. "That only takes you so far, son. Look at Nelson and Wynter. Six years ago, no one would have called them well-suited, or any kind of suited for that matter. He was one of the richest men in America, but half-crippled and crazy with grief, and she was a dirt-poor kid shoveling shit to work her way through college. Well-suited wasn't even in the picture, but love was. There are times in every relationship when it takes a lot more than having similar interests or backgrounds to decide it's worth the effort to rebuild if something goes wrong."

Chris swallowed. "Good advice."

He wasn't sure he could take it. He knew a lot about what love wasn't, but other than a few couples, Nelson and Wynter and his own parents, he seldom saw what it should be. Chris turned around and stared at the people milling around the showgrounds.

"Listen, Dad, if I were trying to find information about someone or something that happened last year, who would be a good source? You know, someone who hears about everything that takes place, on and off the showgrounds."

David didn't even hesitate. "Marcus VanSant."

Chris didn't know why he hadn't thought of him. The man was a freelance writer who covered most of the shows and society parties around northern Virginia.

"Last time I saw him, son, he was over at the hunter ring--where most of the socialites are anyway," the elder man added.

"Thanks, Dad. Listen, I'm going to need to go out tonight." He paused and grinned. "Can I borrow the car?"

David laughed and nodded.

Before Chris headed over to the hunter ring, he flipped open his phone and tried to call Anna, but got no answer. He should have talked to her earlier in the week. Allowing their disagreement to fester had been a mistake. He continued on his way to the hunter ring but was stopped several times along the way to be introduced to people. He smiled and excused himself as fast as possible each time. He recognized VanSant's trademark straw hat right away. The man was close to sixty and had been around the show world for decades. Yes, if there was anyone who would know what happened at that party last year, he would.

Chris called his name in greeting as he approached. VanSant turned and frowned at him.

"Stevenson. I heard you showed up. How's your dad?"

"Doing well."

VanSant eyed Chris. "You look a hell of a lot better than you did last year. I hear you've cleaned up your act some."

Chris felt himself flush with anger and chagrin. He hadn't realized his lifestyle was such a topic of conversation. "That's part of the reason I wanted to talk with you. You have a reputation for knowing everything that's going on or has gone on somewhere."

VanSant nodded and shrugged his thin shoulders. "True. People tell me things, and some things I learn on my own. Some I use." He paused as he studied Chris. "Some I choose to keep to myself. I'm guessing you're here about the latter."

Chris nodded.

"I saw Thea DuQuesne talking to you earlier. Would it have anything to do with her party last year?"

Chris darted a glance at VanSant and nodded.

The older man looked at the hack class in the ring. "Can you come by my house this afternoon? I don't think this is something we want to talk about here."

Foreboding slammed into Chris like a train hitting a stalled car. "Sure. What time?"

"Four. Here's my card. The address is on it." VanSant turned his attention to the ring, dismissing Chris with a wave.

Chris stuffed the card in his pocket and stalked over to the jumpers. Shit. What the hell happened at Thea's place that VanSant refused to talk about it in public?

"Any luck?" his dad asked as Chris leaned against the top railing of the ring.

"I'm meeting VanSant at his house at four."

David turned toward his son. He searched Chris's face.

"Is there something you need to tell me, son? In the years I've known VanSant, I've never known him to invite anyone to his home to talk."

Chris swallowed and stared at the dirt in the ring. He felt as he had when he was about fifteen and he'd wrecked the farm truck after sneaking out at night. Chris ran a hand through his hair and stared off in the distance.

"You know I dumped Sydney here last year."

"Yes, and your mother and I were overjoyed. We'd begun to worry you were going to ask her to marry you."

"I was until I caught her screwing a groom in our tack room."

His dad grimaced, but said nothing. He'd been around the horse world too long.

"I threw her out," Chris continued. "Then I went to Thea DuQuesne's with the sole intent of getting plowed."

"Okay."

"I don't remember much about that night, Dad, except that I woke up the next morning with the worst hangover I've ever had and a feeling there was something I should remember."

"You don't remember anything? And it's never come back to you?"

Chris waved his hand. "An odd feeling here or there, but no concrete memories. Now, the other odd thing is that from the moment I met Anna Barlow, I've had the strangest feeling I've met her somewhere before, but she's never mentioned it, and will hardly talk about her past."

David stared at his son. "You think the two are connected?"

Chris shook his head. "I don't know what to think. Thea kept talking about some girl, Preston Barlow-Barrett from that newspaper family. Everyone kept pushing her at me, but I don't remember her, and she doesn't fit Anna's description." Chris paused and muttered, "Except about one thing."

"What?" his dad asked.

"Being a misfit. Thea said Preston Barrett was the misfit of the family. What little Anna has said, it appears she was a misfit too."

"That's hardly much to go on," David dismissed. "You could be reading way too much into this."

"Exactly why I wanted to talk to VanSant."

"The only thing I will tell you, son, is something must have happened at Thea's party if VanSant would rather no one overhears when he tells you what he knows."

Chris feared the same thing. He tried again to reach Anna before he left for VanSant's house, but still got no answer. He stared at the well-groomed horse and rider on course without seeing them at all. What possible connection might Anna have with something as sordid as a party at Thea DuQuesne's house? He pictured the way she'd looked at Mass the first Sunday, all fresh-complexioned and makeup-free. No way would she have anything to do with a crowd such as the one at the DuQuesnes's. God, if he could just talk to her.

VanSant lived not far from the showground, so Chris decided to walk. He knocked on the door at four on the dot. VanSant answered. He was minus the straw hat, but instead had a pair of reading glasses perched on top of his bald head. He showed Chris to a cluttered study with overflowing bookshelves reaching from the floor to the ceiling.

"Have a seat."

Chris shifted a pile of newspapers and sat in a worn leather chair, feeling like the kid who'd been called to the principal's office. VanSant sat in a matching chair and steepled his fingers in front of him, studying Chris over the top of them.

"You've changed in the past year," VanSant commented. "Grown."

Chris shifted. He hadn't come here to be chastised for his past lifestyle.

"You used to be a pretty shallow prick riding on your daddy's coattails."

Discomfort turned to irritation. "Look, VanSant, I didn't come here to be insulted."

VanSant laughed. "I know why you came. I just wanted you to know what I thought of you, but I have seen you change. You have talent, and you're finally using it--in and out of the show ring. Until now, you had latched onto the wrong crowd, like that whore Sydney. I guess you saw her today. She's reeled in a sugar daddy. Married him last month. They honeymooned in Greece."

"I don't give a shit about Sydney. That was over a year ago," Chris snapped, beginning to lose patience.

"Except she's at the root of why you are here." VanSant stared at him hard. "What do you remember about the DuQuesne party last year?"

"Arriving and waking up the next morning."

VanSant nodded. "Sounds as though they got you too, or you tied one on more than usual."

"Got me? Who? And what do you mean 'they got me?'"

"A group from Loudon. Into drugs and a few other less desirable things. Friends of Sydney who were angry you dumped her in such a public way."

"Are you saying they did something?"

VanSant snorted. "Oh yeah, they did something all right. And according to my source, you weren't the only victim."

Chris stared hard at VanSant. A sudden flash again of deep blue eyes, like Anna's, but this time frightened and confused.

"What the hell happened that night?" Chris snarled.

"Do you remember being introduced to Preston Barlow-Barrett?"

Chris shook his head. There was that name again. "No, but Thea mentioned her too, as if I should know her. Maybe if I saw a picture it might help."

VanSant looked thoughtful. "I don't have any of that night, but there might be something from a few years ago. Preston isn't one to seek the limelight. In fact, I haven't heard a damn thing about her in the past year. Last thing I heard she was going to vet school somewhere."

Chris felt as if someone sucker punched him in the gut. Now this was too much to be mere coincidence. The older man stood and went over to a filing cabinet, where he mumbled to himself as he sifted through it.

"Aha!" He pulled a picture from a file and handed it to Chris. It showed a group of people, tall, blond and athletic-looking. Off to one side was a scowling man and next to him, a short, plump young woman with long straight blond hair. VanSant leaned over Chris and pointed to her. "It's not good, but Preston Barrett was pretty talented at keeping herself out of most of the family photos."

Chris shook his head. The black and white photo told him nothing, and Preston Barrett had her eyes averted. There was something, though, in the mutinous set of her mouth and jaw. No, it wasn't enough.

"I'm sorry. I don't remember her." Chris pointed to the man next to Preston. "Who's that?"

VanSant slipped his reading glasses on his nose. "Oh, her elder brother, Seth."

Ice poured through Chris's veins. His voice sounded faint to his own ears as he pointed to another man who looked similar to Seth. "And this guy?"

"The other older brother, Brandon. Kind of a playboy, shortlisted for the Olympic ski team at one point."

Tension tied Chris's stomach in knots. "Do you by any chance know what Preston Barrett's full name might be?"

VanSant executed a high-speed flip through a rolodex file with the expertise of someone who still held the computer age in infinite contempt until he stopped at one card. "Preston Anna Barlow-Barrett."

"Holy Jesus!" Forget feeling as though he was punched in the gut, he felt as if he'd been poleaxed.

"You remember anything now?"

Chris shook his head. He wouldn't tell VanSant even if he did remember something. "Tell me what you know, VanSant. I don't want to play detective games. I need to know what you've heard."

"What I heard, Stevenson, is this group from Loudon pushed Preston at you. They slipped you both drugs in the booze you were drinking. Someone carried Preston upstairs, and when you admitted you were ready to pass out, they sent you to her room."

Chris felt cold inside. "What else have you heard, VanSant?"

"They stripped her and left her lying on the bed, out cold from the drugs. You stumbled in, thought the obvious, and…"

"…and raped her?" Chris croaked.

"Your words, not mine." VanSant replied. "There's something else you should know."

God in heaven, could this get any worse?

"Someone videotaped the whole thing."

Chapter 10

Anna awoke Saturday morning to banging on her door. She checked the bedside table. Seven, too early for guests to come calling and, besides, there were few people she knew. She ran her fingers through her short curls before throwing on a pair of gym shorts and a t-shirt. Another rap on the door.

"Hang on!" she called as she crossed the living area. "I'm coming." Whoever knocked was impatient. An emergency? She checked her pager as she crossed the room, but didn't see any messages, and there weren't any on the phone either.

Anna pulled open the door. Worry changed to welcome as she squealed. "Seth! What are you doing here? Come in."

Her older brother towered over her. A rare smile softened his harsh features for an instant as he picked Anna up in a bear hug. "Anna love. How are you?"

She pulled him inside the room and shut the door. He was so big, he dwarfed everything around him. She hugged him again, the top of her curly head barely reaching the middle of his chest.

"I've missed you!"

"Are you happy here?" he asked, his voice gruff. His keen golden eyes searched her face.

"Oh yes! I love the job, and I've found a good daycare for Becca. She's got two teeth."

Seth smiled again. "I can't wait to see her. You wouldn't happen to have a cup of coffee, would you? I flew in to Raleigh and drove here without stopping anywhere."

Anna fixed a pot in the coffeemaker. As the water dripped, she turned to Seth with a feeling of trepidation. "Please don't misunderstand. I love having you visit, but why are you here, Seth?"

He stared at her with his strange cat eyes. "You're sure everything is okay?"

Anna shifted. His questions were beginning to make her nervous.

"Yes," she said, drawing the one word out this time. "What's wrong, Seth? You're starting to scare me."

He pulled a small DVD case from his jacket pocket.

"This was delivered to my office yesterday, along with a note demanding money."

Anna came from the kitchen and took the disc from Seth. As she stared at the clear plastic case, a hard knot of fear uncurled in her stomach and left her feeling a bit sick.

"Do you have a player?" he asked as he glanced around the room.

Anna nodded, shoved the DVD into the player and pressed Play. As the images appeared on the television screen, she emitted a hoarse, wounded cry and punched the stop button. She spun like a blind man only to find herself caught in Seth's strong arms. He had always been there for her, even taken the time to fly to State College when Becca decided to arrive before her due date. Seth was the one to smooth her hair and tell her to relax. He was the one to hold her hand when she must have almost crushed it as she bore down and pushed Becca into the world.

Now he held her as she shook with the memory of what she already knew was on that DVD. "Who sent it?" she asked in confusion. "Who would have done that?"

Seth swung Anna into his arms and sat on the couch with her. "Anna," he murmured, "whoever shot it is demanding money, or they'll make it public." He held her away for a moment as he searched her expression. "What that video shows looks like rape, honey. Was it?"

"No. Chris isn't like that."

"Anna, you don't know him," Seth admonished. "You don't know he wasn't part of it."

"No!" Anna insisted. "He wasn't. I know it. I know him."

At Seth's arched brow, Anna bristled. "Stop it, Seth. I know him. His farm is five miles away. He doesn't remember me from that night, but we, we've become friends…"

Seth snorted. "He's promiscuous and a playboy."

Anna shook her head. "He's not like that. He--he's good with Becca. He's had chances to do things," she continued with a blush on her cheeks, "but he's never pushed me. He didn't rape me. Someone did something to both of us that night, I'm sure of it. I don't know what, but something happened. I remember everything that happened. I also remember what happened that's not on that DVD. If it was, you would never even worry that he raped me."

Seth cradled her against his chest.

"I've hired detectives, Anna. I had to. I can't let this become public."

Anna stiffened. "Of course not, it would be another screw up on my part to stain the family honor, right?"

Seth sighed and stroked her hair. "Honor be damned. It might hurt your career, hurt Becca and Stevenson...and, yes, it could hurt the family. I know you don't think much of us, Anna, but I have to."

The beeper on the coffeemaker sounded at the same time Becca began her morning feed-me wail. Seth smiled at his sister. "I'll get the coffee, you take care of the newest generation."

Seth had two mugs in his hand when Anna returned, carrying Becca.

"My, my," Seth murmured. "She has grown a lot since I last saw her."

Anna smiled. "I'll let you hold her in a few minutes. Right now, she's interested in breakfast. Do you mind?"

Seth smiled. "I watched you giving birth. What's a bare breast among family members?"

Anna laughed. She had forgotten how Seth always made her feel better. She sat in the rocker and raised her t-shirt to give Becca access. He laughed as the baby latched on. Anna winced and tapped Becca on the cheek. "No teeth."

She looked at her brother's surprised expression. "I think I might have to wean her soon now that her teeth are coming in. I know some moms keep nursing, but I don't think I can stand it."

"Do what's best for you both, Anna. That's what matters." That's what she'd always loved about Seth--though he was a real bastard about some things, he'd always been her protector and her friend.

As she nursed, he sipped his coffee and told her about the family and her parents, whether she wanted to hear it or not. Seth always stood up for her, but he also tried to make her be more understanding of her parents.

"Tell me about Chris Stevenson," Seth ordered at last. "You know he has a major rep as a playboy."

"He had a reputation. He's changed." Anna was somewhat surprised by her own vehemence in defending him, especially after their last encounter, but she had been as guilty. She had seen aspects of Chris since she'd gone to work here she would never have suspected before. No, he wasn't the mythic hero she'd made him in her teenage fantasies, but neither was he the monster she might have wanted him to be at one time.

He was a man who loved his horses, cared about their…her daughter… and her? She wasn't so sure about the last, but she knew what she wanted.

Seth grunted, with a cynical twist to his wide mouth.

"Oh stop it, Seth. He's no worse than you or Brandon."

"I'd like to meet him," Seth stated.

"You can't. He went to Upperville…with his parents," she added at Seth's raised brow. "Besides, I don't think it would be a good idea for you to meet him."

"Why?"

"You're too much alike."

Seth snorted.

"How long can you stay?"

"My flight leaves tomorrow afternoon. Brandon beat me to the jet, and is on his way to Puerto Rico, so my secretary had to book an airline flight."

"Poor baby! Did you terrorize the flight attendants?"

"No, the flight was too short."

He stayed with Becca while she ran a couple of emergency calls. He took her to dinner in Durham, even talked her into a glass of wine. She tried to get him to use her bed to sleep that night because of his height, but he insisted he would be fine on the couch, even with his feet hanging over the end. He went with her to Mass in the morning, drawing curious and speculative stares from parishioners. Anna cried when he told her he had to leave, and Seth held her against his broad chest.

"Don't worry, honey. I'll take care of it, okay? I needed to make sure what I saw on that DVD was not rape as far as you were concerned. I had to hear you say it." He held her away from him and stared into her eyes. "Do you understand?"

"Yes." She knew if he thought for an instant what he'd seen was rape, he would have hunted Chris and beat him to a bloody pulp. Seth's temper was legendary. Brandon wasn't far behind, his was just diluted with a bit more humor.

After he left, the full import of what was on that DVD struck her. Someone had set them up, then taped Chris screwing her. But he hadn't known she was a virgin, and he was drugged and drunk out of his head anyway, so it looked a whole lot more like rape. Seth had seen the whole thing… Seth and how many others? Had Brandon seen it too? Anna was mortified.

She thought back to that night and shivered. Chris had already been kissing and caressing her when she had awakened, so she had been frightened and confused until she realized it was him. Chris, who had been nice to her all evening. Chris, whom she had idolized since puberty. But this wasn't like her fantasies, those vague dreams she had spun around him, in which he adored her and his every touch was a study in tenderness. In reality, he had been rough and it had hurt the first time.

But that was the thing. It hadn't been one time. Several times, he'd buried himself between her thighs, all with her full consent and participation. He had been patient, even tender after their initial coupling, and the whole tenor of their coming together had changed. It had no longer been about the sex. They had made love to each other, again and again. If she closed her eyes, she could still hear him whispering in her ear in his husky, smoky voice, telling her how much she turned him on, how beautiful she was. Her. Plain, plump Preston Barrett.

And someone had videoed it.

* * * *

Chris headed straight for the shower in his hotel room after his meeting with VanSant. He stripped off his clothes as he went. Someone had drugged them and sicced him on Preston Barlow-Barrett. Anna. His Anna. But she looked nothing like Preston Barrett. Why hadn't she said something? He shook his head. Why would she? Was she like him? Did she even remember what had happened?

He changed into a polo shirt and khakis. He would go to Thea's tonight, and he would learn more. He had to find out about this video. Had to get his hands on it and make sure no one else saw it. He would get hold of the original and destroy it. That was all that mattered. Since no one had come to him looking for money, he hoped--bad as the situation already was--if there was a video, it was only for someone's private viewing. He had a gut feeling VanSant was wrong about one thing. Chris doubted Sydney's Loudon crowd were the only ones involved. If it had happened at Thea's, he would bet his bottom dollar she was in on it too.

Anna. He tried calling her again, but got no answer. He couldn't leave a message, not about this. What had he done to her? It would explain the way she sometimes cringed from his touch, but--did she also not remember? He recalled the way she had responded to him with such passion. If they'd been together…

Chris stumbled and collapsed on the edge of the bed as the next logical thought occurred to him. His hands hung between his knees as he fought back a sudden wave of dizziness. Becca? He did the math on his fingers, but the baby was too old. He felt a rush of disappointment. Unless the baby was early? He shook his head; he was reaching for straws. She had to have already been pregnant that night. He rejected the idea. That didn't fit with the Anna he knew.

He joined his parents for dinner. When his mother commented on how quiet he was, he said he was tired. However, David wouldn't be diverted. When Liz excused herself after dinner, saying she was going to the room to read, his father collared him.

"Join me for an after-dinner drink and a cigarette in the bar," David told his son. It wasn't a request.

His father waited until they were seated at a small table in the back. He leaned across the table and lit Chris's cigarette and his own. After inhaling and blowing smoke at the ceiling in obvious enjoyment, he leveled his steady gaze on his son.

"What did you learn from VanSant?"

He was quiet as Chris relayed the details. To give his father credit, David showed hardly any reaction until Chris mentioned the video.

"Bastards," he snarled. "Sorry, son. I think the real target of this DVD is not you. It's Anna. In the greater scheme of things, our family is small change compared to the Barlow-Barretts. And everyone knows how strict Joseph Barlow-Barrett has always been with his family. We're talking about a Catholic who would prefer Mass still conducted in Latin."

Chris looked thoughtful. "So, I was a bonus? Ruin my career at the same time you blackmail one of the richest families in America?"

David nodded. "That's what I think. The only question is why they haven't done anything with it yet."

Both men were quiet for a moment as they sipped their drinks. David leaned forward and stubbed his cigarette in the ashtray.

"Any idea who might have the original?" he asked Chris.

"VanSant kept talking about this crowd from Loudon, but I have a gut feeling Thea DuQuesne might not be an innocent in this whole deal. The Loudon crowd were friends of Sydney's," Chris explained. "They were into drugs, so spiking our drinks was a possibility, but arranging to video me in bed with Preston, I mean Anna? They would have needed help. They couldn't have arranged that inside Thea's house, at least not without her knowledge."

Chris shook his head and ran his free hand through his thick hair.

"Shit, Dad. Why can't I remember?"

"You were drugged, drunk or both. The alcohol alone might have been enough. And the mind's a funny thing. Sometimes it chooses to block things that are painful in some way."

Chris looked at his dad, his face feeling taut with frustration. "I'm going to that party tonight. I have to see what I can find. I've got to find that video and destroy it somehow." He thought of Anna and her reaction if she discovered what had happened. Did she remember? "If it goes public, it might ruin her career."

David arched one sandy brow. "She's a Barlow-Barrett. It's not as though she needs a career."

"Not true, Dad. She does need a career. She's told me enough about her family for me to know they won't support her." At his father's dubious look, Chris continued, "Tell me, if you knew you had a grandchild, even if that baby was born out of wedlock, wouldn't you want to at least see it?"

"Wild horses couldn't keep me away," his father responded with no hesitation whatsoever.

"Her older brothers are the only family members who've seen Becca or even acknowledged her in any way."

"Damn!" David shook his head in disbelief.

"Exactly."

His father handed him the keys a short time later. "Good luck, and be careful, Chris." With a pat on his son's back, he was gone.

The party was already in full swing when Chris arrived. Cars lined the long driveway, and the huge brick mansion had light streaming from every window. Chris acknowledged the greetings shouted to him as he walked in. It looked like the usual crowd, a mixture of the single riders, trainers, and owners, plus a whole host of groupies and sycophants. Over in the corner, near the bar, he saw Sydney press herself against the tanned arm of one of the newer riders on the circuit, her new husband not far away, and he seemed to have a woman on each arm. That must be a very open marriage.

He cringed as he looked around. Had he really hung with this crowd? There wasn't a genuine bone in the bodies of anyone in the room. He thought of Anna mixed up in this group and couldn't even begin to picture it, but she had changed so much according to what he had been able to see of her in the picture in The Journal.

Had she really been a part of this whole crowd a year ago? Imagining plump little Preston in here was far easier than tiny Anna with her cap of dark curls and her clear, porcelain skin.

"Chris, darling!" Thea DuQuesne purred, interrupting his tortuous thoughts. She was dressed in clingy hip-hugger pants and a silk halter top which better suited someone twenty years younger and twenty pounds heavier. "I have someone I would like you to meet."

Chris smiled as Thea drew a plain-looking young woman forward. In fact, the only things remarkable about her were that she was busty and already well on the way to being drunk.

"Allie, this is Chris Stevenson. Chris, this is Allie Lieberman, you know, of Lieberman Communications. Allie has worshiped you for years, and begged me to introduce you."

Chris smiled and clasped the girl's shaking hand. As he looked into her glazed eyes, he wondered, was this another setup? Had it been the crowd from Loudon, or was it just Thea?

"You two talk," Thea purred. "I'll have someone bring you a beer. Is that still what you're drinking?"

Chris started to tell her no thanks, but decided it would look better if he was carrying something around. He tried to engage the Lieberman girl in conversation, but she was either too drunk or too in awe of him to make much sense. She babbled on until Chris was tempted to tell her to shut up. Thea returned and handed him a beer. Chris pretended to take a sip and saw Thea smile before she turned on her heel.

Chris guided Allie to the side terrace near the drive and found her a seat.

"Are you staying with anyone, Allie?"

She named a prominent horse family Chris knew well. He smiled at her, pulled out his cellphone and dialed the house. The butler answered. Chris quickly explained the situation and hung up. Allie already listed to one side, but the chair should hold her upright.

"Allie, honey, listen to me. Someone will be here in five minutes to pick you up and take you home. You stay here and wait for them, okay?"

She mumbled an okay and waved him away. Chris excused himself. He slipped from one room to another, smiling and laughing, shaking hands and making small talk, but all the while he worked his way toward the far end of the house and the stairway to the basement. He knew Thea and her husband had a mini theatre there. The woman had talked about it at some point. He couldn't remember when and had no doubt shown little interest at the time. Now he was interested to see what was in that movie collection.

Although he had never questioned it before, he now wondered where Thea and her husband derived their income. They never seemed short of cash and were always ready to host a party. Maybe blackmailing wealthy families had become a lucrative business.

He had almost made it to the stairs when a thin, tanned hand with gleaming tangerine acrylic nails twined through the crook of his elbow.

Sydney. Chris groaned. He might have dumped the woman, but he never forgot those nails, or the cloying perfume she wore.

"Chris!" Sydney purred. "It's been such a long time."

He forced a smile to his lips as he turned to look at her. "Sydney. How are you?"

"Haven't you heard the news?" she asked, feigning shock. "I've just gotten back from my honeymoon. Les is into shipping, so we took a cruise in Greece for a month."

"How nice." Chris wondered if whatever Les was shipping was legal, but decided against asking that out loud. He watched in fascinated revulsion as her tongue darted out to wet her tangerine lips, a perfect match for her manicured nails. Her brown eyes dropped to the front of his khaki slacks and she smiled like a cat that had spied a juicy mouse. Chris shifted, feeling repulsed by her blatant stare.

"Les and I have an open marriage," she added in a husky voice as she flitted her fingers across the muscles of his chest outlined by his shirt. "I've told him how...talented you are in certain areas." Her gaze slipped to the front of his slacks again. "And we were wondering if you might be interested in a party? Just the three of us."

It was all he could do to keep from knocking her hand off of him. Chris stepped back with a polite shake of his head.

"Sorry, Sydney. A lot of things have changed since last year. I'm not interested. I wasn't then, and I'm not now."

She stared at him for a moment before her eyes narrowed. "You are a bastard, Chris."

He smiled. "No, sugar, I'm particular. I don't want to plow the same row in what appears to be the community garden."

His head barely turned as she slapped him in the face and stalked off. Once she disappeared, Chris wiped his cheek on the sleeve of his shirt and looked around to make sure no one was watching him before he headed downstairs.

The basement area was finished like the rest of the house, but his luck held because unlike the rest of the house, this area was deserted and, even more fortunate, the first room he tried turned out to be the mini theatre . He ran his hand along the wall next to the door and found the light switch. Chris waited until he heard the click of the door latch before flipping the switch to illuminate the room. The theatre was small. Maybe a dozen overstuffed chairs with a large screen at one end and a VCR/DVD-combo underneath. One wall was lined with a mixture of tapes and DVDs. He scanned them. All traditional movies with a heavy concentration on Oscar winners and some foreign flicks shelved at one end.

Chris gritted his teeth in frustration. There must be another stash somewhere. Hidden someplace. He had heard the rumors, and knew from experience there had to be some truth in them. There was a porno collection. All he had to do was find it. The mistake he had made, he thought with controlled fury, was he'd assumed the porno collection was commercial. Now he knew otherwise, and he had to find it.

Chris began opening cabinets. In the third one, he did find a selection of porno movies, but they were commercial titles with busty women in provocative poses on the covers. He sighed in frustration. Maybe he'd been wrong. Perhaps this was it. He shut the cabinet, bracing one hand on the top as he did. He jumped when he felt something give beneath his fingers with a small click. As he stepped back in surprise, the cabinet turned on a hinge to reveal a set of open shelves.

Pay dirt. Again, there was a mixture of cassettes and DVDs. Chris examined the labels. They were written in a combination of letters and numbers. Damn! How was he supposed to decipher this? He wasn't any detective, but he was determined to get his hands on anything that might have him or Anna on it. He dismissed the videotapes, assuming what he wanted would be on DVD. It appeared the DuQuesnes had made the change to the new format, but had still hung onto their older videotapes.

He paused as he studied the letters and numbers once more. They were not as careful as they might have been. The code was easy enough to decipher...initials and dates. His heart thumped. The tapes went back for a decade! He searched for last year. Those were the DVDs. There, with the initials PBB and the date. One tape was all he saw. He checked his initials, but found nothing. His father was right. Anna and her family were the targets. He was the convenient stud who'd made it possible. Even without looking at it, he felt sick inside.

Chris's hand shook as he pulled the disc case from the shelf and pushed the trigger at the top of the cabinet so it swung once more in view.

He had to be sure before he took it. He looked around and saw a smaller viewing machine at the back of the room. Chris dropped the DVD in, his stomach in knots as he pressed play.

There was Preston, nude and curled in the middle of a large bed. From the varied camera angles, the room was set for the sole purpose of shooting video, and there was more than one camera. He saw himself stumble into frame and begin to strip. Chris closed his eyes and swallowed as he experienced a sick, sinking feeling in the pit of his stomach.

As the scene unfolded before him, he began to understand the meaning of the word violated. As sick as it made him, he couldn't turn it off. His gut clenched until he was afraid he might be sick, and just as his eyes blurred with tears, the tape, mercifully, went to black.

Chris sat for a moment, stunned and horrified. Merciful God, he'd raped her! His hands gripped the edge of the metal cart on which the small viewer sat until the edge almost cut his fingers. No wonder she wouldn't or couldn't remember. He had raped her, and if he hadn't seen the proof with his own eyes, he still wouldn't remember it.

Chris ejected the DVD and shoved it in the waistband at the back of his pants. He worked faster now as he found another disc and labeled it the same as the one he took. He spun the cabinet around once again and placed the dummy case in the slot where he'd removed the video of Preston and himself.

The cabinet clicked into place right before Chris heard voices in the hall. A frantic search showed him a door on the other side of the room. He hit the lights as he went by and slipped inside what appeared to be a closet. The door to the hall opened as he closed the closet door. Chris shut his eyes and steadied his breathing as he tried to determine where he was. He was afraid to move for fear he might knock something over. As he heard the lights click on and the voices outside, he reached in his pocket and flicked his lighter. It was enough to show him what he had stepped inside was no closet, it was a staircase. He smiled. It looked as if he might have an escape route after all.

Chris relaxed and decided to listen. He heard Thea's voice and the deeper tones of her husband. Although their conversation was muffled, the words they spoke were easy enough to understand. They were making no effort to hide what they were discussing, so they must have believed they were alone.

"The Lieberman girl is already about half in the bag. Another drink or two and she'll be ready to go upstairs," Thea commented.

"That's fine, but I think you need to target someone other than Stevenson this time," her husband warned. "The guy's changed in the past year."

"Once a drunk, always a drunk, darling," she purred. "You have to admit, he's hung, and he screws like a porn star…even when he's drugged and doesn't know what he's doing."

Chris felt the bile rise in his throat.

"I think we need to be careful. I haven't had a response from the package we sent to Barrett's office."

Oh my God! They'd sent a copy to Anna's father?

"Seth Barrett won't sit on it long. He's not stupid."

Chris almost sighed out loud in relief. Still bad, but at least the video had gone to the brother, not her father. A new concern though. They'd copied the video. How many were there?

"The original is on the shelf," DuQuesne said, "We can still make more copies if we need to. Cash is getting tight. Let's hope Barrett transfers the money soon because we can't afford to sit on it any longer. We could hit Stevenson, but not for the two mill we asked Barrett for."

Chris felt the hard plastic of the DVD case press against the small of his back. They wouldn't get a damn dime, and he'd make sure of it. With the other videos in that cabinet, it wouldn't take long for the cops to make mincemeat of Thea and Ray DuQuesne. Chris had heard what he needed to. Now all he wanted to do was get away. He put his foot on the first step with care. No tell-tale creak, so he climbed the darkened stairwell. It seemed to go on forever before he reached a door at the top that opened on a small room with a large window overlooking another bedroom. Chris curled his lip in disgust. A freaking viewing room. This was fucking sick. Another door and he found himself standing in an upstairs hallway. It was deserted. How the hell was he going to get himself and the DVD out of the house?

Once a drunk, always a drunk? That's what Thea seemed to think. Hell, he would fit the image they already expected. He pulled his shirt tail from his pants to cover the DVD case, undid a couple of buttons on it and mussed his hair. He practiced stumbling a bit as he'd seen himself do on the tape and weaved along the hall. He smiled like he was drunk at whomever he met and lurched toward the pool area.

The pool was crowded with people in various states of dress and undress. Quite a few were already naked, and Chris wasn't quite sure, but he would swear there was at least one couple having sex at the opposite end of the pool near the diving board. He turned his head and edged toward the gate at the corner of the house. How many times would he have been right there with them?

Once outside in the darkness, he sprinted down the drive to his dad's Volvo. As he reached the side of the car, he stopped, bent over and threw up. He'd never felt so vile in his entire life. As violated as he felt, he could only imagine how Anna might react. He never paused as he tossed the DVD on the passenger seat and put the car in gear.

When he closed the door to his hotel room, it was near midnight. He set the video on the bureau and grabbed a soft drink from the refrigerator.

God, he needed a cigarette. He heard a quiet knock on the hall door, right after he'd taken the first puff.

"Son?" His father's muffled voice came through the door.

Chris opened the panel to his dad who took one look at his face and wrapped Chris in a tight hug. The two men separated and David closed the door.

"I take it you found what you were looking for?"

Chris jerked his head toward the flat case on the bureau. "Yeah. I'm pretty sure it's the original, but I wasn't in time."

"What do you mean?"

Chris relayed the entire story without elaborating on what was on the video. He couldn't talk about that. Some things remained too private, too painful. The scenes on the disc kept replaying in his head the whole way home. It hadn't taken him long to realize something else about what was on that DVD. Preston Anna Barlow-Barrett had been a virgin. He'd taken her in a drunken stupor and she'd never even been with a man before.

Realizing that also led him to the next logical step. Becca was his. And that released a whole boatload of what-the-fucks. How could Anna have kept that a secret? Why hadn't she let him know she was pregnant? He shook his head. Yeah, as if she'd want him anywhere near her. The question wasn't why she hadn't, it was why she would let him know.

"Son," David began quietly. "Did you have sex with Anna?"

Chris frowned and nodded. "Yes. It's on the video."

David pursed his lips as he absorbed that. "What about Becca? You think she's your child?"

For an instant, Chris wished his dad would tell him everything was all right, but that was the trouble with deciding to grow up. Chris would have to find his own way through this mess.

"Yes. There's no doubt. Becca is my child, your grandchild, but I don't know that Anna will ever admit that."

"You could force the issue."

Chris shook his head. "That's not why I did this."

David nodded again and stood. He squeezed Chris's shoulder. "Your mother would like to start home around lunchtime tomorrow. Suit you?"

"Sure."

Chris stared at the DVD for a long time after his father left, rubbing the spot where his dad had touched his shoulder. At last he picked up the case and opened it. With methodical precision, he removed the disc, snapped it in two and broke those pieces once again. No one would ever see it.

He didn't care if it might be evidence. The police could get evidence from some other videos, but not this one. No one else would see this. In his heart, though, he knew his intervention came too late. A copy had already gone to Anna's brother. Surely there were no other copies. Thea and Ray wanted the videos for blackmail purposes. Chances were they only made a copy for their intended target. Maybe Anna wouldn't see it. Ever.

Chapter 11

Seth Barlow-Barrett was not an easy man. In fact, many people who faced him across a negotiating table described him as a Class A bastard who made his father look like a blessed saint. Most of them would pay to see Brandon walk through the door instead of him. Hell, Seth would pay to let Brandon do just that. Seth knew what people thought, and he didn't care. He was who his father had molded him to be. He had taken over Barrett Newspapers four years out of college. Most of those years, he'd traveled the world as a freelance writer. Seth Barlow, as he'd called himself, had covered every political hotspot from Central America to the Middle East, and he had a few scars to prove it.

There was but one soft spot in the armor he'd built around himself. Anna. He and Brandon were the only ones who ever called her that, yet that was the name she now chose to use. He smiled. Little Anna. So different from the rest of them, yet she alone embodied what he'd always felt inside. She was his heart, and he would do anything to protect her.

Now he sat at his desk at the top of the steel and glass monument to Barrett Newspapers snapping pencil after pencil in frustration. Monday morning already, and so far the detectives hadn't given him much to go on.

"Mr. Barrett?" The new secretary's smooth voice came through the intercom.

"What?" he snapped. "I thought I told you I was not to be disturbed this morning!"

The door opened and a slender redhead walked in.

"What the hell is it, Teresa?"

"Tessa," she corrected him. "It's Tessa, sir."

"Whatever."

"You have a visitor, and I think you'll wish to see him."

"Someone gave you permission to think?" Seth provoked her. He knew it. He enjoyed it. That was one of the reasons most of his secretaries didn't last more than a few months, if that. This one tilted her head and glared at him with ice-cold blue eyes.

"His name is Chris Stevenson. He told me he wished to see you about Anna."

Seth stood. He towered over the secretary, but she didn't give ground.

"Why the hell didn't you say so?" he growled.

"Because you didn't give me a chance?" she suggested.

Seth glared at her. She glared back.

"Show him in."

She smiled. "Right away, Mr. Barrett. Shall I bring you both coffee?"

"No, but you might want to have the first aid kit handy." He allowed himself a small smile of satisfaction when he saw he'd rattled her at last.

Chris had just shut the door behind him when he turned and found himself on the receiving end of a punch that snapped his head back and bloodied his nose in one smooth, efficient motion.

"Bastard!" Seth Barrett snarled. "How dare you touch my sister?"

He swung again, but Stevenson dodged the punch with reflexes as quick as a cat's.

"Stop, Barrett!" the smaller man snapped. "I don't want Anna or Becca hurt. I have information that'll help, and I could use your help too."

Seth lowered his fist and tucked his shirt in his pants before straightening his tie.

"Have a seat." Barrett growled and glared at Chris. "Talk. You have five minutes to explain to me why the fuck I should help you before I beat the bloody hell out of you, Stevenson."

He listened in stony silence as Stevenson relayed how he'd met Anna and Becca, and the nagging feeling of recognition he hadn't been able to shake. Seth nodded his head when Chris talked about Anna's reluctance to mention her family.

"She's mentioned you and Brandon. She said you were the only family members to come to her graduation from vet school--that you and Brandon acknowledged Becca, but no one else did."

Seth scowled, but remained silent. He would not air his family's dirty laundry to anyone.

"I decided I had to go to Upperville because everything seemed to center around that party a year ago. I couldn't remember anything about it. I still don't."

Stevenson closed his eyes for a moment in pain. Seth wasn't sure if the obvious look of pain was from his swelling nose, or something else. At any rate, he punched the intercom button.

"Tessa?" he enunciated with added emphasis on the secretary's name. "Please bring two cups of coffee, and a bag of ice. Oh, you better bring the first aid kit too."

"Yes, sir."

Stevenson waited until the secretary came and went. Seth noticed Tessa didn't show any surprise upon seeing the bloody handkerchief the younger man held to his nose. She handed him an ice pack with the same expression she might have worn had she given him a letter to sign.

Seth had to smother a smile. Maybe personnel had at long last found someone able to cope with the job of being his secretary.

"Thanks, Tessa. That will be all."

"Yes, sir, Mr. Barrett." The door snicked shut behind her and Seth swung his gaze to Stevenson.

"Continue."

He listened with increasing interest as Stevenson described the party at the DuQuesne mansion. How he had located the theatre and stumbled on the stash of videos.

"There are more?"

Stevenson nodded and winced. "Ten years' worth, labeled by initials and years. They've turned this into quite a business from what I can tell. I can't believe they've gotten away with it for this long."

"You found the one of you and Anna?" At Stevenson's nod, Seth fired back, "Where is it?"

"I destroyed it," Chris answered.

"It's evidence, man."

"I don't care. No one," he growled, "no one will ever see that video. What I want to know, Barrett, is where is the copy DuQuesne said they sent you?"

"In my safe."

"Destroy it."

"Listen, Stevenson, no one comes in my office and tells me what to do. And no one tells me what to do when it comes to Anna."

Chris Stevenson stood, his gray eyes icy. "I do! Destroy it."

Seth drew back his fist again, but Stevenson wasn't about to back down and faced him without flinching.

"Don't be a fool, Barrett. All we have to do is get the cops to search that place, and there's more than enough evidence without anyone ever seeing Anna. We don't need to expose her to this."

"Don't you mean there's more than enough evidence without your bare ass being exposed as the rapist you are?" Seth spit the words with contempt. He felt a surge of satisfaction as Stevenson's face paled and his gaze fell.

"I'm not the issue here," he said. "I don't care what happens to me. If you or Anna wants to press charges, so be it. I'm a big boy. I don't want her or Becca hurt. All I came here for was to get your help. If you want to have me arrested, fine, but don't hurt Anna to do it."

Something in Stevenson's tone penetrated Seth's anger. He narrowed his eyes to slits as he studied the other man. He looked haunted.

"What's between you and Anna?" Seth inquired.

Chris closed his eyes an instant, then sighed. "A week ago, I would have told you we were friends, maybe even dating in a casual way. Now I'm not sure what to say."

"The baby's yours, you know," Seth inserted.

"I know."

"What do you intend to do about it?" Part of him hoped Stevenson would show himself to be the bastard he was, but another part of him hoped Anna's faith was justified.

"I want to marry your sister, Barrett. If she'll have me."

Seth nodded. Right answer. "Let me call a friend of mine at the FBI. He owes me a couple of favors, so now is as good a time as any to call one in."

* * * *

Chris and Seth Barrett came to an understanding. Both men sat inside Barrett's black Cadillac Escalade and watched from the end of the DuQuesne driveway as the FBI and local officers raided the mansion later that day. Thea and Ray were led out in handcuffs, followed by agents carrying box after box of tapes, DVDs, files and even the couple's computers.

"Thank you," Chris murmured to the man sitting next to him in the driver's seat. "Thank you."

Seth nodded, his jaw tight. "I'm doing this for Anna, Stevenson, not you, but I owe you my thanks. You were the one who discovered who was behind it. I wish Anna hadn't seen it."

Fuck! Cold seeped through Chris's veins. "Anna's seen the video?"

Seth nodded. "I had to know what she knew about it."

Chris pressed the heels of his palms to his eyes and grimaced from the pain in his nose and in his heart. Anna had seen what he'd done. Hell, she must have known all along what he'd done if she knew he was Becca's father. Chris wondered if he would ever be free of the crushing weight of guilt.

"I need to get on the road."

"Stevenson?"

Chris turned and locked glances with Seth Barrett's narrowed golden eyes.

"What, Barrett?"

"If you hurt my sister again, God can't save you," he vowed in such a quiet, even tone, Chris knew Seth meant every word.

The drive from Upperville to Fincastle Farm was long with plenty of opportunity to think. He'd told his parents to go on without him, so he'd rented a car to drive. Now he sure as hell wished he had his dad's company. David had always given him sound advice. Several times, Chris started to call Anna on his cellphone, but what could he say to her?

Hi, Anna, I know I raped you and didn't remember it, but I was drunk and drugged. Say, would you marry me so we can give our child a name?

Or better yet, You sure do look a lot better now than you did a year ago when I took your virginity! Sorry I can't remember you from that night. Can we start again?

Chris left his cellphone on the seat next to him.

He pulled the rental car into his driveway and parked next to the BMW just before midnight. He was bone-tired and knew he looked like hell. His eyes were starting to blacken, and he wondered, not for the first time, if Seth Barrett had broken his nose.

The phone rang early the next morning.

"Stevenson," he mumbled, still groggy from the pain pill he'd taken in the middle of the night.

One of the grooms was on the line. "Mr. Stevenson, Dr. Douglas is here doing the pregnancy checks on the mares. He'd like you to come to the barn."

Chris shook his head to clear it and regretted the action as it set his nose to throbbing.

"Tell him I'll be there in five minutes."

He didn't bother to shave, just threw on clothes and shoved his feet inside a pair of muck boots.

"Jesus!" Jim Douglas exclaimed when he saw him. "What happened to you? Fall off a horse or get kicked by one?"

Chris was about to reply when he saw Anna step from behind the other side of the mare. She gasped and put a shaky hand to her mouth.

"Oh, Chris--I mean, Mr. Stevenson."

Chris studied her, but didn't sense any fear or revulsion coming from her. He had no idea at the moment what to say to her. As he turned to Jim Douglas, he saw her expression go blank.

"I was at the wrong end of a fist."

"From the size of those shiners, boy, I'd say you ended up on the wrong side of a large fist."

"He packed a mean punch," Chris agreed, hoping everyone would let the subject drop.

"H--have you had anyone look at it?" Anna inquired.

"No," Chris replied, cringing as he realized how harsh his voice sounded.

Now he saw emotion in those blue eyes. Irritation and anger.

"I'm sorry. I got in late last night, and I'm not at my best this morning, as you can see," Chris sighed. "What did you need to see me about, Jim?" he asked as he turned to the older vet.

Chris loved the mare, but so far she hadn't settled.

"Your mare here's showing up on the ultrasound as pregnant--that's the good news. The bad news is she appears to be carrying twins."

"Can you pinch one of them off?" Chris asked.

Jim Douglas shook his head. "We can try, but I wanted your go ahead first. There's still a good possibility both foals will be non-viable."

"Can she carry them both?" Chris asked, stroking the mare's chestnut head.

"It's unlikely both, or even one, will live if we don't pinch one. There's also a risk you'll lose her."

"The question we have," Anna put in, "is if you want to let her try to carry the one or if you want us to pinch them both."

Chris stared hard at Anna. "I think you already know the answer to that, Dr. Barlow."

To his surprise, she smiled. "Yes, I do. Well," she continued, "we'll take care of it after we finish checking the rest of the mares. You'll want to keep her in a paddock on her own. It would be better if she didn't roughhouse with the other horses. If you show me where you want her, I'll take her while Sergio brings the next mare for Dr. Douglas."

Chris walked with her as she led the chestnut mare behind her. Once they turned the corner of the barn outside the door and outside the line of anyone else's vision, they halted, and Anna looked as awkward as he felt.

"Anna..." he began.

"Are you okay?" she asked.

They stopped and stared at each other. Chris swallowed, feeling nervous around her as he hadn't before. The timing wasn't right for what he had to say, but Chris wasn't sure there would be a right time. He blurted, "Anna, would you marry me?"

"What?"

That wasn't the reaction he'd hoped to get. "I asked you to marry me. I would be a good father to Becca, and you and I are well-suited to each other."

"Well-suited?" she questioned.

"We get along all right," Chris blundered on, feeling he was making a mess of things but not knowing how to fix it. "And you have to admit, there is quite a bit of passion there too."

"Passion." Anna moved off with the horse again. Chris walked ahead of her to open the gate to the paddock. After unsnapping the lead and turning the mare loose, she walked from the paddock and waited for Chris to close the gate.

"Let me see if I understand you correctly. You want to marry me because you would make Becca a good father, we're well-suited and have excellent sexual rapport. Does that about cover it?"

He had such a bad feeling about this. His head throbbed without mercy, and he knew there was a lot he had left out, but he said, "Yes, that covers it."

"Then no thank you, Mr. Stevenson, I don't believe I'm interested."

"What?"

Anna poked him in the chest and glared at him. "I said, you insufferable, conceited ass... I. Am. Not. Interested."

"Anna! We would be good together," he protested as his head throbbed in earnest.

She spun on him, her blue eyes shooting sparks and spots of color staining her cheeks. "I will not marry a man to supply Becca with a father. I've seen how much fathers can help you through life. I will not marry someone because we 'would be good together.' And I will not marry someone who loves himself far better than he loves anyone else. When I marry, if I marry, it will be to someone who loves me and wants me, not someone who thinks I'm 'well-suited' to be his wife."

Well. Fuck. Chris watched as she spun on her heel and walked off, leaving him standing with the lead shank in a heap at his feet where she'd tossed it. He couldn't have blown that any more if he'd tried.

He bent to grab the lead, setting off a whole new meaning to the word throb as blood rushed into his bruised and swollen nose.

"Damn!" He blinked tears from his eyes. The tears were because his head hurt. He was not about to cry because one small, dark-haired woman had royally dressed him down.

Chapter 12

Anna fumed the rest of the day. How dare Chris propose marriage like that. He would make Becca a good father. Didn't the idiot see he was Becca's father? She resembled him more and more every day. And why couldn't he remember that night? She did. She remembered everything about it. The bad and the good. Why didn't he? Had she meant so little to him? Preston Anna Barlow-Barrett, just another fuck in a long list of sexual escapades by playboy show jumper Chris Stevenson. The questions circled through her brain without end.

Anna rubbed her eyes. Becca had fallen asleep hours earlier. With a sigh, she stood and opened her photo album again. She made herself look once more at the picture of her and Chris taken at the party in Upperville.

She made herself relive what had happened.

She should have been suspicious from the start when Olivia called, inviting her to come along with some of her other friends to the party at the DuQuesnes's. She and Olivia had never been close in school, and although Olivia had never involved herself in any of the teasing Anna received, she had associated with the same crowd.

But Anna had been desperate to escape. She had wanted to do something besides slip around the house trying to avoid her parents.

Her last year of vet school had been a few weeks away from starting. She had been working the summer with a local veterinarian and living at home. That had been a mistake. All summer, she had been on the receiving end of nothing but criticism from the moment she walked in the door.

Seth and Brandon had long since moved out, so they were no longer there to act as a buffer. Anna had agreed to the invitation from Olivia to get away from her parents. Maybe if they thought she had a social life, they would back off.

She had taken pains with her appearance, working extra hard to straighten the curls that kept wanting to pop up in her blonde-streaked hair. She had decided to put on makeup, something she didn't do often because she felt it made her look like a stunted Barbie doll, especially with the big boobs, tiny waist, and generous hips she couldn't seem to get rid of. Anna had hated her figure. In a house full of svelte, lissome blonds, Anna had always stuck out like a serving wench amidst the ladies of the manor.

After vet school was over, she had promised herself, she would go on a diet. One more year before she escaped. She'd already applied to have the name on her degree read "Dr. Anna Barlow." She wanted to make it on her own, like Seth, not as Preston Barrett, Alexander Barlow-Barrett's homely daughter.

She had arrived at the party later than she'd intended. Cars were parked not only in the drive, but along the narrow country road, where she was forced to park, so she had already felt sweaty and disheveled by the time she reached the door. Several minutes passed before she found anyone she knew.

Anna remembered Thea DuQuesne laughing with Olivia and the rest of the crowd and handing her a drink.

"Here, darling, try this. I'm sure you'll like it! And it will do wonders to get that flush off your face from your hike here."

Anna had sipped it with care. She didn't drink much alcohol. Besides being too paranoid about those empty calories, Anna had never developed a tolerance for it. To her relief, the drink had been sweet and didn't taste alcoholic. She had smiled at the older woman and taken a big swallow. Everyone had seemed friendly, so Anna had begun to relax. Maybe this hadn't been such a bad idea.

"Hey, Preston!" Olivia had cooed. "You remember that crush you've always had on Chris Stevenson?"

Anna had felt herself flush under the foundation she wore. Her worship of Chris Stevenson had been the source for a lot of practical jokes. Her laughter held an edge of brittleness. "That was ages ago, Olivia. I'm surprised you even remember that."

"He's here tonight, and he's a free man."

Anna had felt her heart flutter. The last she had read, Chris and Sydney Wallace were an item that looked to become permanent.

"Would you like to meet him?" someone else had asked. Yet another person had pressed a second drink into her hand, and Anna had sipped it too. Meet Chris Stevenson? She coughed as she swallowed more than she had intended. She had wiped at her eyes, forgetting she had mascara on, and then had to run a finger along her lower lid, hoping she hadn't made dark smudges beneath her eyes.

"So this is Preston Barrett."

Anna had turned. Though her heart had pounded, she'd already seen the polite disinterest on his face. Not his type, she had filled in the thought for him: too short, too fat, too plebian. He had already looked about half loaded. Must've been tying one on after the break-up her friends had been more than happy to tell her about.

"So this is Chris Stevenson," Preston replied in the same cool tone, and dismissed him as he had done her.

To her surprise, he'd laughed and put his arm around her shoulders. "A pleasure to meet you, Preston. What a wonderful mimic you are!"

She had giggled then clapped a hand over her mouth. Her mother was always getting on her about laughing too loudly or too freely. Imitating other people was a talent Brandon had helped her develop as a child. He and Seth had always found it funny, and sometimes it helped ease the pain of always being the kid no one wanted on their team because she was rotten at sports.

Anna and Chris had begun talking. He was smart and funny, she realized, not stuck-up as she'd always imagined. Although he was older than she was used to, Anna had found herself more and more attracted to him, not because of an adolescent hero worship, but because he had seemed genuine and nice. They had laughed together. Someone had supplied them with more drinks. She seemed to have a fresh one in her hand all the time.

Anna's memories grew hazy at that point. She remembered struggling to stay awake. Chris had excused himself to go to the bathroom, and Anna had started to droop. As if through a fog, she remembered everyone laughing and someone grunting as they hoisted her like a sack of potatoes over someone else's shoulder.

Hands. She remembered protesting that she needed to get home, and someone saying, "Sleep it off, Preston. We promise you'll feel a whole lot better in the morning." More laughter.

Had she fallen asleep?

The next thing she remembered were kisses. Passionate, but rough. She had awakened to more hands, but this time on her breasts and hips. Her eyes had snapped open and she'd found herself staring into Chris's face. His expression had been intent as if it'd taken his complete concentration to touch her.

Anna had recoiled.

"No!" she'd protested. "What are you doing?"

"Relax. Enjoy it," he'd mumbled.

But how was she supposed to enjoy something that had twisted a dream into a nightmare? This wasn't the fantasy she'd spun, lying in her bed alone while she stared at pictures of him on her wall.

"Preston?" He touched her cheek, but she jerked away.

"Get off me!" she'd sobbed, trying to wriggle from beneath him. What had she done?

"Easy, sweetheart," he'd tried to soothe her. "You were wonderful. I'm sorry I didn't know it was your first time. Relax."

Part of her had recoiled at what had happened, but another part rejoiced. She, Preston Anna Barlow-Barrett, had given a man like Chris pleasure. The feeling had been short-lived. As soon as he'd eased out of her, she'd felt cold and cheap. She'd turned onto her side and curled into a ball.

"I'm sorry," he'd mumbled, breaking the silence a few minutes later. "I didn't know you were here, and then…there you were."

"It's okay," Anna had told him, sitting and pulling the sheet to her chin.

Chris turned. "No, it's not."

He'd touched her with incredible gentleness, caressing her cheek and brushing the hair from her eyes. He'd told her what beautiful eyes she had, as blue as a mountain lake. He'd kissed her this time, with a controlled passion that soon had them gasping for air and looking at each other in surprise.

This time he'd made love to her. He'd taught her how to touch him, making her senses leap with pleasure when he'd moaned in response to her caresses. They'd come together several times throughout the night, but as time passed, she'd sensed he was not all there. He sipped the beer he'd brought with him, but it didn't seem to help. He'd kept fighting grogginess, shaking his head as if to clear it. He'd fallen asleep so deeply he appeared passed out.

Anna had watched him as he'd lain there. It might not have meant anything to a man like him, but it had to her.

Anna shook her head and realized tears streamed down her face. She threw the picture of Preston Barrett and Chris Stevenson in the photo album and shoved them both in the back of the filing cabinet drawer. Those were people she didn't know, didn't even want to know. Neither of them had been at their best.

Yet Anna had never forgotten that night. She closed her eyes to the cynical thought. Two months later, before returning to Penn State for her final year of vet school, Anna had discovered she was pregnant. She'd told no one at first. But she was having such a hard time with nausea and vomiting. She could keep almost nothing in her stomach, and the weight had begun to drop off. When she'd fainted in one of her labs, she'd had to call Seth and tell him. They were admitting her to the hospital to feed her intravenously. She was alone and more frightened than she'd ever been.

Seth had flown out. She'd already lost twenty pounds. They managed to stabilize her weight, so she was no longer losing pounds, but neither was she gaining any. Everyone had assured her it would be all right.

Seth had shown up at Thanksgiving and brought her home. Anna had protested the entire way. Other than her brothers, she did not want to see the rest of the family. She'd discovered when she'd reached the Barrett compound that her parents didn't want to see her either, and above all else, they didn't want any of their friends seeing that Preston Barrett was obviously pregnant.

As small as she was, Preston had started wearing maternity clothes at the end of September. She had even developed that expectant mom waddle sooner than most women. Seth and Brandon had watched her like hawks, making sure she ate and got enough sleep. Seth even moved back to his old room for Thanksgiving. Anna suspected he'd done it to watch over her.

At Christmas, Brandon stayed at their parents' estate, almost as if they'd flipped a coin on who would take which holiday to temporarily move back home. Her parents had made plain they would be unable to attend her graduation. Anna had looked at them as if they were strangers. In a way, she thought, they were.

At the end of February, she had gone into labor a month before her due date. Brandon had been diving in the Galapagos, but Seth had hopped on board the corporate jet and flown to State College to be there. It had been a long labor and an exhausting delivery. The doctors had been about to do an emergency C-section when she'd at last dilated, and they'd told her to push.

And there was Becca.

She more than made up for the pain, and the months of odd looks coming from family, classmates and professors. Anna touched the picture of Becca she'd had taken this week to show off her growing daughter's new teeth. Her eyes were paler than Anna's now. They seemed to be turning gray, and her hair was all Chris, already that distinctive sandy color.

Anna sighed. She desired nothing more than for them to be a family, but she wanted it to be real, not because Chris decided a suitable marriage was what he needed, and she was a good candidate. Anna wanted love. Was it possible to build on what was already there? Maybe she needed to talk to him. Maybe if they both got everything in the open, they could put the past behind them and discover whether they even had a future together.

Her phone rang the next morning. She checked the caller ID as she picked up.

"Good morning, Seth. Couldn't sleep?"

"I thought vets kept early hours," he teased. "Half the day's already gone."

Anna checked the clock. Seven AM.

"You need to get a life, Seth." She chuckled.

"Tessa," she heard him bark into his intercom. "Where's that coffee?"

"Coming," was the muffled reply even she heard over the phone.

"Chasing off another secretary, brother dear?" Anna inquired.

"Anna," Seth admonished her. "Tessa likes coming in at the crack of dawn."

Anna grunted in reply. "What's up, Seth?"

His tone sobered. "I wanted to call and let you know the little matter of the video is settled, thanks to a tip from a very reliable source. Thea and Ray DuQuesne now face some pretty stiff state and federal charges."

Anna sagged with relief, before she ventured, "What about the original?"

"It's been destroyed," he reassured her.

Anna felt a sudden, almost dizzying lightness. The thought that someone else might see what was on that video had horrified her. In addition to being a hideous invasion of privacy, the video had also been misleading. The DVD had shown only what had happened at first. Though it cast Chris in a despicable light, she had to admit some gladness what they'd shared later hadn't been cheapened by being videoed.

"Who gave you the tip?"

The line was silent for an instant before Seth said, "Let's say someone I had good reason to trust."

Discovering the video was no longer a worry started the day off right. After dropping Becca at daycare, Anna called in to the clinic for her list of farm calls for the day. The clinic secretary gave her a list, which she saw included Pheasant Run.

When Anna pulled into the long, Bradford Pear-lined drive in the afternoon, she was bone-tired. The call at the McCauley's cattle farm had taken longer than anticipated, so she'd been forced to call the clinic to let them know to delay her calls and find someone else to take over a couple of them.

Their trainer met her at the door.

"Good afternoon, Dr. Barlow," he greeted her in his still-thick Scots accent. "We've a couple of new horses in that need routine exams done and new Coggins pulled."

Anna smiled. "No problem."

She gathered supplies.

"Anna!" Wynter Anderson called from behind her. "What a pleasure to see you again."

"Good afternoon, Mrs. Anderson."

"Call me Wynter."

"Sorry. How are you, Wynter?"

"Ready for a vacation," the tall redhead admitted. "Nelson and I are taking the kids to the beach for a couple of weeks. Of course..." Wynter laughed. "I'm not sure how much of a vacation that is."

"I know what you mean. Becca cut her first two teeth last week and I thought I would never get any sleep, she was so fussy."

Wynter walked beside her as they entered the barn. They stopped at the first two stalls. "These are the newbies here. We try to keep them right up front and separated until we know they've got a clean bill of health. Of course, these guys should be fine. They came over from Fincastle. Chris dropped them off on his way out of town."

Anna's heart stopped. "Out of town?"

Wynter laughed. "Yep, I guess he couldn't stand the inactivity. He loaded his gelding and the mare he bought from us and said he was going to catch the rest of the shows in the Northeast."

Anna felt a strange sense of loss and hurt. The man asked her to marry him yesterday, and now he'd up and left town? The fact she'd turned him down flat didn't seem to matter in her mind. Somehow, it just seemed like Chris living up to his old reputation. He'd asked, she'd told him no and that was it, he was gone and once more on the show circuit.

"How long is he going to be gone?" Anna inquired, trying to keep her tone casual.

"Sounded as if he plans to stay a couple of months at least."

Anna worked on autopilot as she tried to absorb that bomb, examining each horse and getting the blood samples she needed for the Coggins tests.

Months, not weeks. She bit on her lower lip. He hadn't even seen Becca's new teeth, she thought incongruously.

Chapter 13

The drive to New York gave Chris plenty of time to think before he reached Lake Placid. Anna's words kept beating like a hammer in his brain. When I marry, if I marry, it will be to someone who loves me and wants me, not someone who thinks I'm "well-suited".

Chris ground his teeth in frustration. His father was right. Getting through those rough spots took more than being a good, logical match. Anna, it seemed, already understood that and wouldn't accept anything less than a man who loved her.

Chris rubbed his temples as he entered the showgrounds. Thanks to a couple conversations by cellphone as he drove, he'd managed to get both the gelding and Bittersweet in as late entries. Of course, his stall placement wasn't the best as a last minute entry, and even being Chris Stevenson hadn't been able to change that.

He should feel more excitement. Something instead of…weariness.

Chris decided to take Bittersweet in the Schooling Jumper division; the gelding would do several of the stakes in the Open Jumpers. His assistant trainer met him when he arrived to show him where the stalls were located. A groom was there to get the two horses settled.

After handing off the horses, Chris walked around the showgrounds, greeting people he knew, but he was still distracted. The feeling of excitement he'd once experienced when he competed was missing. It was no longer fun. Even winning had become routine. It was business, a job.

As he tried to immerse himself in the world that had once been at the center of his existence, random thoughts popped into his mind. Really nothing more than feelings. The feel of a snugly diapered bottom resting on his hand and baby hands patting his cheeks. The sight of tousled dark curls and the slender column of a neck, the deepest blue eyes he'd ever seen, surrounded by long, sooty lashes needing no makeup to enhance them. Anna, asleep on his parents' porch as Becca nursed at her breast.

That memory alone was almost enough to make him get in the truck and hurry home. Why had he left?

But Anna didn't want him. She'd called him an insufferable, conceited ass. Did he truly appear to love himself more than anyone else? He mulled the thought over and over during the next several days. He refused invitations to parties. He threw a horse blanket over one groupie who had decided showing up nude in his tack room might be the way to reach him. The pool at the hotel offered some relief if he hit it at odd hours when he could swim, or when the only people around seemed to be moms and their kids, but that had its own set of drawbacks.

From behind dark sunglasses, he watched the mothers with their children. He'd never paid much attention to kids or babies. He now saw how each of them, no matter how young, was already developing a distinct personality. As he sat in New York, he would miss those changes with Becca and miss sharing them with Anna.

Chris grabbed his towel and his key card and climbed the stairs to his room. He didn't want to call her. He was afraid she would hang up on him because it seemed to him every time he opened his mouth around her, what he wanted to say came out wrong. He dropped his glance to the hotel stationery lying on the desk. Maybe he should write to her. It sounded old-fashioned enough he almost convinced himself otherwise, but after a couple false starts, the words flowed. Without stopping to think, he folded the pages, sealed them in an envelope and sent the letter inside another envelope to his dad since he didn't know Anna's address. God, he hoped she wouldn't think he was an idiot.

If nothing else, writing the letter had made him feel better, and an improved mood helped in the show ring. Morning shadows lay long across the ground as he warmed Bittersweet up. She was spooky to begin with, taking in the sights and sounds of a busy showground with wide eyes, but as the week went on, the level-headedness he'd noticed in her from the beginning came to the fore, and she settled in like the pro he knew she'd become. Domino, his gelding, was his usual workmanlike self. He would never have the pizzazz of a Grand Prix star but always managed to be in the money somewhere and had racked up some pretty decent earnings over the years.

Between rides, Chris checked on some of his students, glad to see they were in the ribbons under the tutelage of his assistant trainer. Chris smiled as he watched one of the pony jumpers. She was the rider whose chaps Anna had borrowed, and he'd had to make the waist smaller. He shook his head. Amazing how much woman was packed inside such a tiny frame.

"What's funny?" Chris turned to find Danny Adams, his trainer, standing at his elbow.

"Thinking about the new vet at Redfield," Chris replied.

"The girl?" Danny asked. "Haven't met her yet, but someone told me she was pretty sharp. One of those big, horse-faced girls, huh?"

Chris stared at Danny for an instant, then burst out laughing. "Not hardly. She borrowed Sara's chaps to ride with me."

Danny laughed. "Okay, a tiny, horse-faced girl."

Chris smiled. A picture of Anna came to mind. "Not horse-faced either, Danny. Anna has black hair, eyes as blue as the ocean, skin like fine porcelain and the most kissable lips." He trailed off in embarrassment when he saw the way his trainer eyed him in open-mouthed astonishment.

"You sleeping with her?" Danny asked.

Chris's jaw tightened. "She's not like that. And it's none of your business."

"I heard she had a kid, never been married," the trainer supplied as if that were a brand identifying her as a crazed nympho ready to put out for anything with a penis. And where they were from, Chris realized, people would think less of her.

Chris's hands tightened on the rail of the ring. Only the many years he'd known Danny prevented him from spinning on the man and decking him. Damn. Gossip sure made the rounds fast, and it appeared Anna had already become a target of it.

"Becca. The baby's name is Becca." He paused and took a deep breath. "And if you're going to think less of Anna, then put me down for some of that criticism too. Becca's my daughter." God damn, that felt good to say.

Danny squinted at Chris and held his hands in front of him. "No shit? I'll be damned."

Chris stared at the ring, not paying attention as more riders completed their rounds. Did people really say such things about Anna? Did they think she was cheap? He swallowed the thick knot in his throat. Was that what he had set her up to face because of one shared night? He'd left her alone to face things by herself. A small, angry voice in the back of his mind whispered, "But I didn't know. I would have stood by her if she had told me." Why wouldn't she tell him? Had what he'd done to her been so awful? The conclusion he reached left him feeling half sick.

* * * *

Late Saturday afternoon, Anna and Becca were in the backyard, where she was curled on a platform rocker reading, while Becca gurgled and played with some toys on a blanket Anna had laid on the grass.

"Anna?"

At the sound of the deep voice, she nearly jumped out of her skin. For a moment, it reminded her so much of Chris she thought she'd brought him to life from her thoughts. She wasn't concentrating on her reading. She sat up and spun around. Chris's father stood a few feet away at the corner of the house.

"Hi, Mr. Stevenson. What brings you here? Would you like a glass of tea?" Anna knew she babbled, but he was the last person she would have expected, with the exception maybe of his son.

He smiled at her. "No thanks. I just stopped by to bring you this."

Anna tilted her head and gave him a smile, puzzled. "A letter?"

"It's from Chris. He wasn't sure of your address, so he sent it to our house with a note asking me to bring it to you."

Anna took the envelope and stared at it. She swallowed around a lump in her throat. He had written her? She blinked and blinked again. Curiosity and fear mixed together as she held the thick hotel vellum between her fingers. Did people write letters anymore in this age of cellphones and email?

"Anna?"

She looked at David, who had a sheepish look on his tanned face. "Do you mind if I visit with Becca? I love kids," he added as an explanation.

Anna smiled as she continued to glance at the envelope in her hands, not paying much attention to the tension on the older man's face. "Go right ahead," she murmured as she ran her fingers over the envelope. "She has two new teeth, if you can get her to smile at you."

She itched to open the envelope, but smoothed her hand over it as she glanced up. When David stretched on the grass with the baby and played with her, Anna laughed and watched for a few minutes, but the envelope grew heavier and heavier with the weight of her curiosity. She could stand it no longer. She slipped one finger along the edge to break the seal and pulled two pages of Chris's scrawl from inside.

Dear Anna--

I'm sorry we didn't part on better terms. You said some things at the time I thought were pretty harsh, but I think I know why now. I couldn't seem to put into words what I wanted to say to you, and to be honest, my head hurt like hell and it came out badly all the way around. I felt like a freaking idiot, as if I was some tongue-tied high school kid. So, yeah, I'm sorry for that.

There were a lot of things I needed to tell you, and didn't. Things I still need to tell you.

The first bombshell. I know about Becca.

Anna dropped the letter in her lap as if she'd been burned. Her heart skipped a beat and her throat closed, making her almost breathless with panic. She must have made a sound, because David looked at her. "Are you all right, Anna?"

She nodded and made herself pick the letter up. Was he going to demand custody? Was that what this was about? She shook her head. No, not his style--but it certainly put his marriage proposal in a different light.

I kept thinking I knew you, but I couldn't remember from where. I tore apart my office looking at old issues of The Journal and anything else I got my hands on, but I never found any mention of you or a picture of you anywhere.

There was one blank spot in my mind, a night I didn't remember and still don't, but in a sense, it was also a night I never forgot. Deep inside me, I think I knew something happened that night, and it changed me, Anna.

Last year at a party at Thea DuQuesne's my world shifted. I just didn't know why. So I went to Upperville to find out. I had to discover what had happened there. I did. There were plenty of rumors. There always are on the show circuit. I sat with Marcus VanSant because he always seems to know everything, and he seemed keen to bend my ear about this.

Anna cringed. She had never liked VanSant. She knew he did a great job covering horse events, but there always seemed to be a vicious edge to the social columns he wrote. She turned her attention to Chris's letter, her hands shaking.

He'd heard about a video. I know you found out about it, and you've seen it. Shit, Anna. I never would have wanted you to see that for a million years. I went to the DuQuesnes's and I found where they had it stashed. If you never believe me about anything else, I want you to know I found it, sweetheart, and destroyed it. No one will ever see it again.

Last year was a set up. You were the intended victim, I happened to be the "stud" they chose. Given my reputation, I'm sure they figured I wouldn't have a problem with what occurred even if I did happen to remember it.

I don't expect you to forgive me for what I did to you. Why would you? I saw what was on that DVD, but I don't know if I did anything else. I wish I could remember, if only so I would know. If I did anything else to hurt you, all I can do is beg your forgiveness.

I'm sure more than booze was at work that night. Someone, and I don't know if it was the crowd from Loudon or Thea, drugged us. I know how angry and violated I feel right now. I can't even guess how you must have felt...how you must still feel.

Figuring out Becca was a result of that night was the next logical step. I'm sorry you had to face your pregnancy alone. If there's any comfort in this whole thing, it's knowing something as beautiful as Becca came from it.

I get why you wouldn't want to marry me, but please don't shut me out of Becca's life. Hell, I promised myself I wouldn't go into this. I wish I'd told you everything in person, but I can hardly face myself right now, let alone look at you and talk to you about it. I tried to make it better by offering marriage. But I guess I made the offer for all the wrong reasons, and now things are only worse.

I think of you day and night.

Chris.

Anna folded the pages and put them in the envelope. She stood, not sure where she planned to go, and then remained in place, staring off into the fields behind her house. A gentle hand on her shoulder, the warm smell of saddle soap and tobacco--both combined to comfort her.

"Are you okay, Anna?" David's voice was quiet and steady.

Force of habit made her nod before she brought one hand up to wipe her eyes and shook her head no. She wasn't all right. She wasn't sure any of this could ever be made right. Strong arms turned her and held her, comforting her as she had always wished her own father would.

"Do you know?" Anna asked in a muffled voice against David's chest.

"Yes," he replied as he continued to hold her and pat her back with his gentle hands.

"I'm sorry," she choked on a sob. As much as Chris seemed to be assuming all of the guilt, she had a major slice of it to shoulder too. "I didn't want to keep Becca from any of you. I think that's part of the reason I tried to find a job around here, even if I wouldn't admit it to myself."

She rested her head against David's chest. "My parents have never even seen her. They don't want to see her, and I guess I hoped way deep inside, I hoped maybe you would."

* * * *

David's jaw clenched as he stared over her shoulder to the baby lying on the blanket. Anna's last comment was more in the nature of a question. She hoped? How could anyone turn their back on this young woman and a baby as sweet as Becca? David swallowed the lump in his throat as his own eyes clouded for a moment. He crushed Anna to him and closed his eyes. One tear slid along his cheek.

"Anna, I can't think of anything that would make Liz and me happier than to be able to tell the whole world Becca is our grandchild. Liz doesn't know yet. I didn't feel my place is to tell her. That job belongs to you, or Chris, or both of you."

He set Anna away from him and pulled a large white handkerchief from his back pocket. "Wipe your eyes and blow your nose, kiddo, and if you don't mind, I believe I'll have that glass of tea if the offer's still open."

Anna sniffed and smiled at him. "Always."

He spent the afternoon with her. She was a good mother, but not selfish. She was more than willing to watch and let a proud grandpa play with his newly discovered grandchild. As the baby began to get drowsy, he cradled her.

David grinned self-deprecatingly as he rocked Becca. He had always had a reputation of being tough as nails while he was on the show circuit, and there'd be plenty of people who wouldn't believe what he was doing right now.

He looked up to find Anna studying him. When he raised a brow in inquiry, she said, "Thank you."

"For what?" he asked.

"For being the grandfather I would have wanted for my baby."

He tested the word in his mind and smiled. "No matter what, Anna, Becca has a place to belong. You do too."

As the hour grew late, David cuddled Becca and kissed her cheek before handing her to Anna.

"I need to get home. Will you join us for breakfast after church tomorrow?"

Anna hesitated. "Are you sure?"

"Yes. And I leave it to you to think about telling Liz. Remember, she only looks tough on the outside. I know she will be overjoyed to learn she has a grandchild, but I'll leave the telling to you."

* * * *

Anna dressed both herself and Becca with care for church the next morning. Becca wore a pink sundress and a matching bow in her hair. As usual, Anna left the baby's feet bare. Becca had already made it known she did not want anything cramping her style when it came to wiggling her toes. The choice was more difficult for Anna. The new and improved Anna found she liked short skirts, but she didn't want to go to an extreme. She settled on a sundress that hit above the knee.

David and Liz both smiled at her when she arrived at church, but she sensed an added twinkle in David's eye as he moved over to give her room next to them. He even took Becca from her as she settled all of her gear on the pew. In a few minutes, Anna noticed, Liz cradled Becca and let her grab hold of her finger. Anna smiled. Did Chris know how lucky he was to have two such wonderful people for parents? Best of all, they were Becca's grandparents, by blood and by choice.

After church, the priest once again reminded Anna that she needed to have Becca christened. She smiled at him.

"Not yet, but soon. Okay?"

The priest shrugged and nodded.

Anna followed the Stevensons to Fincastle. As she drove past the main barn, she thought of Chris. A wave of longing shafted through her so strongly it was almost painful. Did he not remember how he had loved her that night?

When they reached the house, David came over to her SUV to help. Anna looked at him and arched a brow. "Would you take Becca? I want to talk to your wife."

David squeezed her shoulder.

"Liz, sweetheart," he called, "why don't you take Anna onto the side porch. I'll take Becca inside and get her fed and changed."

His wife slanted him an odd look, but smiled and led the way around to the porch. Anna remembered Chris standing near the railing, his eyes averted, as he waited for her to cover herself after nursing Becca. She had sensed the longing in him, but had written it off as masculine curiosity about a process he couldn't share.

"Have a seat, Anna," Liz invited. "I have always loved this porch. It's my own private retreat. David added the honeysuckle vines after Chris's sister was born."

Anna blinked in surprise. "I thought Chris was an only child?"

Liz smiled with just a trace of sadness. "Constance was premature. She lived just a few days."

Anna's eyes widened and filled with sudden tears. "I'm sorry."

"David was away when I went into labor. I endured a tough delivery and the doctors warned us not to have any more children after that. We were devastated. We love kids and we had dreamed of a large family." Liz paused, glancing around her. "That was part of the reason David built me this house. We had hoped to fill it to the brim with children."

Anna looked at Liz with new respect. There was no bitterness in her voice, just nostalgia and an acceptance of what life had given her. Liz watched Anna. "Now that job is up to Chris."

Anna tilted her head and gazed at Liz's gentle expression. With a flash of insight, she asked, "You already know, don't you?"

Liz chuckled and patted the space next to her on the bench swing. "Sit, Anna." She waited until Anna had settled herself then continued, "I knew almost from the moment I saw your baby in church the first Sunday." At Anna's surprised look, she waved her hand in the air. "Oh I don't know any of the details, but she is the spitting image of Chris when he was her age. I don't know what has gone on between you and my son, or what is going on. If you want to tell me, fine. If you don't, that's all right too, Anna. The relationship between a man and a woman should be private. It is the most intimate relationship in the world, and every couple has to find their own way through it. I get the feeling you and Chris haven't gotten there yet."

Anna shook her head and bit her lower lip, which seemed to want to tremble. "I'm not sure we can."

Liz smiled at her. "You've made a start. You've created a beautiful little girl together, and no matter what, she will always be a bond."

Anna stared at Liz and began in a halting manner, "I want you to know what happened. I need to be able to tell someone. Please don't think badly of me or Chris."

"I would never think any less of you," Liz reassured her. "Remember, Anna, I also spent my share of time around the horse show world. There's nothing you can tell me that will make me think you or Chris are anything but the wonderful, loving people I know. Believe me, I have seen plenty over the years, so whatever you tell me won't shock me."

In slow, painful fits and starts, Anna told her story. She omitted the more intimate details. Those were for her and Chris alone. When she finished, they both sat without speaking for a moment.

"Do you love my son, Anna?"

"I think so, but I don't trust it yet," Anna whispered. "That may sound silly to you, but as a teenager, I had a crush on the rider Chris Stevenson.

I hero-worshiped him. But as a woman, I feel like I'm still trying to figure out who he really is, and separate him from his public image."

Liz nodded. "Fair enough, but you've made a move in the right direction. Your choice to come here to work rather than return home shows me you have a desire to explore what there is between you." Liz stood. "Come on, child, let's eat so I can spend time playing with my granddaughter!"

Chapter 14

Chris hadn't expected a letter from Anna. In fact, after he'd sent his letter, he'd kicked himself twenty times for being a fool. Who wrote letters anymore, for God's sake? Why couldn't he pick up the phone and talk to her like any normal red-blooded American male? Or better yet, talk to her in person instead of blundering through a marriage proposal like some Neanderthal?

He held the envelope with her handwriting on it as if it were a snake. She'd sent it to him in care of the show office at Lake Placid.

"Who's your letter from, Chris?" one of the office workers asked. Chris sensed the curiosity. He was sure they didn't get personal mail for exhibitors often, but he was far from willing to trot out his business.

"A friend," he replied, and turned to go back onto the showgrounds. He would save it. He couldn't open it now, not with classes to get through today. He would read it later, after the day was done.

He thought about it all day. When he put on his show coat, he shoved the envelope inside his breast pocket. He touched his gloved hand to it before taking Bittersweet into the ring. He'd bumped her to higher fences. The mare responded magnificently. She had personality and style on top of the talent. He was quickly realizing Bittersweet was a world-class jumper.

He rode his gelding in a stakes class that night and pocketed several thousand dollars at the end of the evening. On a professional level, it had been a wonderful day. He touched the letter one more time. He thought about waiting until he reached his hotel but couldn't. The showground emptied and the noise in the barn area settled into the peaceful rustlings of horses munching hay or moving around their stalls, with just the occasional burst of music or laughter far from his area. He closed the door on the tack room and exchanged breeches and boots for jeans. Leaving the tail of his dress shirt hanging for comfort, he slipped his bare feet inside worn loafers.

The envelope was in his hand. He licked his dry lips and broke the seal. Nestled between the single page of paper on which Anna's letter was written was a picture of his parents holding a laughing Becca between them. She was waving a rattle in one chubby hand and he saw two perfect teeth peeking at him from behind her lower lip.

Chris touched the picture with one finger, and to his horror a gut-wrenching sob tore through him. Relief, regret, and utter longing to be anywhere but where he was, to be home was behind the outburst.

He set the letter and picture aside as he braced his elbows on his thighs and pressed his head into his hands. His breathing was rapid and shallow as he fought to get control. He still had to read what Anna had written. He raked a hand through his hair and took a deep breath. He was losing it. Chris picked up the letter once again with a hand that shook.

Dear Chris,

I see you every day. Each time I look at Becca's face, I see your hair and, more and more, your eyes. I would never exclude you from her life. You're a part of her, and I hope you'll be an important part of her life. Our baby deserves to have both of us there for her.

I've told you bits and pieces of my childhood. Now that you know about the party, you must know my full name. I don't feel much like Preston Barrett anymore. I had already decided to use the name Anna Barlow before I got pregnant. I wasn't trying to hide. Anyway, it's hard sometimes for people to believe someone born as one of the mighty Barlow-Barrett family can have a life so miserable.

Even I sometimes wonder if I blew it out of proportion. You know, the whole poor little rich girl routine. I hoped when I discovered I was pregnant my parents might change, might be able to accept Becca, even if they wouldn't accept me or what I'd done. But they couldn't. That hurt for a long time, but not anymore.

Your parents are everything I hoped Becca would have in grandparents and, yes, if you've looked at the picture you can see for yourself. They know. Of course you already knew about your father. What you didn't know was that your mother guessed the first time she saw Becca.

They've opened their hearts and their home to both of us, and I can't even begin to tell you how their generosity makes me feel. Other than Seth and Brandon, I've never experienced so much love.

I want you to be a part of Becca's life. I wanted you to see her new teeth in person, but you were already gone, so I'm doing the next best thing and sending you a picture instead.

She signed it, Anna.

Chris stared at the letter. His heart beat like a drum in his chest. She wanted him to be a part of Becca's life. In spite of what he'd done to her, she was willing to share Becca with him. It was a start and more than he had dared hope.

The letter buoyed him for the rest of the week. Monday morning, he pitched in with Danny and the grooms to pack everything and load horses. The next show was two weeks away, but they would be traveling from New York to Kentucky. The temptation to go home was great, but he wasn't ready to face Anna yet. He needed to come to some kind of terms with himself about what he'd done to her. Instead, he called a friend of his near Lexington to see if they could layover there for a few days.

Chris was exhausted after pulling up at the barn and unloading. He'd driven most of the way without a break, following the Fincastle tractor trailer rig. Martin Davenport was waiting when they pulled in early in the morning. Chris felt as though he was about to drop from exhaustion. Davenport took one look at him and shook his head.

"Let the grooms take care of getting everyone settled. Damn, man, that's what you pay them for. They've been sleeping most of the way. You need to learn how to delegate."

"Bite me, Martin," Chris mumbled.

"Go inside. First door on the left at the top of the stairs. Go to bed. I don't want to see your ugly face until afternoon at the earliest."

Chris managed a smile. "Bossy as ever, I see."

Davenport snorted. "I run a racing stable. You're lucky I'm making room for your fancy show horses. I'll see you at dinner, since you should sleep until then."

Fatigue pulled at Chris as he climbed the stairs inside the imposing brick mansion and opened the door to the spacious room. He eyed the king-sized bed with longing. He wanted sleep, but not quite as badly as he wanted a shower and a shave. A half-hour passed before he dropped into bed. He woke a couple times during the day and rolled over.

Exhaustion gave way to vivid dreams. Anna, no Preston, and the scene from the DVD played back. Even in his sleep, Chris experienced a bone-deep feeling of revulsion, wanted to wake up but couldn't. This was different than the video. He comforted her. She felt good, rounded and ripe like a peach ready for picking. So different from the lean, bony women who always wanted to turn sex into an Olympic sport. Preston was lush. He buried his face next to her ear, whispering to her. His dream Preston relaxed. He used his fingers to stroke and caress between her thighs, creating a liquid heat that turned her breathing ragged with need.

Her shyness was evident in the way she touched him. The heat of her hand sent shockwaves through his body. Now he gasped with need and surprise. He'd never had such an instantaneous response to any woman. He stared into eyes of such a deep, intense blue and saw the same wonder he felt reflected in their depths. Wonder, not fear.

He woke up.

Anna.

Chris looked at his raging hard-on and stroked himself as he let the dream play through his mind over and over. But even after he came, his relief was only physical. A shower helped, but he was still restless. He prowled the room, at last sitting at a small desk near a window overlooking the front paddocks.

He found paper and a pen and began to write. The letters had become therapy. This time he put Anna's address on the envelope. He had memorized it from the one in which her letter had arrived.

Chris tucked the picture of Becca and his parents in the edge of the bureau mirror as he dressed for dinner. He knew Martin. Tradition was big for the Kentucky blueblood, so dinner dress would be a coat and tie at this house. Sure enough, Martin was already in the living room, pouring himself a Scotch at the dry bar in the corner.

"Can I get you anything, Chris?"

"Bourbon, Martin. I never have understood how a native Kentuckian would dare to drink Scotch."

Martin chuckled. "I haven't liked any bourbon I've tasted since Granddaddy quit buying it in back of the church on Sunday afternoons."

"Back home, we North Carolina rednecks call that 'shine, and I've had some pretty smooth stuff." He took the bourbon from his friend, swirled it and sipped. "Mmm. This takes the cake. Now this is a real sippin' whiskey."

Martin's wife, Veronica, joined them a few minutes later. She kept the conversation light during dinner. They adjourned to the veranda for coffee and after dinner drinks. Chris lit a cigarette and leaned back.

"I appreciate this, y'all. The timing between Lake Placid and Lexington wasn't enough to get everyone home and make the drive here. The horses would have been exhausted, not to mention everyone else."

"No problem, you know that, Chris," Martin responded, with a glance at his wife. "You've helped us over the years placing horses that weren't cutting it on the track. How's your breeding program coming along?"

"Everyone we bred has settled, although I did have one mare carrying twins."

"Didn't you have the vet pinch one of them off?"

Chris nodded. "I knew the chance of getting two viable foals was next to nothing, but I'm still hoping to get at least one. This mare took years to settle. I'm afraid to abort and try again. We're keeping her under constant observation." Chris shrugged. "So we'll see."

"How about you?" Veronica asked. "I heard you split with Sydney some time ago. Anyone new on the horizon?"

A vision of Anna flashed through his mind and he smiled.

Veronica's laugh had the clear tinkle of a bell, musical and light. "Ahh, that is almost answer enough, but I insist on some details. At least a name."

"Dr. Anna Barlow. She's a local veterinarian." Chris didn't want to mention the Barrett family connection. He knew Martin and Veronica both traveled in those circles, but Chris wasn't ready to expose Anna to that. There were things he had to take care of first, things they needed to settle between them.

"What's she like?" Veronica asked.

"No bigger than a mosquito." Chris chuckled. "I first met her when she came to stitch my stud's hip. She had to use a mounting block to get enough height to work on him." Chris drew on his cigarette. "She's beautiful inside and out."

Martin arched a brow as he looked at his wife. Veronica smiled as if she knew some secret and wouldn't tell.

"Why are you here instead of wooing your doctor?" Martin demanded. "You might have flown back and forth. You know I would've housed your horses and crew."

Chris stubbed his cigarette and stared off in the distance. "We still have some things to work out. I asked her to marry me, and she said no. I believe she also added a few things about my being an insufferable, conceited ass."

"Ah, it sounds like true love." Veronica laughed again.

Chris stared at her. "You are kidding, right?"

"Oh no!" she assured him. "I hated Martin when I first met him."

"I believe she called me something more along the lines of boorish, blue-blooded bastard. At least it had nice alliteration."

Chris laughed and relaxed. The dream of Anna had made him uneasy and tense, but Martin and Veronica were good therapy. Having Anna herself by his side would be even better.

Chapter 15

Becca was cranky, and Anna suspected the baby might be sprouting more teeth. Between the teething and the uncertain routine of pumping, Anna wondered how long she could continue breast-feeding. As she pulled into the driveway, she realized she was beyond tired, and to top it all off, she was on call this weekend too.

Juggling the baby and diaper bag in one hand, she grabbed the mail from the box at the end of the driveway and headed inside. After putting Becca in her swing, she sifted through the stack of mail. Her heart thumped as she saw Chris's untidy handwriting. Another letter. Seeing it in the stack of mail made her heart lift.

Becca chose that moment to begin her I'm-hungry wail, so Anna set the letter aside with a last, lingering touch to shower before she nursed her daughter. The baby would nurse for a bit before breaking off and fussing, shove a fist inside her mouth and gum it.

"Poor thing," Anna murmured. "This one is bothering you, isn't it?" She rubbed some analgesic on Becca's gums. The baby finished nursing and drifted into an uneasy doze. She was flushed and felt a bit warm, but Anna wasn't as concerned as she had been the last time. A slight fever seemed to be one of Becca's teething symptoms. She set the baby in her swing and turned it on. Maybe the rocking would help relax her. As the baby continued to doze, Anna poured herself a glass of water, added a twist of lemon, and curled at one end of the couch.

At long last, she picked up the letter bearing Chris's now-familiar handwriting on the outside. She didn't fear this letter as she had the first one. Instead, she looked forward to it.

She opened the envelope and removed three sheets of paper. She smiled. Who would have guessed Chris was a letter-writer? Getting personal mail was so rare in this day and age that it felt even more precious to her.

Anna's fingers trembled as she unfolded the pages, then lingered as she smoothed them flat.

Dear Anna,

We arrived in Lexington, Kentucky early this morning. I would've liked to come home for a few days, but I was afraid the horses would be too tired. We're laying over with friends of mine, Martin and Veronica Davenport.

Anna remembered them as a pleasant couple who'd attended one or two parties at her parents' home.

I dreamed of you and that night. What I experienced was different than on the DVD, and I want it to be true. You were so sexy, lush and round and womanly. It was the most incredible turn-on. In my dream, you responded with passion when I touched and stroked you. Watching you climax was an incredible gift.

Anna's hands shook as she turned the page. Was this a dream, or did he remember? Reading it now made her breasts ache and her core throb.

I whispered to you and you responded, touching me. Your hands on me were like fire. Anna, I know you didn't think much of yourself, but you were beautiful to me. I looked into your eyes, as blue as a mountain lake, and I was lost. I still am every time I gaze at you.

Anna put her hands over her face and pulled her knees to her chest. He did remember. Those were the same words he'd said to her that night. In his dreams, he was remembering what it had been like.

I think of you and Becca all the time.

How's she doing? Her teeth are perfect. Does she fuss when she teethes? I've heard parents complain about that. You're good with her, I know you can handle it. Still, I wish I was there. If it gets to be too much, remember Mom and Dad are more than happy to help if you need a break. Please don't exhaust yourself.

It'll be more than a month before I'm home. I want us to talk. It's hard for me. That's why I haven't called you. I want to be able to see you when we talk, not try to get this in the open over a phone line.

You know I told you about the DVD. What I didn't tell you was I went to your brother, Seth, for help. He's the one who gave me the busted nose and black eyes, but I think we've come to an understanding. I couldn't have done it without his help. He loves you so much. I'm glad he was there to look after you when I wasn't.

--Chris

Anna smiled. She imagined Seth's reaction to Chris. That must have been the source Seth mentioned. Anna laughed. Her journalist brother, always protecting his sources, or maybe he just hadn't wanted her to know. Chris would have had a much easier time of it if Brandon had been the one he'd seen.

Anna folded the letter and tucked it in the envelope before going inside her bedroom and sliding it in the nightstand drawer right under Chris's first letter. Her fingers lingered on them before she removed her hand and shut the drawer. She smiled as she realized some of her exhaustion had faded.

Anna called Liz the next morning between farm visits. Saturday was shaping up to be busy, and she couldn't drag Becca, who seemed miserable with this latest tooth, along with her.

"Liz? It's Anna."

"Is there anything wrong, dear?"

"I'm passing by Fincastle on my way to another emergency call and wondered if I might drop Becca off. I have to warn you, she's teething and not happy."

Liz laughed. "She's welcome even if she is cranky. You bring her on. David and I will entertain her for the day. Come back at dinner time, and we'll fix you something."

Anna could have cried with relief. What a difference it made to have people she could count on for help. Becca smiled and waved her arms at her grandparents a few minutes later as Anna arrived in the clinic truck. What a manipulator, already putting on a show for Grandma and Grandpa.

David kissed Anna and the baby before handing Becca to Liz, then collected the rest of the baby's things.

"Don't worry about a thing Anna, we'll take good care of her," David assured her.

"I know you will. Thank you both," Anna said. "You are such a great help."

Anna spent most of the afternoon helping a family whose mare had been in labor since morning. Things weren't progressing and the mare was weakening. When Anna arrived and checked, she saw why. The foal had twisted at an odd angle. From the position of the foal and the lack of movement, she was almost positive the baby was dead.

She looked at the mare and decided they still had a chance to save her. The daughters cried when Anna broke the news the foal was dead, but she would do everything in her power to save the mother. When the only response she got was renewed tears, she suggested to their father it might be a good idea to send the girls away while she repositioned and removed the foal. He looked at her stupidly for a moment.

"Oh. Oh yeah. Sorry, Doc."

Anna watched as the girls ran to the house before she turned to her work. Patiently waiting to reposition the foal between the mare's contractions was difficult and sweaty. The mare's exhaustion actually made it easier because she was too tired to be panicked, but her fatigue was the next problem Anna would have to deal with. Once the foal was out--it had been a black colt--Anna made sure the afterbirth was delivered.

"Mr. Harrison, I hate to ask you to do this, but I need for you to dispose of the colt and the afterbirth while I wash and start hydrating this mare. She's on the verge of going into shock."

He loaded the remains in the bucket of his tractor and headed toward a back part of the farm to bury it. Anna washed and gave the mare IV fluids. She checked the temperature and pulse of the exhausted horse and began to hope she would live.

Anna shook her head in frustration. She doubted she would have been able to do anything to save the colt, but she would have been a lot surer of saving the mare had the Harrisons called earlier.

As she waited to see which way the mare was going to go, she used her cellphone to call the Stevensons. David answered and she explained the situation to him.

"I'll be at least another hour, and then I'll have to go home to shower and change. Please don't wait dinner on me."

"If there's anything we can do, let us know."

Anna reassured him she was fine and hung up. She knew David meant every word of what would have been an automatic response from many people.

She turned her attention to the mare. The horse's body functions were recovering. Anna wanted to see her get on her feet and try to eat and drink before she would even consider leaving her.

"Come on, honey," she coaxed her. "On your feet. You might have lost your baby, and I'm sorry about that, but I would prefer to get home to mine."

It was about fifteen minutes later that the mare shifted, put her front feet in front of her and stood. She was stiff and uncertain, but stayed on her feet. Mr. Harrison and his family were alongside the stall to watch. After a few more minutes, the mare lowered her muzzle to sniff at the flake of hay in the corner of her stall. She lipped it before walking over to her water bucket and taking a long drink.

Anna smiled and patted the mare on the neck. "That's a good girl. I know you must be hurting, but it will pass." She turned to the Harrisons.

"This was an unfortunate situation in which the foal got into the wrong position during birth. It's not your fault, and it's not the mare's. You'll want to check with your breeder. Most of them have a live foal guarantee, so you should be able to get another stud service. I would recommend waiting a few months, or until next spring to breed. Your mare needs a rest. If you do decide to breed again, be aware by the time most of us know a mare's in labor, she's in hard labor. If she doesn't deliver within about an hour, you need to call because a problem could be developing. Okay?"

"Thank you, Dr. Barlow," Mrs. Harrison muttered. "I'm sorry we couldn't save the foal, but I can't thank you enough for saving Sassy. The girls would have been lost without her."

Anna smiled. "I feel the same way about horses. I'll pack and get out from under your feet. Y'all have a good evening."

Anna was dog-tired as she headed to her house to shower and change clothes before going to the Stevensons'. She would have preferred to stay home, but she needed to pick Becca up. She was also getting close to the point where she either needed to nurse or pump. Once she'd dressed in some khaki slacks and a lightweight sweater, she hopped into her own SUV since she wasn't on call and made the short drive to Fincastle Farm.

Chris's house was dark as she went past. Anna thought again of the letter he'd sent her. Aside from everything else, what he'd written was downright erotic. She marveled again at his description of her as round and lush and womanly. To her, it had been fat. Had he meant what he said? Anna never wanted to return to the way she was, but it amazed her Chris had thought her sexy.

If someone pushed her, she might still be inclined to say she was heavy, a leftover, she supposed, of having been told that her entire life. Now she was slender, although by no means bony, she still didn't see herself that way. In a lot of ways, she would always be chubby little Preston Barrett.

David answered Anna's knock.

"Come in, sweetheart. You must be whipped. We have a plate warming in the oven for you. Becca is asleep right now, so do you want to go ahead and eat before you nurse her?"

Anna smiled. "That would be nice."

She'd never felt so welcomed anywhere, including her own family home. Liz and David took everything in stride. Anna couldn't even imagine her father referring to her need to breastfeed. Chris's parents joined her at the kitchen table. While she ate grilled chicken and a delicious salad, they sipped cups of coffee.

"Chris called earlier," David told her as Anna munched on salad. "He's moved Bittersweet to intermediate level classes and she's doing great. He also won a mini-prix on Domino, so he's excited."

Liz looked at Anna. "You know his birthday is this coming Saturday. We thought about surprising him by flying to Lexington. Why don't you come with us?"

Anna stopped eating and stared at Liz. Fly to Lexington to see Chris? She swallowed, afraid to hope.

"I would have to bring Becca with me."

"Of course." Liz smiled. "We can help with that. And you know a visit from his daughter would be the perfect birthday present."

Anna giggled. She couldn't remember feeling so light and happy. The whole idea was spontaneous, so unlike anything her family ever did, excepting Seth or Brandon. That spontaneity would have made them as shunned as her, except they were boys, and of course, tall and blond, just like her father.

Anna floated through the following week. She avoided sending a letter back to Chris on purpose. She would deliver his newest picture of Becca in person. Becca had sprouted two more teeth, the two front ones on top.

"Now you resemble a bunny rabbit," she told her daughter. Becca showed off her new teeth with a big smile, waving her arms and kicking her legs. "Do you have any idea how much your mommy loves you? I can't wait to show you off to your daddy."

Wow, that felt good to say.

Chapter 16

"It's a small party," Veronica explained to Chris, "in honor of your birthday."

"All right," he replied, but his mind was already on the jump course he would take Bittersweet through later in the day. The design would be more complicated than what they had attempted before, and she'd seemed on edge when he schooled her early that morning. Concern he might be pushing her too much kept him distracted.

When he wasn't obsessing over Bittersweet, his thoughts turned to the silence from Anna. No letter from her this week. Had his last letter scared her? Shocked her? Had he misjudged what they'd shared? Chris kicked himself several times after sending it. What had he been thinking? True, they'd created a child together, even shared an afternoon of passion, but when it came right down to it, they hardly knew each other. How could he have written with such detail about his dream?

He knew the answer. He was desperate to know what had happened, and hoped his dream was more than just wishful thinking.

"Everyone will arrive around seven," Veronica continued. "Martin said you would be done early today."

Chris turned to her and smiled. "I'm sorry, Veronica. I'm distracted. Thank you for thinking about me. Seven sounds fine, and I do appreciate the thought."

She smiled at him. "Oh, I think you'll be pleased with the party."

All in all, the day had been a bust. His gelding was off in the right front that morning, so Chris scratched him. Bittersweet was on edge and temperamental. He wondered if she was going into season. After all, the decision to show her had been a last minute idea, so he'd not put her on anything to regulate her cycles.

Chris and the young mare entered the ring. Thank God they were at least not in the Rolex arena, but even this one, on a hill and closer to the barns and the tourists at the Horse Park, was spooking her today. As he stopped to salute, the mare jigged beneath him. Within the first line he knew he needed to retire her. He was not going to risk blowing her mind by allowing her to continue to topple rails and possibly injure herself. Chris pulled up, saluted again and trotted from the ring.

As soon as they exited the gate, Danny took the reins when Chris vaulted to the ground, shaking his head.

"Her mind's not right today," Chris grumbled. "Have one of the grooms cool her. I'll try her again tomorrow."

Chris headed to the tack room and changed clothes. As he walked to the covered aisle in front of the stalls, he saw his father lounging against one of the roof supports.

"Dad!" Chris strode forward, and gave his father a bear hug. "What a surprise!" He stepped back and looked around. "Did Mom come with you?"

"She's relaxing at Martin and Veronica's, or if I know your mother, she and Veronica are both huddled together planning this birthday party for you. By the way, happy birthday, son."

Chris leaned against a stall door. "Let's hope the rest of the day looks up, so far it's been a bust. Domino was off this morning, so I scratched him and retired Bittersweet. She was out of sorts today."

"It happens," his dad said. "Sometimes we have bad days, sometimes they have bad days. You just hope the two don't happen together, and more often than not, you both have good days at the same time. She'll get over it. The mare's got a lot of talent."

They watched some of the other classes, leaning on paddock rails as they assessed the horses entering and leaving the ring. Chris relaxed. This was what he'd needed. Family. His dad had always been able to calm him.

"Whaddya say we head on back to Davenport's place?" David suggested. "I'll drive."

"It's early yet to get ready for the party," Chris commented.

"You might want some time to relax and talk to your mother before the evening gets under way," David suggested.

Chris nodded. He was tired. Maybe a nap by the pool would be a wonderful idea. Veronica met them at the door when they arrived, which Chris thought was odd.

"Hey, Veronica." He smiled. "Anything I can do to help?"

"No, darling. The caterers have everything in hand. Your mother's by the pool, if you want to join her there."

"Good idea. I'll go say hi to her first."

As he walked through the French doors onto the deck next to the pool area, he saw his mother seated at a table under an umbrella on the far side of the pool. She was talking to someone, but his view of the other person was blocked. He decided to sneak up and surprise her, but when he got within twenty feet of them, he was the one who stopped in surprise.

Anna. She reclined on a lounge chair with Becca playing with toys on a blanket next to her. Chris swallowed and blinked back the tears that sprang to his eyes. His hands shook, so he dug them in the pockets of his khakis, embarrassed by how much the sight of her affected him.

"Mom. Anna?" His voice sounded hoarse. He cleared his throat as he hurried forward. "What are you doing here?"

He looked from his mother to Anna, searching her face for any clue of her feelings, but she wouldn't hold his gaze.

"We brought your daughter," his mother murmured. "Happy birthday."

Chris grinned as he reached them. He squatted next to Becca, hesitating as he reached for the smiling baby who kicked and waved her arms at him. "May I?"

Anna looked almost pained for a moment. Was she reluctant, he wondered? He hoped not. Right now, Becca was about as much woman as he thought he could handle, although he and Anna would have to talk.

"Of course you may, Chris. You don't need to ask my permission. She's your daughter."

That was the second time he'd heard those words in the past minute. He picked Becca up, holding her away from him as he stared into her gray-blue eyes with a feeling of wonder. The baby gurgled and flashed another smile.

"Oh," Chris breathed and glanced at Anna. "Two more teeth."

Anna laughed. "The better to bite you with."

His heart pounded. His daughter. His. He drew the baby close to him, inhaling her sweet scent as he nuzzled her ear and enjoyed the feel of her firm, diapered bottom resting on his hand. Becca stuck a fist in her mouth and patted his chest with her other hand.

"Hmm. I'm afraid I can't help you there, darlin'. You need Mommy for that." God, how wonderful those words sounded to him. "Anna?"

She ran her hand through her dark curls as she sat up and raised the back of the lounger. After grabbing a lightweight towel to throw over her shoulder, Anna reached for Becca, and Chris settled her in Anna's arms.

"I'm going in to check on your dad," Liz said and walked inside the house.

Chris smiled and watched his mother leave. He was alone with them. Just Anna, Becca and him. A family? Anna had covered herself and Becca. He watched for a moment, feeling an incredible longing, and touched the towel.

Raising his eyes to Anna's face, he murmured, "May I?"

Anna looked around, but there was no one else nearby and the pool was surrounded by tall shrubs.

"Yes," she replied in a small voice.

Nothing, he decided, was more beautiful than watching Anna nurse their child. His child. His Becca. He swallowed past the lump in his throat as he touched the baby's sandy curls, the tips of his fingers brushing the side of Anna's breast. He met her gaze.

"Happy birthday," she said.

"Thank you," he whispered back. God, she was beautiful. So many emotions flooded him, he feared he would frighten her. He wanted to take her into his arms and cradle her as she cradled their daughter. He wanted to kiss her until she gasped in passion. Instead of doing any of those, he took a deep, shaky breath and stood.

"I'll be back. I--I'm just going to change into swim trunks." He spun on his heel and hurried away, afraid he might make a fool of himself. Afraid he might frighten Anna again, like the night he'd met her. Guilt crushed him.

* * * *

Anna watched him leave. She nibbled on her lower lip. That hadn't gone well. In fact, it had been a disaster. Chris seemed glad to see Becca, but she wasn't sure about herself. She swallowed, blinked and looked at the baby's head. Her head still ached from the flight, and now her heart ached too. She had wanted this to be perfect. Maybe surprising him hadn't been such a good idea. Hadn't she already learned from his letters how awkward he felt when he was unprepared? The way he oozed so much confidence in the show ring but was unsure of himself when it came to dealing with anything serious still amazed her.

Anna tried to relax, but she knew Chris sensed her reserve when he returned. He was still nervous, uncertain how to behave toward her. How could they have this beautiful child between them and yet be such strangers?

"Chris," she said, drawing his gaze to her. "If you're uncomfortable with us here, Becca and I can find a hotel and catch a flight home tomorrow."

He scowled. “No. I mean, if you want to leave, I’ll understand.” He paused, sighed and raked a shaky hand through his golden hair. “Do you?”

“Do I what?”

“Want to leave.”

She shook her head, watching him shift as if he were ill at ease. “It’s just, it doesn’t seem as though you want us here.”

He shifted his gaze to meet hers. “I do want you here, Anna. I can’t help but think about what happened, what you must think. Shit. I’m not any good at this. I’m not prepared.”

Anna felt herself getting defensive. “You mean you’re not ready to work at it instead of having someone just fall into bed with you?”

“Not fair,” he retorted.

Becca finished nursing and yawned. Anna stood with the baby and looked at Chris.

“I’m going to take her in for a nap. She had a tough time on the flight with the pressure changes.”

“Will you come back or is this an excuse to run away?” he asked.

“I don’t think so. I have a bit of a headache. If you think that’s running away, I’m sorry, but that’s all I’ve got to offer right now.” She wanted to cry, and not just from her head aching. She had pictured a fantasy in which he would tell her he loved her, that he’d meant every word about how sexy she was, and she would tell him the same thing. Yet here they were, still feeling like strangers in so many ways.

* * * *

Chris nodded, turning away from her in frustration. They didn’t seem to be finding any common ground, unless he counted being able to write letters to each other. What a joke. What a fuck-up he was. He was beginning to wonder if they ever would find a way to come together. There was Becca, but was a shared baby enough?

He dove into the pool and swam back and forth, hoping the physical exertion would distract him. Somehow, he had to get past how they’d started. She had to get past it too. And that might be even more difficult for her because, from what he gathered, she actually remembered what happened. What if there hadn’t been more than what he’d seen on DVD? If he felt like a victim, he could only imagine how Anna must feel.

In actual fact, they were both victims. Fuck. What a mess.

* * * *

Anna watched him from the room Veronica Davenport had given her and Becca. What was wrong with him? This wasn’t the same man who’d written to her with such passion. She rubbed a hand across her eyes. She had a splitting headache. Becca had whined and fussed the entire flight. She glanced over at the dressing room to see the baby had settled without a problem in the travel crib they'd picked up on the way over from the airport.

Anna stripped her bathing suit off and headed for the shower, hoping it would ease the headache nagging at her. She assessed herself in the mirror after she showered. Slender arms and legs, full breasts, a tiny waist flaring into slim hips and a belly that was, for the first time in memory, almost flat. It should have been an attractive picture, but Anna still coouldn't identify with what she saw in her reflection. Inside, she was the young woman she had been before her pregnancy: more than pleasingly plump, with an awkwardness around people she was unable to overcome. The latter, at least, was gone. Anna no longer cared what other people thought. She had been forced to toughen up in the past year.

Sliding her arms inside a thick silk robe, she snugged it around her waist and went in to the bedroom to lie down. Her eyes felt heavy…

* * * *

Chris went in search of her just after six. When he got no response to his knock on her door, he turned the knob and entered the room. She was stretched on her side, her soft mouth parted. Her robe had also parted, revealing the slender length of her leg and a bare, rounded hip. Chris swallowed as he approached the bed. He did not want to startle her. As he sat on the edge, the shift in the mattress caused her to open sleep-clouded eyes.

"Chris?" she murmured. She touched his sleeve.

"Are you feeling better?"

"Mmm." She smiled and stretched. Chris exhaled as her movements tightened the silk across her full breasts. "Much better."

One kiss, he told himself, that's all he would take. Her eyes widened, but the smile never left her lips as he leaned forward and tasted her. Their breaths mingled as they drew apart, then came together again. This time he slanted his mouth across hers with all the hunger and longing he had stored, and she answered him with a hunger of her own. Anna grabbed the lapels of his jacket and she pulled him to her.

Chris groaned deep in his throat as he continued to kiss her. He felt his need start to spin out of control. She was so soft, so willing. And he was so amazed. He glided his hand over her silk-covered breast. A soft moan escaped her and made him shrug out of his jacket. He braced a hand on either side of her head and kissed her again, teasing her lips with his tongue until she opened her mouth. From there, he moved along her neck to the hollow of her throat and lower. With one hand, he brushed the silk of her robe away from her breast and lowered his head, laving the hard, dark nipple.

"Chris!" His name came out of her mouth as a plea or a prayer. Her moaned response brought his already aroused body to full readiness. He sucked her nipple inside his mouth, drawing on it until he tasted her. He would embarrass himself if he didn't get inside her soon.

Sliding his hand over her belly and between her thighs, Chris groaned when he found she was already swollen and wet. Holding her gaze, he sat up. Her dark blue irises were filled with hot desire. He moved his hands to his belt before Becca interrupted with a cry from her crib. Chris fought to surface from the desire coursing through him, while Anna blinked as though she were awakening from a trance.

A soft knock sounded on the door. They broke apart. Chris jumped up and turned away, grabbing his jacket and holding it in front of himself. Shit. What was he doing?

Anna scrambled off the bed, adjusting her robe to cover her swollen breasts.

"I'll get the door," she said awkwardly. "Would you get Becca? She's hungry."

Chris nodded, angry with himself for having let things get out of hand. He tossed his jacket on the bed and turned toward the dressing room. As he bent to pick up Becca, he heard Anna answer the door.

"I'm sorry, Veronica. I overslept."

He couldn't hear Veronica.

"Yes, Chris came by to wake me. He's getting Becca ready."

Anna paused as Veronica said something. "Yes, thank you. That was thoughtful."

Chris heard the door shut, then the rustle of silk as Anna stepped inside the small dressing room. He held Becca in one arm and had a diaper dangling from his hand. What he truly hoped was now that Veronica was gone, Anna would take Becca.

"I think she has a bigger problem than being hungry right now," he muttered.

Anna arched an eyebrow at him. "Well, change her diaper, Daddy."

He sniffed the air. Whoa. He didn't want to even go there. "Anna," Chris tried whining. "Come on, it's my birthday."

"Right," she said with a giggle. "And Becca's given you a present."

"Very funny." But now he laughed too.

"Come back in the bedroom and I'll show you what to do."

In a matter of minutes, the bed where he had been about to make love to her had become a diaper changing station. Chris watched as Anna showed him how to change the diaper before she let him practice getting the new diaper on and fastened. He smiled in satisfaction.

"There."

Anna took the baby from him and sat in the overstuffed chair near the bed. As she loosened her robe, Becca rooted at her breast. Chris sat on the bed and watched, enjoying the picture they made.

"Is it wrong to feel jealous of a baby?" he inquired.

Anna looked at him, saw that he was teasing and giggled.

"Chris! That is sooo wrong!"

"But I'm hungry too."

Anna blushed. "You'll have to wait for the adult drinks."

Chris waggled his brows and sobered. "Do you want me to go?"

"Not if you don't want to," Anna whispered.

He realized he still stared when Anna glanced at him and blushed. "I'll wait until you finish nursing. I take it Veronica found a sitter?"

"Yes. One of the hot walkers will keep an eye on her in the den down the hall. Go ahead and take her things there. When she's through, you can take her to the sitter while I change."

Chris smiled. It sounded like a normal family. He gathered the portable crib along with Becca's diaper bag, a blanket and some toys, and disappeared out the door. He set everything in the small upstairs family room before returning to Anna's room. He hesitated before walking on in. Anna was closing her robe.

"I'll burp her," Chris offered. When Anna handed the baby to him, he felt a sense of family again. If they worked things out, that's what they would be. He wanted them to be more than Becca's parents. He wanted Anna with every breath he took.

* * * *

Anna smiled after handing him Becca, and entered the dressing room. This felt so right, and she wanted it to stay this way between them. She heard the door shut after Chris as she looked through her clothes. At the last minute, she had thrown in a simple black cocktail dress. Anna had bought the dress, which was cut in a deep V in the front and back, with a skirt ending at mid-thigh, on impulse the week before when she'd found it on sale at a small shop in Durham. Never in her life had she worn anything that daring. She had never had the figure for it, and still wasn't convinced the purchase was right for her.

After slithering into the dress, she fluffed her curls, added the sapphire pendant Brandon had shipped to her for her vet school graduation and slid a pair of black high-heeled slingbacks onto her slender feet. She looked in the mirror and added a touch of lip gloss.

Chris came back to the bedroom after dropping Becca off. Anna needed some reassurance. This was the first time she had dressed for anything fancy since her pregnancy. She emerged from the dressing room, uncertainty dogging her footsteps.

“Is this okay?” she asked.

Chris’s eyes widened. “You take my breath away, Anna.”

“Take your breath away good, or take your breath away bad?”

He hesitated, staring at her intently as if working a puzzle. His expression transformed. “You have no idea how beautiful you are, do you?” He crossed the room to her and slid his hands up her bare arms before tilting his head to kiss her on the forehead. “You will be the most beautiful woman there, with the possible exception of Becca, but she won’t be downstairs. And if I don’t get my hands off you, we might not make it either.”

It helped ease Anna’s tension and she chuckled. “Spoken like a true father, at least the part about Becca.”

“I’m working on it. Now, if you will allow me to escort you.”

As they descended the wide staircase, Anna realized Veronica hadn’t been truthful when she’d told them she had invited just a few people. An absolute crush of guests awaited them. When their sudden appearance descending the stairs made everyone fall silent, Anna tensed with growing embarrassment. In her experience, quiet always preceded someone making her the target of a putdown.

“Smile, Anna,” Chris whispered. “You are the most beautiful woman here, and the only woman I want on my arm.”

She glanced at him and saw only softness in his gaze. Her tension eased, replaced by warmth…and it felt right.

Chapter 17

A quick glimpse around made Anna realize there were few people she recognized, and even more importantly, none of them appeared to recognize her. Since Martin and Veronica introduced her to everyone as Dr. Anna Barlow, it gave her a sense of freedom she seldom had in a social setting. Always before, she'd been Miss Preston Barlow-Barrett, a ponderous name more weighty than the extra pounds she'd carried.

Chris stayed close to her for the first hour, but then the flow of the party sent them in different directions. Anna found herself talking equine medicine with racing owners and trainers from some of the neighboring farms and comparing baby notes with another new mother. For the first time she could remember, she felt confident and comfortable socializing.

At some point, music flowed from the back terrace. Chris materialized at her side and took her sparkling water from her hands. "Come dance with me. Martin and Veronica insist we open the dancing."

"Chris!" Anna hissed as he pulled her along with him. "I haven't danced since cotillion, and I was a miserable dancer."

He chuckled as they reached the edge of the dance floor. "Then we should be perfectly suited. I asked them to play a waltz, and I happen to be an excellent dancer."

He swept her into his arms, holding her closer than necessary.

"Relax, sweetheart, and follow my lead. It will be over before you know it."

He caught and held her gaze as the music began. Anna stared at him in desperation at first, and as the music ebbed and flowed, she relaxed and followed with more ease. He was a wonderful dancer and made sure nothing happened to her. Other dancers joined them on the floor, and Anna felt almost heady. Chris guided her around a corner of the terrace where the sound of the voices and music dimmed. There was no one there. The music in this dark corner was a background to the hum of the cicadas. The scent of freshly mown grass mingled with the perfume of the flowers growing in profusion just off the terrace.

The music slowed, and Chris pulled Anna closer. He kept one strong hand entwined with hers while his other hand caressed her bottom. Would he realize how little she wore beneath it?

"Anna," he whispered as he rested his cheek near the top of her head. "Good Lord, what are you not wearing under here? You feel all but naked, and I want you so badly I ache."

She looked at him and was not at all surprised when he kissed her. They stopped dancing. She wrapped her arms around his neck as he cupped her buttocks and lifted her against him. It gave him easier access to her mouth, but it also brought every hard plane of him in close contact with her softness. Most of all she felt the rigid length of his cock against her hip. He tasted her mouth, traced her lips with his tongue. When she responded by opening to him, he plundered it with a hunger that left her gasping for breath. His chest pressed against hers, his movements stimulating her already hyper-sensitive breasts until she moaned and trembled in his arms. He stepped back, leaning against an outside wall of the house, and let his hand glide along the hem of her skirt and up her thigh.

"Chris, we should stop. Anyone could walk up on us."

In answer, he swung her into his arms as if she weighed nothing at all and walked even deeper toward the back of the terrace, where he found steps leading to the flower garden. There was no hesitation in his stride as he headed straight for a gazebo at the corner of the large yard, only stopping once or twice to kiss Anna with a slow thoroughness that made her body weep for him.

"What are you doing?" she protested.

"I want to unwrap my birthday present," he groaned, pressing his lips once again over her mouth before traveling along the column of her throat. He stepped inside the seclusion of the gazebo and lowered her to her feet. After taking his jacket off, he loosened his tie and set them both aside. He pulled her close again, shifting his hands to either side of her waist and under her skirt.

"Chris." Anna wasn't sure if she said his name as a protest or not. She was on uncertain ground. He aroused her so completely with his touch she felt already as if she were on the verge of a climax. When he used his fingers to brush aside the wispy silk underwear that barely justified the name and slipped between her thighs, Anna gasped.

"Christ!" Chris growled, and she felt his hips surge against hers. "You're already wet."

"Kiss me," she whispered. "I want you to kiss me again."

He led her to a small loveseat, where he sat and pulled her, half-sitting, half-reclining onto his lap. Grasping her wrist loosely in one hand, he brought her hand inside his shirt, sighing with pleasure as her fingers tangled in the golden hair covering his chest and lightly teased his nipple. He pushed the shoulders of her gown down until her unfettered breasts sprang free.

"You have the most gorgeous breasts. You have no idea how they turn me on."

He caressed her, tweaking her sensitive nipples until she gasped with pleasure. He lowered his head to gently suckle her. Shafts of pleasure rocketed through her. He drew on her firmly, sucking, then licking as her milk let down. Chris caught her unrestrained moan with his own lips. He turned her until she straddled his thighs.

"Touch me, Anna," he muttered with an urgency she couldn't ignore. "Please touch me."

There was such raw need in his voice, she hurried to comply. Still, her fingers felt clumsy as she found his belt and loosened it before opening his suit pants.

"Chris?" Uncertainty made her hesitate. Other than that one night and their afternoon together, she had no real experience in pleasuring a man. As if sensing her unease, he shifted and freed himself. Once again he brought her hand to him. This time she closed her fingers around the hard length of his cock and moved experimentally.

He groaned in pleasure. "Easy, Anna," he murmured against her mouth. "I want to make this good for you. I want to last."

"Chris," she mumbled. "We can't. I don't… You don't…"

"Have any protection?" he finished for her. She nodded against him.

"I'll be careful." He kissed her again, deeply and lingeringly before pushing her gently back against the cushions. He stared at her breasts, then lowered his head and sucked strongly, lapping at the drops of milk that beaded on her nipples. "Do you have any idea how erotic that is?" he growled as he drew her dress down even further, sliding it over her hips and raising her bottom to draw it completely off. He laid it aside and sat back for a moment to stare at her. Even in the dark, she saw the heat in his gaze.

She was clad in only the wisp of black silk and the high heels.

"Stand up," he ordered in a quiet voice. Anna rose and stood in front of him. He let his gaze float from her feet along the length of her legs to the apex of her thighs, still hidden by the lacy silk underwear, over her flat stomach to her breasts and finally came to rest on her expression. She trembled. "You are the most beautiful woman I know, Anna."

"Chris," she begged on a sigh, wanting to believe him, needing to believe what he told her. They were words she'd feared she would never hear.

He moved forward and pressed his face against her belly, drawing in the scent of her skin. Hooking his fingers in her underwear, he eased it along her thighs until she stepped out of it. She stood before him, completely nude save for the high heels, and felt wild and wanton.

Seeing his hot gaze and desire-filled expression, she teased, "You've unwrapped your gift. Did you want to play with it?"

If possible, his gaze burned even hotter. He thrust his fingers between her thighs, stroking and kneading until she had to put her hands on his shoulders to keep from falling. Somehow, she wasn't quite sure how, she was lying on the cushions and he knelt between her thighs. He caressed her stomach with his mouth, inching lower, his breath hot on her as he inhaled deeply, savoring her scent. When he touched his tongue to her, Anna thought she would go insane. He loved her with his mouth and fingers until she slipped over the edge into a world filled with pleasure that seemed to go on and on.

She felt bereft as he leaned away from her. With little heed for his clothing, he stripped off what remained. In the moonlight, his lean athletic body shone pale in the silvery light. Anna looked at the hard thrust of his cock and licked her lips.

"Let me touch you," she said, holding out her hand.

His eyes met hers and he stepped closer. Anna dropped to her knees in front of him and stroked his lean hips, then along the length of his shaft.

"Oh, sweet baby," he groaned, twining his fingers in her curls. She thrust the silky head of him between her lips and all his breath escaped on a moan of pleasure. As she moved him back and forth in her mouth, she felt him tremble. "Easy. I want to be inside you," he mumbled.

She licked around the ridge of his shaft and lay on the settee cushions. He needed no more invitation, bending to push her thighs even wider apart. She reached to guide him, loving the size of him, and knowing how good he would feel. Their gazes locked as he pushed forward, burying himself deep within her.

"Anna, sweetheart," he groaned. "Hold still."

After a moment in which she felt his body shuddering, he moved in a rhythm as old as time. The gentle groan of the settee kept beat with his movements. Anna stroked through his sandy hair, wondering if he saw the depth of her feelings. She built once again to a powerful climax. Her head fell against the cushions and her mouth opened on a cry of pleasure. She felt Chris stiffen and he abruptly withdrew, his breath coming in harsh gasps as he spilled his seed into the handkerchief he held in his hand. He collapsed next to her and gathered her close against his chest.

"You are the most incredible birthday present!"

They lay together, lethargic and replete. Anna stirred first when the coolness of the evening began to give her a chill.

"We should go back." She sighed. "Someone will miss us."

"I know you're right, but I wish we could stay here the rest of the night." With another sigh, he collected his clothes, putting them on as he went. After he shoved his shirttail in his pants and zipped and buckled his trousers, he helped Anna dress, reassuring her she looked fine. He straightened his tie and put his suit coat on.

"There's a side door to Martin's study," Chris said quietly. "We can use that to go in and no one will be the wiser."

They laughed as they snuck across the darkened yard and back to the terrace. Chris held the door for her. As they stood near the hall door, he kissed her hard on the lips. "You go ahead, and I'll follow in a few minutes."

Chapter 18

Anna slipped through the hallway and back amidst the crush of people toward the front of the house. She felt loved, and she loved in return. She would rather sneak up the back stairs but, deciding she was hungry, headed toward the buffet arranged in the large dining room. The tinkle of glasses and silverware on plates grew louder as she approached. Anna had nearly made it to the dining room when someone said in a rich, soprano voice from beside her, "Preston? Preston Barrett?"

She felt as if she had stepped into the middle of one of those commercials in which someone mentions a name and the whole room goes quiet and stares. It might have been an exaggeration, but several people looked her way. In the far corner, she swore she saw a woman who looked just like the woman Chris had been hooked up with last year. What was her name…Sydney? But surely she wouldn't be at a birthday party for Chris after he had dumped her.

Pasting a smile on her face, Anna turned. Next to her was Taylor Tisch, a former college sorority sister, and Veronica Davenport. The latter looked momentarily stunned, but recovered quickly. She looked as if she was about to say something, so Anna stepped in before things really got awkward.

"Hello, Taylor. It's Anna now. Dr. Anna Barlow. I dropped the Preston."

"And the Barrett too, I see." Taylor laughed. "You always did seem to find that more of an albatross around your neck."

Anna felt more than the weight of her name. All those old insecurities returned, as if she had somehow tacked on about fifty pounds and a plethora of putdowns.

Chris walked in at that moment. Anna wanted to run to him and beg him to take her out of there. Anywhere would do as long as it was far away from Taylor. He smiled pleasantly, but Anna picked up on the sudden narrowing of his eyes and knew he sensed something was wrong.

Anna saw confusion on Veronica's face, but she was far too polite to voice it in public.

"Oh, Chris," Veronica smiled. "I was looking for you. Everyone wants to sing Happy Birthday to you on the terrace."

Chris draped his arm around Anna's waist. "Will you join me?" he asked her.

Anna nodded gratefully and leaned against him before she glanced at Taylor. "So nice to see you again."

As they headed to the terrace, Chris remarked, "It was bound to happen, Anna. You can't keep running away from the fact you're a Barrett."

She stiffened, wanting to rail at him that he could never understand, but her polite smile never wavered as she retorted, "I am not running away from it. I walked every single step of the way."

She stood by his side, still smiling, as the band played and everyone sang the birthday song, but inside she roiled with a mixture of confused emotions. Chris accepted the congratulations and the slaps on the back, and as he did, Anna slipped away. She needed time alone. Between the intimacy in the gazebo, then seeing faces from her past right on the heels of it, she was simply too raw to handle anything else.

* * * *

A few minutes before Chris realized Anna was gone, he had seen the insecurity on her face when he found her with Taylor Tisch. It dawned on him Anna had been replaced by the old, insecure Preston. Would she never be able to accept who she was? How could they build something together with Becca if the shadow of her family always stretched between them? There had to be some way to resolve it.

This was one area where he knew he would have to push. They had come too far to let her retreat now. And there wasn't just the two of them to consider.

He found Anna upstairs in her room. She was seated in a chair near the window, her head bent to Becca as she nursed the baby. She looked up as she heard the latch on the door click shut.

Chris stood inside, hands jammed in his trouser pockets.

"I'm sorry, Anna. I know I've made you angry, but I don't know why. Was it saying you need to face your family?"

She glanced over at him before turning her face to stare out the window. The sounds from the party drifted to them, but the room was remarkably quiet, like being wrapped in a cocoon.

"You have no idea, Chris," she began. "You have two parents who have always wanted what was best for you, and happily, it fit right in with your family tradition. You've met Seth. He is the epitome, in looks, of the rest of my family. They are all tall, blond, and athletic. I stuck out like a sore thumb."

"Anna," he interrupted, but she cut him off.

"No! Listen. My whole family sails. Brandon was the captain of his team at Harvard. It's a Barrett tradition, but I get seasick. The rest of my brothers and sisters rowed in school. I read. I have never fit in, and rather than even attempt to accept that, my mother and father spent years trying to make me fit in."

She paused as she adjusted her clothing and switched Becca to her other breast. "I've told you my parents packed me off to summer camps, but I didn't mention what kind. These weren't traditional camps, they were camps for fat kids where they all but starved the weight off of us. After three summers of that, my parents finally gave up. I thought I had won." She hesitated before she went on in a pained whisper, "But my father still found a way. I was an excellent rider. Finally I excelled at a sport no one else in my family did. My school wanted to put me on their show team, but my father refused. He promised he would consider it if I 'slimmed down.'"

Anna turned to look at Chris. "I tried. I starved myself, but I would get so hungry I would eat everything in sight, and I would feel guilty so I would make myself throw up. I lost twenty pounds, but it wasn't enough. Nothing," she continued vehemently, "nothing was ever enough for them. I consistently brought home top grades, but that never compared with the sailing trophies or sculling medals.

"Once," she muttered, "just once I wanted my parents to look at me and say, 'We love you exactly the way you are, Preston. We're proud of who you are.' It never happened. Becca was the last straw as far as they were concerned. They turned their backs on me, but I would not let them do that to my baby. My beautiful Becca. I'm not running from my family, Chris. I walked away from them for the sake of my daughter, our daughter."

Chris listened in horror. His Anna. His beautiful, damaged Anna.

"I don't know what to say."

She looked at him, her expression shuttered. "Don't say anything. Go enjoy your party. I'll put Becca to bed and come downstairs."

"You don't have to if you don't feel like it." His voice was gruff. She looked almost defeated.

She gazed at him and he saw some other emotion in her blue eyes, what, he wasn't sure. "It's your birthday, Chris, of course I'll return."

He slipped out the door and closed it quietly behind him. Her parents had a lot to answer for, and he decided he was going to start getting some of those answers.

* * * *

Anna laid the now-sleeping Becca in the travel crib and hummed to her softly until the baby settled into a deeper sleep. She checked on the sitter in the den and told her she'd left the door open a crack so she could hear the baby in case she cried. The teenager grinned at her, showing a mouthful of braces.

"Okay, Dr. Barlow. She sure is a pretty baby and happy. My sister's baby is forever crying."

Anna smiled. "Becca has her moments too."

As she prepared to go downstairs, she paused in the hallway at the top and took a deep breath. She had revealed more to Chris tonight than she'd told anyone, including Seth or Brandon. Even they never knew about her bout with bulimia. Anna watched what she ate, but she had quickly found nursing Becca, combined with a physically demanding career, had its benefits. She was keeping off the weight she had lost while pregnant.

Straightening her spine and squaring her shoulders, she descended the long, curved stairway. She deliberately mingled with the other guests, and kept space between her and Chris. She needed some distance. Her emotions were too close to the surface, and she was too close to losing it. Occasionally, she caught him looking at her, but he would shift his gaze immediately someplace else. She did not regret her decision to come to Kentucky with Chris's parents. After all, he did deserve a chance to see his daughter. And now she was lying to herself. She'd come because she needed to see him, needed to see if they could be good together. They were…and she had no idea how to handle it.

Her attention shifted as a man called from the den in a brash voice, "Hey, folks. We have some video of the birthday boy riding his new mare in Upperville, if anyone wants to see."

If there was one given with horse people, they would gather like flies to watch any kind of horse-related video. Anna suddenly found herself pushed forward until she stood next to Chris. He looked at her with a grimace, but reached to casually rest his arm around her waist and draw her against his side. They both saw an older man straightening away from the DVD player, a smug smile on his mouth as video popped up on the screen.

Anna felt Chris stiffen and jerk his arm away from her as he rushed forward. Everything seemed to move in slow motion. As her eyes lifted to the TV, she saw the first images from that night. Her gasp was one of many in the room. At the same time, Chris swore like she'd never heard him before. His fury shook the room.

"You Goddamn son of a bitch!" He reached for the TV, but Martin Davenport beat him to it, quickly flicking a button on the remote that turned the set off. Chris's attention turned completely toward Sydney's middle-aged husband. "You have just pissed off the wrong North Carolina redneck!"

In one smooth motion, he swung his fist and slammed it into the other man's face. As the other man swung back and missed, Chris went after him again. From somewhere, Anna saw Sydney appear, her face filled with spite as she rushed at Chris. Oh God! Anna wanted to shrivel up and die. Could this possibly get any worse? The room was in chaos. Women were screaming and trying to flee as Sydney picked up an expensive looking ceramic figure to throw it at Chris. That was all Anna needed to see. Narrowing her eyes, she rushed forward and caught Sydney's arm on the backswing, quickly twisting it behind the taller woman. If there was one advantage to being a large animal vet, it was the upper body strength it had forced her to develop.

"Try it, you skinny bitch!" Anna whispered in her ear.

Sydney turned shocked eyes on her. "Preston?"

Anna yanked her arm. "The name's Anna Barlow and don't you forget it."

From somewhere, David came to grab the half-conscious older man whose nose was bleeding and strangely shifted to one side, while Martin Davenport, his patrician features arctic, grasped Sydney firmly by the arm.

"Allow us to escort you and your spouse from my home. Perhaps if you hurry, you'll manage to miss the police officers. However, I can assure you that should you still be anywhere on my farm within the next three minutes, I will see you both behind bars."

Anna turned to see Chris popping the DVD out of the player and methodically breaking the disc into pieces. His jaw worked and his movements were faintly jerky.

"Chris?" Anna murmured. She went over to him and touched his arm. He was as tense as a coiled spring and she had just a moment to glimpse the pain in his gray eyes before he dropped the disc shards to the floor and pulled her into his arms. He buried his face against her dark curls and held her in a nearly crushing embrace.

"I'm sorry, sweetheart," he choked. "I'm so damn sorry. I thought I had taken care of this. I didn't want you to see. Never wanted anyone… How could anyone…" He sucked in a deep breath. "How can you even stand to have me around you?"

Anna clung to him. Yes, she was shocked, but she wasn't in nearly the pain he was because she truly remembered the entire night. "It's all right, Chris," she soothed him, knowing they needed to clear the air about the past.

He continued to hold her, rocking from foot to foot as if he were trying to calm them both. They were alone in the room. The other guests had gone. Anna had heard Veronica suggest to everyone they should leave in order to give them some privacy. Anna still felt the tension in Chris. His body trembled with anger and his breathing was ragged.

"How can you ever forgive me?" he muttered at last.

Anna rested her head against the firm wall of his chest. "Every time I look at Becca, I thank God for that night."

Chris's arms tightened so much around her Anna thought for a moment her ribs might snap, but then he relaxed. "Thank you for that."

Chapter 19

Anna had long since headed upstairs, her whole demeanor telling Chris she was too exhausted in body and mind to handle anything else. Chris was still too tense, but there was another reason he was still up. He felt he owed his hosts some explanation. He saw the understanding in his parents' faces. They already knew what had happened.

Chris found Martin and Veronica in Martin's study, a cozy book-lined room with portraits of past Davenport champions gracing every available space. The couple looked at him as he came into the room.

Martin raised a brow. "Brandy?"

Chris nodded. "That would be great. I want to apologize for what happened tonight…"

Veronica waved a delicate hand to dismiss what he was saying. "We're sorry it happened. I should have left better instructions to turn people away who had not been specifically invited. It certainly wasn't the surprise I envisioned."

Chris took the snifter from Martin's hand and swirled the amber liquid in the bottom of the glass before sipping it, and savoring the smooth heat as it slid down his throat. "I needed that." He paused. "Thank you for hosting a party. And thank you even more for inviting my family." He turned a smile on both his friends.

Veronica chuckled. "It seems the real surprise was for us… Dr. Barlow?" She arched a delicate brow at Chris. "And you also didn't mention the tiny surprise she brought with her."

Chris felt his cheeks flush. "If there's one thing I know about Anna, she's full of surprises. Look, I'm sorry I didn't mention it. Anna has been protective about Becca and about using her full name. I know it seems strange, but she did not want to be known as Preston Barlow-Barrett. It's a long story, but it's her story to tell."

"And Becca?" Veronica asked in her quiet, but persistent way. "Where does she figure in this picture?"

Chris was not going to deceive his friends. He had known Martin and Veronica a long time and trusted their discretion. He set his glass on a nearby table before blowing his breath out. "You saw at least the beginning of what was on that DVD. Becca's my daughter." Briefly, he told them what had happened, without going into detail about Anna's parents' reaction. But he didn't have to. Veronica had grown up in the same circle.

"Have they disowned her?" she asked. "Or is she just getting the cold shoulder?"

Chris sighed. "The latter, I think, except for her two older brothers. They may be the only ones who actually know what happened."

Martin chuckled. "Seth has always been a bit of a rogue, despite being the spitting image of his father at that age. Brandon's even worse. What Seth gets through sheer bull-headedness, Brandon charms out of everyone."

"Where do you go from here as far as Becca is concerned?" Veronica asked.

Chris picked his glass up and sipped his brandy. "Anna wants me to be a part of Becca's life. Beyond that, we haven't had a chance to talk."

Veronica nodded as she sipped her own brandy. "She was quick to stop Sydney from beaning you tonight, but remember one thing--for all she rails against the Barrett traditions, I have yet to meet any member of that family who isn't stubborn in their own way."

"Trust me, Veronica, I've already discovered that firsthand." Chris finished his brandy and excused himself. He needed sleep so he could be at the Horse Park early to check on Domino. He paused outside the door to his room and looked across the hall. Anna. He wanted to go to her, even if just to hold her. He closed his eyes for a moment before turning and slipping inside his room.

Things had gotten away from him tonight. He had wanted to make their lovemaking something special. Instead, he'd practically screwed her on the dance floor before at least having enough sense to drag her to the gazebo. But, God, she was exquisite, so incredibly, mind-numbingly sexy all he'd been able to think about was burying his cock inside her. And she let him. Not only let him, but responded so passionately to him he thought they might both go up in flames.

That gave him hope. Surely she would never have responded in such a way had she harbored any fears from what happened last year. Then

Sydney and the bastard she married had decided to take their own revenge. It tarnished what had happened earlier.

They needed time to breathe. It had been an emotionally charged day. Chris felt drained. He stripped his clothes off and tossed them on a nearby chair before slipping between the cool sheets. He'd already decided to fly east after tomorrow to pay a visit to Barrett Newspapers. The time had come to get some answers. And God forgive him, but he wasn't mentioning it to Anna. Far easier to ask forgiveness than permission.

He heard Becca early the next morning. At the sound of her cry, Chris came instantly awake. He slipped on a pair of jeans and padded across the hall barefoot. As an afterthought, he tapped on the door.

"Anna? Can I get you anything?" he whispered.

"Chris?" came her muffled reply. "Come in, please."

She was propped in the bed with Becca nursing hungrily. After smiling briefly at his daughter, Chris raised his eyes to Anna's face. She looked pale and had dark circles under her eyes.

"What's wrong, sweetheart?"

"Migraine," she whispered and winced. "There's medicine in my toiletry bag in the bathroom. Would you mind loading the syringe? The vial's single dose."

Chris was already halfway to the bathroom by the time she'd finished speaking. He returned with the syringe and offered it to her. She pushed the blankets aside and uncovered her thigh.

"Thank you." Each word was spoken slowly as if she had to concentrate to articulate.

She took it from him, checked it automatically then jabbed it into her thigh. After she handed him the syringe, Chris tossed it in the waste basket.

"What can I do?"

"Stay, if you can, and take Becca when she's done." Anna raised pain-darkened eyes to him. "I'm sorry. I haven't had one in ages. It might have been the flight yesterday."

"Shh." Chris pulled a chair next to the bed and sat, watching Becca push at Anna's breast. "You're both beautiful. Do you know that?"

He touched his daughter's sandy curls then stroked Anna's cheek. She responded by leaning her head against his hand and closing her eyes. Becca released Anna's breast and waved her arms around. Anna handed her to him.

"Burp her, and I'll let her nurse on the other side."

Chris patted Becca's back and was rewarded with a small burp. He handed the baby back, watching as she rooted hungrily at this new offering and latched on. Anna let her head fall against the pillows. Her eyes were closed and her skin still looked pale. Chris watched her quietly and saw her breathing begin to even out in sleep. Becca too was getting drowsy. As her mouth slipped from Anna's breast, Chris took the baby in one arm and covered Anna. His daughter lay heavily against his shoulder, one of her hands tangling in the hair on his chest.

Chris let her lie there as he eased from the room and padded downstairs in search of a cup of coffee. His father and Martin were both in the kitchen. They smiled as they saw Chris walk in with Becca nestled against him.

"Coffee?" Martin asked.

"Please." Chris sat and leaned back, letting the baby get more comfortable. "I was going to go to the Horse Park early, but I think I'll wait awhile. Anna's suffering with a migraine. She can use some help with Becca, and I don't have any classes until after lunch."

"I can go," David volunteered. "I'll take a look at Domino to make sure he's okay and get Bittersweet and move her around too."

"Thanks, Dad." Chris smiled.

When he took Becca upstairs, Anna was curled on her side, asleep. Some of the color had come back to her face. Chris took the baby into the dressing room and changed her diaper as Anna had shown him. The baby laughed at him as Chris tried to remember everything he was supposed to do.

"Yes," he whispered. "Daddy is very funny. I don't suppose there's an instruction manual anywhere with you either." Daddy. He liked the sound of that.

When he finished closing the new diaper, he found Becca fresh clothes, gathered the baby, a blanket, and some toys, and took her across the hall to his room. That way, he could get ready and Anna could get more sleep.

Once he had the baby settled on the floor, Chris went into the adjoining bathroom and left the door open so he could hear Becca if she cried. As he shaved, the baby watched him, her big eyes never wavering. Once he turned to adjust the shower, the baby resumed mouthing and playing with her toys, laughing and gurgling as she did.

Chris showered quickly, reluctant to have her out of his sight. He wondered how Anna managed to get everything done. Hell, he wondered how she managed to get anything done. It seemed as if there were a lot of things to remember. He had stepped out of the shower and wrapped a towel around his hips when he heard the bedroom door open.

"Chris?" Anna called, concern in her tone. "Oh!" He heard the instantaneous relief as she saw Becca. "There you are! Hi, sweetie."

"I brought her in here so she wouldn't disturb you. Are you feeling better?"

Anna nodded, her gaze skittering away from his bare chest. "Yes, thanks. Shouldn't you be at the Horse Park already?"

"Dad went with Mom, to allow me to stay with you longer. You and Becca can ride with me. That is, if you want to go."

"I do. Will you be riding Bittersweet?" When he nodded, she glanced at her robe. "I need a shower. It will take me a few minutes, if that's okay?"

Chris tilted his head quizzically. "Of course it's okay. I wouldn't leave without you."

* * * *

Anna sprinted to her room. No one had ever changed plans before for one of her migraines. As a girl, she'd grown accustomed to being left behind with the household staff, since it always seemed that the headaches hit when she was home from school. She was ready within fifteen minutes.

Anna enjoyed the ride to the Horse Park. Many of the narrow roads around Lexington were overhung by huge oaks, sycamores and maples with a few cottonwoods mixed in. There were of course the inevitable cedars, like North Carolina, but not nearly as many pine trees. Running along the edge of the roads beyond the trees were huge pastures, filled with mares and foals, some with weanlings already playing together and surrounded by miles and miles of fencing, everything from board to woven wire, and even stone walls. When they finally turned into the Horse Park, they were immediately waved around to the exhibitor parking near the barns.

"If you want to leave most of Becca's stuff for now, I'll get one of the grooms to carry it to the ring in a bit."

Anna smiled gratefully. She was even more surprised when Chris wanted to carry Becca.

"What if she gets something on your tie?" Anna protested.

Chris laughed. "I'll put on a different one. Don't worry about it. Maybe baby drool will give me good luck. I haven't had much here yet."

Chris seemed completely oblivious to the looks they received as they walked through the barn area, but Anna wasn't. Surprise and speculation colored some reactions, and even here and there outright laughter Chris Stevenson was toting a baby on his arm. Anna finally had to join in when they reached the Fincastle stable area and a couple grooms actually dropped brushes. A braider, patiently plaiting one of the hunters, inadvertently stepped back and almost lost her footing on the stool on which she stood when she saw Chris and Becca. The baby was patting his cheeks and gurgling at him, and then looking off to wave at the horses they passed.

David was in deep conversation with a shorter, older man at the end of the aisle. As Chris and Anna came to a halt next to them, David turned to the older man.

"Danny, have you met Dr. Barlow?" The man shook his head, so David performed the introductions before turning to Anna. "We need a professional opinion here, if you don't mind. I think Chris's gelding is fine. Danny seems to think he's still shortening slightly on his right front. Would you mind?"

Anna smiled. "Of course not." She glanced at the aisle. "If you would trot him away and back to me right here. If he's still a bit off, it will show on this asphalt as well as anywhere." This was the one area of her life where she felt complete confidence. If only she could approach everything in the same manner. Anna looked at all three men. "I think he's sound. When's his first class?"

Chris looked at his watch. "An hour."

"I'd give him a good long warm-up on the flat so we can see if he starts to shorten under saddle." She reached to take Becca from him. "Thanks, Chris. I'll take her so you can get ready."

He smiled at both of them before leaning to kiss Anna and Becca on the forehead. Life was filled with moments, Anna thought, and this was another one. The entire barn area seemed to hush for a split second as if everyone held their breath before the usual noises resumed of people yelling back and forth while horses stomped and munched on hay.

"Hey, Dad," Chris called over his shoulder as he headed to the tack room. "I was going to get one of the grooms to take Becca's stuff to the ring. Can you do that?"

"I'll do it myself since I know where your mother is sitting."

The afternoon passed quickly. Chris's luck seemed to be turning today. The big gelding was fresh and ready to go. Anna grinned from ear to ear as Chris managed to win the first class based on his speed round. Bittersweet was his next ride. As the mare entered the ring, Anna found herself on edge, but the young horse seemed to have settled today and sailed effortlessly over everything Chris pointed her at. They took second after the speed round by less than a second. Anna knew Chris was trying to go slowly with the horse and not overface her.

She was overjoyed to see Bittersweet in the show ring where Anna had always known she was meant to be. After Chris handed the horse to a groom, he came around the side of the ring where Anna and his parents were seated. Flopping next to her, he smiled.

"What do you think?"

"She's marvelous! You were both marvelous. Oh, Chris, thank you!" Anna leaned over and kissed him, taking Chris by surprise. His gaze flared with heat before he remembered where they were. He smiled at her.

Chapter 20

Chris accompanied them to the airport. He hugged his dad, kissed and hugged his mom, then he came to Anna and Becca. He lifted the baby and nuzzled her close, drinking in her sweet baby smell as he closed his eyes. But even focused on Becca, part of him was still conscious of Anna. Always Anna. He stared at her, hesitating briefly before tipping her chin and kissing her lingeringly on the lips.

"I'll be home in two weeks," he murmured for her ears alone, "and I want us to talk. Really talk." This was not the time or the place to tell her how he felt, and besides, he wanted to talk to her family first. He wasn't telling her that. "I'll be in Indianapolis next week, then I'll be home."

Anna's blue eyes were dark with emotion.

"I'll be waiting," she told him in a soft voice.

Chris watched them go, waving at them as they made their way through the security checkpoint. When they climbed out of sight, he rubbed a hand on his chest, but the ache there wouldn't go away. He had already told Danny to make arrangements to drive the truck and his trailer to Zionsville. He would be leaving Lexington the next morning for Washington, DC--and, he hoped, a meeting with Alexander Barlow-Barrett.

Chris ate an informal dinner with Martin and Veronica that night. They sat on the back terrace, sipping iced tea to go with the sandwiches and pasta salad the housekeeper left for them.

"Anna and Becca are absolutely adorable, Chris," Veronica said. "You are going to ask her again to marry you, aren't you?"

"Yes," Chris admitted. "I want to as soon as I get home, but there are some things I want to take care of first. I'd like her family to be there for our wedding, especially her parents."

"That doesn't seem like such a tall order," Martin commented.

"Bigger than you think," Chris remarked, "because the first thing I want them to do is apologize to their daughter for the way they've treated her and Becca."

Veronica raised her delicate brows and pursed her lips. "Now I see some potential complications."

Martin laughed. "Yes, the biggest one being Alexander Barlow-Barrett."

Chris recalled that comment as he stared at the steel and glass monument to Barrett Newspapers. He rubbed his nose in reminiscence of his last visit. This time, Seth Barrett was helping him get in the door instead of using his fist to punch his head through the door. He was amazed how fast doors opened when he mentioned Seth's name, surely a testament to how much power the eldest of the Barlow-Barrett children had already taken over from his father.

"Good afternoon, Tessa," Chris greeted Seth's assistant, surprised from what he'd heard the last time that the woman was actually still there.

She smiled slightly. "Have a seat, Mr. Stevenson. I'll let Mr. Barrett know you're here."

As she opened the door to Seth's office, he heard the other man bark, "Damn it, Tessa. How many times today have I told you to use the intercom?"

"Ten," she replied imperturbably. "That's the same number of times you've told me not to bark at you over that 'squawk box.' Mr. Stevenson is here."

"Send him in."

Tessa poked her head back out the door. "Mr. Barrett will see you, but I suppose you already heard that. Oh, his brother's in there too."

She laughed as she held the door open for Chris, who simply shook his head as he walked through.

Seth Barrett was standing over a large conference table on the far side of his office, another man standing next to him who was just as tall, but looked infinitely more approachable. They were poring over a series of blueprints. Seth let the pages he was holding fall to the table and came around to shake Chris's hand.

"How are things going between you and my favorite sister?" he asked with a raised brow.

"That's why I'm here. I'd like to speak to your father about Anna, but his secretary wouldn't give me an appointment."

Seth chuckled. "We can work around that." He punched the intercom. "Hey, Tessa, get in here."

Chris looked at Seth quizzically. “Do you always talk to her like that?”

“Like what?” Seth asked.

Brandon laughed, coming around the table to shake his hand. “I’m Brandon. Looks like your nose has healed.” He glanced at Seth and back. “And to answer your question--yes, he does.”

Tessa closed the door behind her and stepped inside the office. “Yes, Seth?”

“Mr. Stevenson needs an appointment with Barrett Senior.”

Tessa walked over to Seth’s desk and casually sat at his computer as if it were something she did all the time. “Today or tomorrow?” she asked as she looked over her shoulder at him.

Chris glanced at Seth and back to Tessa. “Today would be great.”

Brandon nudged him with his elbow. “Watch this.”

Tessa made a few mouse clicks and swiftly punched a few keys.

“All done. Barrett Senior is expecting you in one hour.”

“How…?”

Seth clapped him on the back. “You really don’t want to know. I discovered Tessa has some unique talents, but I’ve found it’s a whole lot better not to know how she gets things done.”

Tessa rolled her eyes as she left, shutting the door noisily behind her.

“Would you like moral support?” Seth asked. “Or do you want to face the lion on your own?”

“Will he punch me?” Chris responded.

Seth laughed, a big, booming sound. “No, but he might verbally flay all the skin from your hide, rip your head off and laugh. Besides, if it’s moral support you need, Brandon’s your man. Every now and then, we suspect our father actually likes him.”

Brandon winked. “Seth’s just jealous.”

Chris shook his head. “I’ll take my chances.”

They chatted about Anna’s visit and how Becca was doing. Chris showed both brothers pictures from their visit in Lexington and discovered Martin and Seth were fairly well acquainted, something he hadn’t known. Fifty-five minutes later, Tessa poked her head in the office.

“Would you like me to take Mr. Stevenson to Barrett Senior now, Seth?”

“Yes,” Seth said and actually looked at the young woman. “And, Tessa, you can go on home for the day after that.”

She smiled. “Thank you.”

Tessa led the way along the hallway and paused outside the double doors at the end of the hall. She looked at Chris and coached, “His secretary thinks you're the son of an old family friend. Be vague. She'll probe." Tessa checked her watch. "But she's only got one minute. Barrett Senior hates tardiness, so she'll let you through to make sure his appointment schedule stays on track."

Chris nodded and walked through the door. Tessa had not lied when she described the elder Barlow-Barrett's secretary. Her look alone would be enough to sink a battleship, and he found it easy to believe she had no idea whatsoever about the meaning of the word joy. Nevertheless, Chris managed to smile his way through the short space of time before she grudgingly arose to announce him to Alexander Barlow-Barrett. Chris straightened his tie and ran a hand over his sandy hair before he walked into Anna's father's office.

The elder man looked up from the papers he was reading. His glasses were perched on the end of his long, almost too-straight nose, a nose Chris immediately recognized. He'd seen the smaller, feminine version of it on Anna. So much for her not looking anything like the rest of her family.

"Good afternoon, sir," Chris began.

Alexander Barlow-Barrett set his papers on the desk and removed his glasses. He looked fit and tan. Chris supposed that must come from plenty of time on the water sailing. Right now, he raised thick gray brows to peer inquiringly at Chris.

"Miss Tallmadge must be getting near time for retirement, I do believe."

Chris paused at this apparent non sequitur. "Sir?"

Alexander Barlow-Barrett waved Chris to a seat as he proceeded to explain, "She seems to think you are the son of an old family friend, but I can assure you, I have never heard your name before, nor do I know any of your family. What exactly is it that you want, Mr. Stevenson? A job?"

Chris crossed one leg over the other and leaned back in the chair in which he sat. He kept his arms and hands relaxed where they rested on the arms of the chair.

"No, sir. I have my own career and my own business, which more than occupy my time. Since you're being frank, let me be as frank with you. I am here to ask permission to marry your daughter."

If anything, Alexander Barlow-Barrett's eyebrows rose even further. "Don't you think you're a bit too old for Morgan?"

"Morgan?" Chris repeated. "I'm referring to Anna--uh, Preston."

Chris watched in amazement as Alexander Barlow-Barrett's haughty expression changed to a frown, followed by a carefully blank expression.

"You hardly need my permission to marry Preston. She chose her own road in life a long time ago." The older man drummed his manicured fingernails on his desk. "Nothing her mother and I tried to do for her has ever had any effect on her decisions..."

"Oh, I beg to differ," Chris interrupted, drawing a censorious look from the older man. "Let's see, where should I start? There was her bout with bulimia in boarding school while she tried to 'slim down' enough that you might allow her to show horses like the rest of her classmates. There was her drive to excel in school and college in order to gain some notice since she didn't excel in the traditional family endeavors. You might even say her 'blonde' years were an attempt to fit in with the rest of the family. Pardon me, Mr. Barlow-Barrett, but that hardly sounds like someone with no regard for what you wanted."

Chris paused, trying to control his anger before he allowed it to get the better of him.

"If you're through, young man, you can see yourself out," Barlow-Barrett said, but Chris interrupted him.

"No, sir, I am not through. Anna's life aside, I am here for another reason, too, and that is our daughter. She has a right to know her family."

"Preston's bastard?"

"Our daughter. Rebecca." Chris stood and flipped a snapshot he had taken in Lexington of Anna and Becca onto the older man's desk. Anna was holding the baby and smiling. Becca was laughing and showing off all four of her new teeth.

He watched as the Barlow-Barrett reached for it out of reflex, but stopped himself. How sad, this man had such control over his emotions when it came to his children. "Preston has made her decisions," he stated. "She must live with them. Her mother and I have nothing to say anymore about what she does with her life."

Chris clenched his jaw in frustration.

"I'm sorry you feel that way, sir. In the part of the South I come from, we place a high value on supporting family no matter what. I am proud to say that Becca already has two wonderful grandparents who love her for who she is, and not the circumstances of her creation. They also have plenty of love to give Anna. I hope to convince her to become my wife. I had hoped you might be there to give her away, but either way, she is a woman I would be proud to have at my side, if she will have me."

Chris turned for the door, but he stopped and faced the older man again. "Becca's christening is in two weeks. Seth will be her godfather. You and your wife are both welcome to attend. He can give you the details should you choose to be there." He saw no reaction from Alexander Barlow-Barrett and sighed. "Good day to you, sir. I wish I could say it's been a pleasure to finally meet Anna's father, but even my southern manners don't allow me to lie for the sake of politeness."

Chris shut the door quietly behind him and smiled at Miss Tallmadge, who glared at him ferociously, making him wonder how much of his conversation with Alexander Barlow-Barrett she had listened in on.

Chapter 21

Anna had finished getting Becca settled for the night when her cellphone beeped. It had been a long day and she hoped there was no emergency. She wasn't supposed to be on call this evening, but that didn't always mean she wouldn't get a call. She flopped on the couch at the same time she flipped the phone open.

"Hello?"

"It's me. I miss you."

Anna smiled at the sound of Chris's voice. She had hardly spoken to him on the phone, and it felt strange now.

"Where are you?" she asked softly.

"A hotel in Indianapolis. I flew to town this evening from DC."

Anna frowned as she idly traced the pattern on the couch's upholstery with one finger. Why would he have flown to DC instead of coming home? As she formed the question, Chris continued.

"I went to see your father."

Anna felt the blood drain from her face.

"You did what?" Anna asked, incredulous. "Why would you do that?"

"I hoped I might get his blessing on asking you to marry me."

Chris suddenly sounded reserved, but imagining her father's reaction, she was so furious she chose to ignore it.

"That must have been a joke. Did he even remember who I was or did you have to remind him?" Anna inhaled sharply before continuing. "How much of the 'we've tried to do everything for her, but she won't listen' story did he give you?"

"Anna…"

"No. I don't even want to hear it. How could you go to him, Chris? How could you? Let me guess. Did the words 'Preston's bastard' figure in this conversation at any point?" She paused, and when Chris didn't reply, Anna laughed bitterly. "They did. You don't have to even say it."

“Anna,” Chris began again in a tone he surely meant to be soothing but only increased her fury. “I was trying to think of Becca too.”

“Don’t do us any more favors. She’s better off without them. I don’t want her turned into an Aryan automaton to satisfy their perverted sense of family.” Anna felt her emotions starting to spin out of control. “You obviously don’t believe what I’ve told you about them, so talk to Seth or Brandon.”

“Seth got me in to see your father.”

Anna was speechless. Seth and Chris. Why would the two of them betray her? And that was what it felt like. Anna’s throat tightened with unshed tears. Seth was her protector, her champion. Chris had shown her more love than she had ever felt from anyone except Becca. Why would the two of them do this?

“Brandon was there too. Anna? Are you still there?”

“I don’t want to talk anymore,” she said in the polite, boarding school tone she had been taught to use. “Goodbye.”

Her hands shook as she put the phone down. Images of her father with his cool, patrician voice saying “Preston’s bastard” to Chris churned through her brain. She saw once again her parents’ reactions when she’d broken the news she was pregnant. Her devout, religious mother looking at her as if she was some sort of serpent, and her father simply saying in a bored tone, “You will of course take care of it, I trust, Preston.”

Anna was shaking all over by now. As her stomach turned, she rushed to the bathroom and retched miserably into the toilet. She sat on the floor in the confined space, knees drawn to her chest. She cried, her body shaking with gut-wrenching sobs, yet she never made a noise, something she had learned to do well over the years. Crying had usually gotten her slapped at home. After all, Barlow-Barretts were never supposed to show any untidy or demeaning emotions. At school it had brought ridicule from classmates and teachers. So she had learned to hide her misery. No one wanted to see rich girls cry. What did they have to cry about?

Chapter 22

Chris stared at the hotel phone after Anna hung up on him. Hell, had that even been her hanging up? There'd been no slamming of the phone. She had even said goodbye, but there had been something in the cool, polite tone that wasn't Anna at all. It sounded like a girl who was well-schooled in making the correct response. There was the soft click, the sound so much more final than a loud crash. Chris picked up the phone again to call her, but changed his mind. They were both tired. It might be better to let it rest.

Saying he needed to let it rest and actually doing it were two different things. Anna's polite, frozen tone unnerved him. He couldn't dismiss it all the next day. He tried calling her cellphone, but got only her voicemail. He called the house and left a message there too. The clinic explained she was on farm calls. In frustration, Chris called his father.

"How are things going in Zionsville?" David asked.

"Okay. Everyone seems to be on for this one. It must be the prospect of a couple of month's rest before Washington in October, but that's not why I called."

"Something wrong?" his father asked, always quick to pick up on Chris's tone.

"It's Anna, Dad. Could you drop by and check on her this evening?"

"Sure, son. Anything I need to know?"

Chris hesitated before telling his father about their conversation of the night before. "I'm worried, Dad. She didn't sound like herself. Maybe she's just angry with me, it's hard to tell. In all fairness, we don't know each other as well as I'd like, and I guess this time I screwed up. I have to tell you, I've never met anyone quite like Alexander Barlow-Barrett."

"What do you mean?" David asked.

"Could you even fathom referring to a grandchild as 'Preston's bastard'?"

“Not in a million years, and I’d likely horsewhip anyone who did.”

“Exactly. It was all I could do not to reach across the desk and punch him in the nose, even if he is Anna’s father.”

“Hmmph.” David’s grunt was more than enough to reveal his feelings. “Don’t worry about her or Becca. I’ll swing by to invite her for dinner.”

“Thanks, Dad.”

Chris felt somewhat better after he hung up the phone. Still, he was frustrated, and the week looked like a long one. During free moments, he read and reread the letter Anna had sent him in New York. He had another copy of the picture of Anna and Becca he had left with Anna’s father. This picture, he kept in his wallet with the letter. At night, though, his dreams were only of Anna. He would awake aching and aroused, longing to feel the real Anna nestled against him. By Saturday evening, Chris was done. As he changed from his riding clothes to jeans and loafers, he shouted for Danny. When the older man entered the tack room, Chris turned.

“I’m through, Danny. Scratch me from the classes tomorrow.”

“What’s up?”

Chris jammed his shirttail inside his pants and ran fingers through his hair. “Things I need to take care of at home. Domino and Bittersweet both did great tonight, and I need to get home. I’m gonna catch a late flight and see if I can’t connect to Raleigh. Have one of the grooms drive my rig home.”

“No problem, boss,” Danny responded and added, “Good luck.”

Chris swiveled his gaze to the smaller man. For a second, his temper flared as he recalled Danny’s comments in New York. As Danny continued to look at him with a calm, kind expression, Chris’s tension eased. “Thanks, man.”

Chris called a transport service to take him to the airport. The last thing he was in the mood for was a chatty groom wanting to carry on a conversation as they gave him a lift there. Once inside, he stretched his long legs on the van seat. There was only one other passenger, and he seemed to be in the same kind of mood. The ride was silent, giving him plenty of time to think about the conversation he’d had with his father after David had been to see Anna.

“She’s thrown up some pretty serious walls, Chris. I did get her to agree to let us keep Becca Saturday night since she’s on call. That way she won’t have to worry about waking the baby if she gets called on an emergency.”

If he caught an early enough flight, he would make it to Anna’s in time for them to be alone. Luck was with him. He got the last seat on a jet headed to Cincinnati, and from there he would be able to make a connection to Raleigh. As he waited for the flight to be called, he used his cellphone to book a rental car in Raleigh. Still, the clock read one AM by the time he pulled into Anna's driveway. The house was dark except for the glow of a lamp in the kitchen. Chris spotted the tail end of the truck around the corner of the house, so at least she was home and not on an emergency call.

He knocked on the door and waited. It seemed to take forever before he finally heard Anna approaching the door. When it still didn't open, he called, "Anna, it's Chris. Open up please. We need to talk."

"I don't wish to speak with you. Go home, please."

Chris rested his balled fist against the door. Amazing, he thought, how much she sounded like her father right now, her enunciation both cold and precise.

"Don't shut me out. Don't shut the door on what we have," he urged her. "Anna, I love you. Please let me in."

He rested his forehead against the door. He wouldn't force this. There had already been enough of that between them, even if some of it had been unknowingly on his part. The door stayed shut for so long he finally lifted himself away from it. He wanted to pound something. Instead, he jammed his hands in his pockets, and his shoulders sagged. With one final look at the closed door, Chris walked to his rental car. Even once he slid into the driver's seat, he still waited, hoping she might open the door. But it remained shut.

"Shit!" Chris slapped the heel of his hand against the steering wheel and ground his teeth. Life had been a whole lot easier when all he was looking for was a good screw from a busty blonde content with a few fancy dinners and being able to say she was 'dating' Chris Stevenson. He started the car and reversed out of the drive before heading home.

A good stiff bourbon was what he needed. In fact, several or a whole bottle might be just the thing. After parking the rental car, Chris grabbed his duffel bag from the backseat and sprinted up the steps to the house. He dropped the bag inside the door and went straight to his study. After grabbing a glass and the bottle, he stretched on the plush leather sofa, then set the glass on the table and hefted the bottle.

That last night in Upperville over a year ago had been the last time Chris got drunk, but now he swallowed the bourbon with the single-minded intention of tying one on. After a third of the bottle, he finally felt some of the welcome numbness for which he searched. By half the bottle, he was no longer stretched out on the couch, he was sprawled. His shirt was unbuttoned and hung loosely from where he'd pulled it free of his jeans, and his bare feet hung over the end of the couch. As much bourbon as he'd drunk, oblivion still eluded him. He kept replaying all the ways in which he had screwed things up when it came to Anna.

Chapter 23

Anna leaned with her back against the door even after she heard Chris's car leave. The silence that remained echoed with his plea. Anna, don't shut me out. Don't shut the door on what we have. She still heard the words Chris whispered through the door. Anna, I love you. Please let me in.

Her fingertips pressed against the wood of the door and she shut her eyes. Images of her childhood played in her mind. "I love you, Mommy. Please don't send me away." She had begged her mother not to make her go to boarding school. She had been only eight years old. Seth had added his pleas to hers, but in the end it hadn't mattered. The chauffeur had driven her to school, and Seth had spent most of the semester grounded. After Thanksgiving and her attempt to hide, they had packed Seth off to school too.

Anna had done everything in her power to get away from school, even gone so far as to stow away on an Amtrak train headed to Seth's military school. He and his roommates had hidden her for one night, but the next day, Seth had been caught. She had been shipped back to school, but Seth had never admitted what had happened to him.

How many times over the years had she begged to be let in to the golden circle of Barlow-Barretts? That big group of golden-haired, statuesque children she had never quite belonged to. Only Seth and Brandon had made her feel as if she was a part of the family.

Now the tables had turned. She was the one shutting someone out. And why? What had Chris done other than try to fight the same fight she had given up the day her parents' refusal to attend her vet school graduation had arrived in the mail?

Anna, I love you. Please let me in.

The words haunted her. The man she had hero-worshipped as a teenager now told her he loved her, and she refused to open the door to him. She remembered the first night she had seen him again inside his barn. Even then, the ways he'd changed were obvious. He was leaner, less dissipated-looking. Then he'd cradled Becca with such curiosity and uncertainty, held onto her and accepted her even without knowing she was his daughter too. Anna smiled. Chris had opened his heart to both her and Becca, and she had refused to open the door to him.

If she gave up on him, on what they had together, it would be the biggest mistake of her life. She knew that now with an unshakable certainty. Anna pushed away from the thick wooden front door and jumped in the shower. After fluffing her short curls with a blow dryer, she pulled on a pair of slim-fitting capri pants and a matching square-necked button-up top. She was just slipping her feet into a pair of sandals when her beeper went off.

"No!" she choked. Not now. Please not now. She checked the beeper. The clinic answering service number flashed. When she checked in, her heart sank as she took the information and directions and repeated them. Someone coming in late from a horse show with a horse showing signs of colic. Anna grabbed the sandals and instead slipped her feet into her barn clogs as she raced out the door. By the time she reached the boarding stable where the owners kept the horse, the barn manager had walked off most of the problem. Anna did a routine exam to reassure herself the gut noises were normal, gave the horse Banamine, and reassured the owners.

As she headed toward Fincastle, the clock glowed nearly three in the morning. Anna turned into the main drive and passed the barns, heading for Chris's large stone house. Through the trees, she saw a light still on toward the back of the house in what she knew to be his study. After pulling the truck next to his rental car, she hopped down, stripped off her clogs and her coverall and tossed them on the backseat before once again slipping her feet into the sandals she'd brought with her.

She knocked on the door and waited. No answer. After the second time knocking, she tried the door and found it unlocked. The heavy wood opened silently on its hinges. Anna looked around.

"Chris?" she called quietly.

No answer.

Anna shut the door behind her and slipped along the hall to the study. As she neared the door, she thought she heard a faint sound from the couch. Chris lay on his back with one arm flung over his eyes. She stopped. The half-empty bourbon bottle and an empty, overturned glass stood on the floor next to him.

"Chris?" she whispered, almost afraid to speak any louder.

He moved abruptly, swiveling his head to look at her with red-rimmed, bleary eyes. He wiped his eyes with one hand and blinked at her. “Anna?” he asked in a voice that was more than a bit slurred. “Wha are you doin’ here? Can’ you shee I’m bishy?”

“Oh, Chris!” Anna hurried around the couch. Moving the bottle and glass aside, she knelt in front of him and took his hands, which hung limply between his thighs. “I’m sorry. I’m sorry.”

“An’ I’m sooo drunk.” He grinned at her as he listed to one side on the couch. Anna’s hold on his hands was the only thing keeping him upright. He raised his sandy brows and tried to focus on her face. “Are you really here or am I ’maginin’ things agin?”

“I’m here, and I’m not leaving unless you kick me out.”

He shook his head. “I’d never kick you out. I love Preshton Anna Barrlow-Bart Barth Barrett,” he finished, and his smile faded. “You know?”

“Yes, Chris. I know.”

“You’re so pretty n’ soft. I loved you even that firs’ night. I changed for you. I wanned to be good.” His expression clouded over and he frowned. “But you don’ want me.”

Anna watched in horror as his eyes filled with tears. As the first glistening drop slipped along his unshaven cheek, Anna pushed forward between his thighs and pulled his head to her shoulder, patting him soothingly with a hand on his muscular back and one curled into his disheveled hair.

“I do want you,” she whispered against his ear. “I have wanted you longer than I can remember. I love you, Chris. I love you.”

“Anna?” he mumbled. “I’m too, too drunk.”

He leaned back and once again wiped his hand across his eyes. He blinked again several times as if trying to clear his bourbon-clouded brain. For a moment, he looked at her intently.

“I need sleep. Stay with me?”

Anna nodded.

“Help me. Bedroom’s down the hall.”

Getting him there wasn’t easy, but somehow Anna managed to half support his long, lanky frame, and they weaved their way to the master bedroom. It reflected the same casual elegance that characterized the rest of the house, nothing stuffy or formal about it. The house revealed how much he cared about preserving its history.

She helped Chris to sit on the edge of the high four-poster bed.

He looked at her once again with an expression that told her his mind was at least momentarily clear. "Get me…glass of water…ibuprofen. Biggest glass of water you can find."

"I'll be right back."

She left him shrugging off his wrinkled Oxford cloth shirt. Anna hurried to the kitchen. She found the glass of water in no time at all, but it took a couple of minutes to locate the ibuprofen. When she returned to the room, Chris was on his back with his hands resting limply on the front of his unbuttoned and unzipped jeans. His eyes were shut and he snored gently.

Anna smiled and sighed before setting the glass of water and the pills within easy reach on his nightstand. As if she'd done it a hundred times, she tugged his jeans from his hips and over his muscular thighs. She swallowed as she shifted her gaze to the swell of his cock inside his snug-fitting shorts. Down girl, she chided herself. When she had his pants off, she pushed his legs onto the bed and rolled him over slightly so she could pull back the covers. By the time she had him tucked in, she was slightly breathless. He sure was a lot heavier than he looked.

She stared at his sleep-softened features and felt a lump in her throat. What on earth had she done to deserve this man? For all his past playboy reputation, Anna had only seen a side of him since coming here that was beyond reproach. He was a devoted son, he worked hard at what he did, and he showered her and Becca with care and attention. Anna looked at her watch. Four AM. She shrugged before taking off her clothes and carefully folding them. After setting them in an overstuffed chair, she pulled open the drawers in Chris's bureau until she found a clean t-shirt. She pulled it over her head and climbed into bed next to him.

As she snuggled against the warmth offered by his muscular body, he sighed and turned toward her.

"Anna?"

"I'm here. I'm not going anywhere, Chris."

"I love you."

She pressed a soft kiss against his lips. "I love you too."

"I want to make love to you." His voice was sleepy. "But I had too much to drink. Things aren't working right."

Anna smothered a chuckle and reassured him instead. "They will. There'll be other times."

"That's nice." Chris settled her against his side and nuzzled her hair. "You promise?"

"I promise."

While Chris continued to sleep, Anna awoke to the knock on the door the next morning. She padded to the bedroom door, still clad only in a t-shirt, and found Liz standing there dressed for Mass. Anna felt herself blush, but Liz only laughed softly.

"I must say, though this is an unexpected sight, it's certainly not at all unwelcome."

Anna grinned. "I'm afraid it's not quite what it looks." She glanced at Chris's softly snoring form. "Suffice it to say I don't think Chris will make it to Mass. In fact, he might be hard-pressed to do much of anything today except nurse a hangover."

Liz arched an eyebrow. "We can certainly keep Becca for a while longer, if needed."

Anna shook her head. "If you don't mind, I'll stay with Chris for now, but I'll need to nurse Becca when church is over. I can't go much longer without either nursing or pumping."

Liz looked over her shoulder at her son. "Do you have ibuprofen?"

Anna nodded. Liz smiled and waved goodbye as she headed for the door.

Chapter 24

Chris awoke with monumental reluctance. His head pounded like a bass drum in a marching band and he felt as if an entire herd of camels had camped in his mouth overnight. Gradually he became aware of the small, soft form of a woman curled into his side. He eased one eye open and saw Anna lying with one arm and one leg thrown across him. Her face nestled against the curly, golden hair of his chest. He racked his brain, trying to remember what had happened after he left her house. For a moment, a sick feeling of deja vu overwhelmed him before logic and at least some memory won.

He had returned home by himself, which meant she had to have come over on her own.

He turned his head slowly in the other direction and spotted the glass of water and ibuprofen. Trying hard not to wake her, he eased into a sitting position to scoop the pills into his mouth and swallow several mouthfuls of water.

"Chris?" Her voice was husky with sleep. He'd never heard anything more beautiful.

"Mm."

"How do you feel?"

He closed his eyes against the dull throbbing in his temples. "I've had better mornings."

She stroked her hand over his flat stomach to the waistband of his shorts. His body came to instant life.

"You feel fine to me," she murmured against his chest.

Chris swallowed. His head might hurt, but other parts of him felt fine. "You might want to stop that, Anna, unless you have something more in mind."

"I might." She paused. "If you think you're up to the job."

Chris smiled in spite of his hangover. "Oh, I think I might be able to get up for the job."

Letting her fingers slide even lower, she gently touched him through his shorts. His hips moved with her caresses, leaving neither of them in any doubt about whether he was capable of the job they both had in mind. Anna pulled off the t-shirt she'd slept in. Chris dropped his hot gaze to her full breasts, with their nursing-darkened areolae and puckered nipples. He swallowed thickly and closed his eyes as he tried to calm his breathing and the overwhelming need to bury himself in her. He wanted to make it good for her.

"Anna, you're incredibly sexy," he laughed shakily. "I'm as horny as a teenager."

Her answer was to smile, her eyes darkening even more with passion. Chris was fascinated as the tip of her pink tongue touched the corners of her mouth. Unable to stop himself, he leaned forward and brushed her lips with his. When he started to draw away, she pushed him back until he lay on the pillows, and knelt next to him. Anna stroked his cheeks with her delicate hands, then slowly lowered her mouth to his, reversing their roles so she became the aggressor. She tasted him, tracing the curve of his lips with her tongue.

He was content to let her take the lead. As she finally pulled his shorts off and wrapped her hand around his erection, Chris could stand it no longer. He moaned her name.

"Anna, I don't have a whole lot of control here."

"Shh."

He watched in amazement as she straddled his hips and guided him inside the tight, wet heat of her. This time his groan was loud and unrestrained. She felt damn good. He reached for her hips, but she pushed him yet again with a small smile and undulated her hips on him. Her head fell back and she closed her eyes. His breathing exploded in short, sharp gasps that matched her tempo as she rode him. She was incredible. He grabbed her bottom in his hands and thrust deeply several times before pulling out, groaning with the most amazing release he'd ever experienced. They laughed as they cleaned each other up, then collapsed onto the bed.

Chris gathered her against him, holding her along his body as they relaxed. He furrowed his fingers through her short curls. When their eyes met, he saw the wonder in hers and felt tenderness well inside him.

"I never seem to say the right thing, Anna," he murmured. "I truly bungled it the first time, but please let me try again."

He felt her body go still, making him more nervous, and his hands trembled as he held and stroked her. He took a deep breath.

"Will you marry me?" When she opened her mouth, he put a trembling finger against her lips. "Not because we're well-suited. Not for Becca or because it's the right thing to do. Marry me--" His voice cracked slightly. "Marry me because I love you, Anna Barlow. I love you, and I want to spend the rest of my life loving you."

She responded, but in his anxiety, what she'd said didn't register.

"I know we didn't get off to the best start. I know we've done things backward…" He paused. "What did you say?"

"I said yes, Chris. I said yes," she added with more volume.

His hands stilled and his silver eyes widened. "Really?"

Anna laughed. "Yes, really. I can't think of anything I'd rather do."

"I thought you were angry with me," he commented, suspicious. This seemed far too easy.

Anna blushed. "I was until I stopped to think about it. I know you were only trying to do what you thought best for Becca and me. Once I gave it some thought, I realized how stupid I was being, how stupid it would be..." She paused, and this time her voice broke. "...to turn my back on a man who would go to the lengths you have to show me you love me. My family has never done that, but you showed me what a family can be like. I want that for Becca, but I'm also selfish. I want it for me, Chris. I want to make more babies with you and fill your parents' house with grandbabies even if it couldn't be filled with their own brood."

Chris lowered his mouth to her and kissed her deeply and thoroughly. He pulled her hips to his and cupped her buttocks, pressing her against him.

She drew back slightly. "Again?"

"Again," he growled.

He took his time, caressing her from head to toe until she gasped with pleasure. Only after he was sure she was satisfied did he grab a condom and fit himself snugly inside her again. He continued to stroke her even as he rocked against her in an increasingly urgent rhythm. There was no withdrawal this time, no need to.

"Yes!" he growled.

Chapter 25

They broke the news to Chris's parents over brunch. David clapped his son on the back and Liz smiled, although Anna thought she saw tears in the older woman's eyes. A momentary feeling of envy washed over her until David came around the table to hug her and kiss her gently on the forehead.

"We are so happy, Anna," he reassured her. "We already think of you as a daughter. This will formalize it."

She blinked sudden tears back. "You have no idea how much it means to me to hear you say that."

David squeezed her shoulder. "Oh, I think I do. You are our daughter. Never think anything else."

This time her lips trembled. She saw Liz and Chris watching them. Anna smiled and had to blink back her tears.

"If you don't mind," she commented, "I would like us to get married as soon as possible."

Chris arched a brow in question.

"I'd like us to be married when Becca is christened." She laughed at herself and shrugged. "I guess I'm old-fashioned for these days, but I would like us to be husband and wife as well as mother and father."

"Don't you want any of your family present, dear?" Liz asked quietly.

Anna hesitated only a second. "Seth and Brandon. I'd want them to come if they can, but if they can't make it until the christening, I don't want to wait."

She called Seth that afternoon and reached him on his cellphone. It seemed to take a long time for him to answer and there was a lot of noise in the background. It sounded like hammers and saws.

"Seth here."

"Seth?" Anna questioned him, "What's going on? You sound as if you're in the middle of a construction site."

"I am."

Anna rolled her eyes heavenward as he didn't elaborate. Sometimes his taciturn nature was annoying "And?" she prompted.

"Uh, it's a Habitat House. We're framing." She detected a tone that sounded almost like bemusement.

A Habitat House? He was framing?

"Wouldn't it have been easier to just write the check as usual?" Anna drawled.

"Uh, no. Not this year."

"And why not?" she prompted.

"Can't talk about that right now. What did you need?"

He couldn't talk about it? This was getting stranger and stranger, but she'd have to deal with that one later. She had something more important on her mind.

"I'm getting married. Would you give me away?"

There was a choking sound on the other end of the line.

"This is a bit sudden. Is it Stevenson?"

"Yes. Chris," she said pointedly, "has asked and I've accepted. There's one hitch."

"Yesss?" Seth stretched the one word into a question.

"We'd like to do it Wednesday."

"Wednesday. What time?"

"When can you be here?"

"Hey, Tessa," she heard him yell from the other end of the line. "My sister in North Carolina's getting married Wednesday. Can I be there?"

Anna grinned at the pause before Seth assured, "She'll clear my calendar. Make it right before lunch and I'll take everyone somewhere."

"Bring Brandon," she added casually, "or anyone else who wants to come."

"No problem."

She hung up the phone and looked across Chris's den to where he was flopped on the couch with a dozing Becca resting comfortably on his flat stomach, her hand curled around a wad of his shirt.

"Seth is working on a Habitat House."

Chris chuckled. "I sense the hand of Tessa somewhere in there."

"His secretary?" Anna asked in amazement.

"I'm not sure who's the boss in that relationship."

Anna shook her head. "No, that can't be. Seth eats secretaries for breakfast and picks his teeth with their bones."

Chris arched one thick blond brow at her. "Not this secretary. He couldn't even make her blink. And besides that, she appears to know more about how Barrett works than anyone...including your father's secretary."

Anna's mouth formed an 'o' of surprise.

Monday, Anna and Chris went to work. First they squared everything away with a license and visited the priest, who obtained special permission to go ahead with the marriage quickly in light of the circumstances. Liz offered her wedding gown, which was easily altered by simply shortening it, much to Anna's amazement. David worked the phone to call some of their closest friends. By Tuesday afternoon, the wedding Anna had envisioned as being just a civil ceremony in front of the magistrate became a church service complete with a string quartet. She stared at the Stevensons in amazement.

"How on earth did you get all this done?"

Chris and David laughed.

Chris volunteered to pick Seth and Brandon up at the airport while Anna relaxed with Becca, but she found it hard to do as she waited for her brothers to show. When the BMW finally pulled in the driveway, Brandon got out, followed by Seth who held the door open for a petite redhead. Anna didn't wait any longer. She ran to give both her brothers hugs.

"I'm glad you could make it." She stepped back to look at them. Both Brandon and Seth possessed more than their fair share of the Barrett genes, and they towered over her and the redhead standing next to Seth.

"This is Tessa," Seth offered in explanation. At a look from the cool-eyed redhead, he added, "My assistant. Tessa, this is Anna, my sister."

The two women smiled at each other.

"I understand you hold the official record for surviving Seth," Anna commented casually.

Tessa arched one brow at her and smiled. "He can't live without me."

Anna laughed.

The morning passed faster than Anna could have imagined. Chris excused himself to get ready and said he would see them at the church. Brandon was on the floor playing with his niece, but Anna was even more interested in Seth and Tessa. When he wasn't barking at her, something the younger woman seemed to coolly let go in one ear and out the other, he was staring at her broodingly. She worked on a laptop at the kitchen table while he dictated correspondence.

Anna felt claustrophobic between the size of both her brothers in her small house. Like Chris's house, hers had the low ceilings characteristic of the oldest construction in the area, so Brandon had already whacked his head on the ceiling fan, and Seth nearly sent the kitchen light fixture into the next room with a gesture as he barked information at Tessa. She retreated to her room to dress.

When she re-entered the living room, this time garbed in her wedding dress, everyone stopped talking. Seth hurried over to her and gazed at her, his golden eyes twinkling.

"You look great, Anna," he complimented her. "You are a beautiful bride."

Brandon got to his feet and stood behind Seth's shoulder. "I'll second that, Sis. You look stunning."

Tessa cleared her throat. "It is time to leave, Mr. Barrett, or we will be late."

Anna peered around her two brothers to see the ever-efficient Tessa already had everything ready to go, including Becca, who was neatly dressed and strapped in her carrier seat.

Anna looked at Seth and whispered, "You need to marry her." She was amazed when a dark flush stained his cheeks and he frowned at her.

"Brandon," Seth barked. "You drive."

Anna was surprised at the number of people crowding the small church. She recognized many of the stable staff and clients at Fincastle. There were also Wynter and Nelson Anderson seated near the front. Brandon escorted Tessa to the front of the church. The redhead had taken firm charge of Becca and all her belongings.

Seth curved Anna's arm through his. She smiled at her older brother and felt her lips tremble. "Thank you for coming, Seth. You've always been there for me."

His gaze softened and he smiled one of his rare smiles at her. "I could do no less. You are the Barrett who makes the rest of us human."

Anna tilted her head at him, but he just squeezed her arm gently with his other hand and stared along the aisle. As the music changed, everyone rose and they started the walk to the altar.

Anna gazed only at Chris. He looked handsome standing near the front of the church, his dad at his side as best man. Seeing his nervousness made her calmer. The man she had idolized as a teenager had turned out to be not some remote fantasy hero, but a flesh and blood man who had his faults as well as all the qualities she desired in a husband and a father. Seth transferred her hand to Chris's with a barely audible growl, "Take care of her Stevenson," before returning to the pews to sit next to Tessa.

The ceremony itself passed in a blur. Anna knew they made all the appropriate responses, but the most important vows they made with their eyes alone. She had seen the tears in his and again felt awed that this man who had such a reputation as a playboy was nothing at all like what she'd thought. Instead, he was tender and loving, a man concerned and considerate of his family. He was everything she'd ever wanted. And he loved her.

Chapter 26

As they walked along the aisle together after the ceremony, Chris didn't remember a thing. He knew he must have made the right responses, but he felt nervous and uncertain. Anna looked beautiful, so bright and brilliant, and the most amazing thing was she loved him. He accepted the handshakes, hugs, and slaps on the back with a grin of happiness. Anna laughed and sparkled, lovelier than he'd thought possible in his mother's wedding dress. Both his mother and father seemed choked up as they hugged and kissed them.

Seth stood to one side, deep in conversation with Nelson Anderson, Tessa standing attentively at his side, no doubt taking mental notes, Chris thought. The woman appeared to be a living, breathing Palm Pilot, or in this case a Seth Pilot. Chris chuckled and Anna glanced at him.

"What's so funny?"

"Your brother, Seth. I haven't figured out yet whether there's something going on there or he's just still shell-shocked to find his female counterpart."

Anna laughed. "Yes to both, I believe."

Seth had arranged to have a catered lunch at Fincastle, complete with a wedding cake. When Chris said something to him, he shrugged and pointed at his secretary. "It's Tessa," he said again with a note of bemusement in his voice. "I don't even want to know how she accomplishes some of the outrageous things I ask her to get done, but she does. I can't get rid of her. I've never had a secretary like her."

Chris's mouth twitched and he raised a brow at Barrett. "Maybe she's a witch," he suggested.

"Hmph." Seth snorted. "There's no maybe about it. The woman's evil."

Chris nodded. Seth had it bad. He just didn't know it yet.

He watched as Anna hugged everyone at the end of the day, including Tessa, who actually grinned when Anna thanked her for everything she'd done. "It's nice to meet a normal-sized Barrett, in ego and build."

David volunteered to take them all to the airport so Chris, Anna, and Becca could settle in. Chris had directed some of the workers to set up Becca's room at his house while they celebrated. They would gather the rest of Anna's things later.

He helped Anna out of her wedding dress and watched in awe as she sat in a rocker in his--their room, he corrected himself--to nurse.

"I'll have to wean her soon," Anna said wistfully. "My milk supply is starting to decrease."

Chris's hand brushed against Anna's breast as he touched Becca's soft, golden curls. His gaze shifted and locked with Anna's. "We could always give her a brother and sister."

Anna smiled. "Are you sure you want to add another child so quickly?"

Chris laughed. "We would certainly have fun trying."

And they did.

* * * *

The week leading to the christening flew by. Seth and Brandon had promised to return for the service the following Sunday. Chris's mother unpacked the christening gown that had been in the Stevenson family for several generations. Pride swelled when Anna looked ecstatic at being able to use it.

Brandon and Seth flew in Saturday morning. This time Tessa was not with them. Anna had prepared the guest room for them. The two brought the restless energy which had always unnerved Anna at home, surrounded by even more Barlow-Barretts, all with the same temperament.

She discovered Chris was at heart a quiet man, quite unlike the playboy from the show circuits. He spent much of his day at the barns. In the evening, he enjoyed nothing more than listening to music and reading or simply playing with Becca. Anna would come home from rounds to find Becca already playing happily and dinner in the works.

She had begun to relax into this new routine when her brothers arrived. Brandon was the worse, younger than Seth and still restless. He was the thrill-seeker in the family. His escapades had left him stranded on mountains, negotiating rapids in streams that were supposed to be off limits, or sitting in the middle of the ocean on a slowly sinking, capsized sailboat. Seth had purged most of his unbound restlessness traveling the world as a reporter. Too many close calls in some third-world hotspots had left him with a lot more calculating approach to life. This weekend, though, Anna thought he looked particularly morose.

While Brandon gushed to Chris over the kayaking trip he was planning in Alaska, Anna walked over to where Seth sat on a lounge on the patio, idly swirling the whiskey in his glass.

"Everything okay, Seth?" Anna asked as she sat on the end of the chair.

"Tessa's gone."

"What?"

Seth glanced up, his golden eyes dim as if the light had gone out of them. "An independent audit turned up some missing funds while I was on a trip. Dad confronted her and she said nothing to defend herself."

"But why would he think of Tessa?" Anna asked.

Seth swallowed the whiskey and stared into the glass. "The accounts involved are two only she and I have access to."

"I'm sorry," Anna whispered and leaned over to rub his arm.

Seth looked away and swallowed, silent for a moment longer before he added, "Me too." He turned his head to her and shrugged. The brittle veneer in him she had come to hate was back in place. He grinned lopsidedly. "What's one more secretary, right? I eat them for breakfast and pick my teeth with their bones, isn't that what you've always said?"

He stood and pulled Anna to her feet. "Chris," he called across the patio, "Anna tells me you bought her horse from her and gave her back. Bad business practice, man."

Chris laughed. "Oh, but I still get to campaign her, and since I married Anna, I guess the mare becomes community property."

They decided to go to the barns to take a look at Bittersweet before they went out to dinner. Liz and David had agreed to keep Becca for the evening so they could enjoy themselves.

By the time Brandon and Seth were ready to come home, both Anna and Chris were yawning. They had pushed the christening to a later service, so at least they wouldn't be getting up at the crack of dawn.

Heading for church so late in the day felt strange, Anna thought the next morning as they all piled inside the BMW. Heads turned as they walked up the aisle, Anna and Chris holding Becca, followed by two blond-haired giants, then Chris's parents. The service was just beginning, and the last few late arrivals still straggled in. Anna heard someone slip into the pew behind them, but paid it no attention. Becca was fussing at the unaccustomed amount of clothing she wore since the christening gown was extremely long. Anna bounced her idly against her shoulder until time to stand up with her. As they stepped into the aisle, Anna turned to hand the baby to Seth, who would hold her during the christening. She nearly dropped Becca from suddenly nerveless fingers as she saw her father seated in the pew behind them. Seth took Becca, nodded at his father and turned away.

Chris had to take Anna's elbow. As he did, he inclined his head at the older Barrett and said quietly, "Good morning, sir."

Anna was hardly aware of the christening going on around her. She supposed she made all the right responses at the appropriate times. All she could think of was the fact that Alexander Barlow-Barrett had shown up after all for his granddaughter's christening. Her mother was nowhere to be seen, but he had shown up.

He waited for them outside the church. His hair glinting with gold and silver highlights in the summer sun. Anna looked at him as she hung back, still holding Becca protectively against her. Seth, Brandon, and Chris flanked her. Chris bent to her ear and murmured, "Go to him, Anna. Take Becca. He's a proud man, and he's already made the first move."

Anna swallowed and walked the few steps to the edge of the sidewalk where her father waited.

"Daddy?" Anna choked in a voice just above a whisper.

She saw a muscle twitch in his jaw.

"Anna." He smiled with what appeared to be a trace of self-consciousness. "You know that's the name I wanted you to have. Preston was so heavy-handed for such a tiny little girl… I'm glad you're using Anna instead."

Anna blinked. "I never realized." Something hard inside her began to loosen. "This is Becca. W-would you like to hold her?"

"The only thing I can think of I'd desire more than holding my granddaughter is to hold both my daughter and my granddaughter."

And for the first time she could remember, Alexander Barlow-Barrett opened his arms and gathered her close to him.

Meet the Author

From the moment Rhett walked out on Scarlett, Laura's been hooked on romance. Deciding truth really is stranger than fiction, though, she chose a career path in journalism. Laura now teaches English and has returned to her first love--writing fiction.

She lives with her husband and son in central North Carolina along with a menagerie of animals that includes two rowdy Jack Russells and a gentle white mare named Tweed. When she's not reading or writing, Laura enjoys riding, photography, and baking the best darned carrot cake you've ever tasted.

Laura's Website:
www.LauraBrowningBooks.com
Reader eMail:
LauraBrowning613@yahoo.com

Turn the page for a special excerpt of Lauar Browning's

Balancing Act

He has high expectations. And she exceeds every one.

Seth Barlow picks his teeth with the bones of secretaries he's chewed up and spit out. Except Tessa Edwards. She's completely unruffled by his bad attitude--and completely undone by his touch.

But Tessa is balancing on a high wire with no safety net. Her job is the only thing that keeps her from losing custody of her little brother to her money-hungry aunt and uncle, who care less for the dyslexic child than for the hefty trust fund that comes with him.

When ten thousand dollars goes missing from Barrett Newspapers and shows up in Tessa's personal bank account, not even her budding relationship with Seth can help Tessa keep her job...or her little brother.

On sale now!

Chapter 1

Tessa stared at the steel and glass monstrosity that housed the headquarters of Barrett Newspapers. It reminded her of the blue-blooded snobbery she had vowed to leave behind, but in the end, a job was a job. Right now she was in need of a steady, well-paid position as opposed to part-time social work with juvenile offenders. Not only did she need to be the picture of stability, but also the additional income working for Barrett Newspapers would provide.

She entered the building at barely seven AM, but a security guard already sat with his elbows propped on the reception desk. Tessa hadn't batted an eye when the personnel director told her how early she would be expected to arrive. She had yet to work any job with truly traditional hours. If the bear of the Barrett family was an early riser, well then, so was she.

"Good morning. I'm Tessa Edwards, Seth Barlow-Barrett's new executive assistant."

"Should I congratulate you or commiserate?" the guard asked.

Tessa tilted her head. Another confirmation of what she'd already heard. The company's chief operating officer had a reputation other employees were more than willing to share. Even the personnel director who hired her warned her in advance. Seth Barlow-Barrett was dictatorial and demanding. He was cruel and cantankerous. The bottom line of everyone's description was he was impossible to work for, and he had a history of secretarial resignations to back that up, so much so they didn't even bother to have him interview any of the candidates anymore. They never lasted long enough for it to matter.

She would be different.

She grinned at the security guard. "May I get back to you at the end of the day?"

He snorted. “If you’re still here by the end of the day, you’ll have outlasted several of them. Elevators are just ahead. The express elevator’s the one on the far right in case you want to leave in a hurry.”

Tessa glanced at the tightly sealed steel doors and shuddered. “No thanks. I like to take the stairs. Keeps me fit.”

She dashed up the steps to the ninth floor. Used to the exertion, she was barely out of breath when she stepped from the stairwell into the carpeted luxury of Seth Barrett’s floor. Well, Seth and his brother Brandon’s. It appeared sole occupancy of a floor was reserved for the patriarch, their father. Tessa sniggered.

The personnel director had told her where her desk would be and what her duties were. She’d also warned her Seth Barrett normally arrived around six in the morning, so he would be there already, and she should introduce herself when she arrived.

It seemed odd that no one really wanted to face him. Only the favorite son in a family-owned empire could get away with such terrible behavior in this day and age, but surely no one was that bad--even the lordling of the mighty Barlow-Barrett empire.

After setting down her belongings, Tessa checked her appearance in the small mirror she kept in her purse. She’d pulled her hair back in a smooth chignon at the base of her neck. It made her look mature and conservative, the image she was trying hard to project. Young and inexperienced was not the impression she wanted to make. Taking a deep breath, she knocked on the partially open door.

“What is it?”

What not who, as though he were too busy to be bothered by ordinary mortals. Tessa raised her brows at the decided bark in that deep voice, but when she stepped into his office, she’d composed her expression.

“Who are you?” The man standing near the windows eyed her with a mixture of irritation and impatience.

The first thing that struck her was how big he was, not fat, just big. He had to be somewhere around six-foot-five, give or take a couple inches, and possessed incredibly broad shoulders that tapered down to lean hips and long, long legs. Not a bear in his den, as she’d been led to believe, but a different animal entirely. His appearance reminded her of a sleek and dangerous lion, ready to attack at any moment.

“I’m your new secretary, Tessa Edwards.”

Even the eyes were feline. The color of gold, they still managed to be cold as they assessed her. “Coffee, Teresa.”

"Tessa," she corrected with amused patience. No way was she going to bite on his deliberate baiting.

"Coffee, Tessa." The deep voice dripped sarcasm.

She kept her expression controlled until she left his office, and then she smiled. He was as bad as everyone said. Maybe worse. He had the personality of the building in which he worked, she decided. All glitz and sharp edges, but no substance. Expensively cut hair, hand-tailored suits and the arrogant air that went hand-in-hand with his name. No wonder the man went through so many secretaries. But she--Tessa gave herself a pep talk--would not be one of them. She knew his type. She had grown up around a dozen or more people just like him, and she could handle his blue-blooded arrogance. She might avoid her father's relatives, but that didn't mean she hadn't learned from them over the years.

She needed this job too much to let some old-money ogre scare her away. If she had to pull out her own pedigree to do it, she would. In court next month, she had to represent the epitome of security and stability because if she didn't, she could lose custody of Zach.

Her smile slipped for a second. Public school last year had been a disaster for her little brother, but she'd found a school that could help him. Now she had to make sure they stayed together. The job with Barrett would provide enough money to pay his tuition, and help keep Aunt Kathleen and Uncle Edwin at bay.

As long as she could prove she was providing the best home for her brother, they didn't have a leg to stand on. She knew the only reason they wanted custody was because of the trust her parents had left behind. If they had guardianship, they could tap it for expenses. She could imagine how expensive Zach's lifestyle would become.

All Tessa had to do was wait it out. One more year, and she would be old enough to use the trust as her parents had intended--for her brother. The problem was, and always had been, that her aunt and uncle could access it right now, but only if they were Zach's legal guardians. If she could show the court how secure her employment was, they would never dream of taking him….

"Is that coffee arriving by mule from Colombia, Tina?" Barrett barked over the intercom.

Tessa grimaced at the speaker. Who on earth still had one of those squawk boxes, in this day and age?

She hadn't asked him how he liked his coffee. She looked at the supplies next to the coffee maker. The creamer was untouched. She checked the small fridge right next to it. Mountain Dew lined the shelves. The man must be a caffeine addict, though he hardly seemed to need anything that would make him testier. No sign of cream. He must take it black. The sugar had been opened and some had spilled. Shaking hands trying to get the ogre's coffee ready? Tessa made a face and added one teaspoon of sugar. He would want it sweet, but not too sweet. Maybe that was to help make up for a very sour personality.

She pushed down a button on the intercom and said, "Coming right up, Mr. Barrett."

He sat behind a very large, cherry desk with a gleaming finish. The papers on it were arranged with almost pinpoint precision. He looked up as she approached his desk, his scowl locked in place. Did the man never smile?

"It's about time. What secretarial school are you from…the Slowpoke Rodriguez School?"

"I didn't attend secretarial school, sir. I graduated from Smith," Tessa replied. That seemed to give him pause for a moment, and she managed not to laugh out loud. Oh, yes, his snobby background was showing now. She'd bet he had a girlfriend named Muffy or Priss filed neatly somewhere in his life. A small chuckle escaped.

For the first time that morning, her new boss slowed down to really look at her.

"I amuse you?"

"Not at all, sir."

His glittering, golden gaze lifted and bore into her this time instead of skating over her. Tessa could now understand how he made other secretaries uncomfortable, but she was not other secretaries and she would not be intimidated. If this was an undeclared war, she was more than willing to plant her flag and stand her ground.

He looked her up and down. "What was your major?"

"Social Work."

"Ah, a do-gooder," he dismissed her. "Why are you here? Has personnel decided I need counseling? Someone who can ask open-ended questions and get me to reveal how society has damaged me? Are you here to save me from myself, Tessa? Help me reveal my inner child?"

She kept her temper under control. "I think you credit them with way too much interest in the position as your secretary. You have a job. I need one. As to your inner child, I believe that answer should be obvious to you. It seems to me you need no assistance with that…sir."

One thick brow slowly arched. "Can you type?"

"Seventy-five words a minute."

"Dictation?"

"Transcription…while you talk."

"How are you with computers?"

Tessa shrugged. "I do well enough."

No way would she tell him about hacking into her high school's computer system when she was fourteen and changing the principal's appointment book so he showed up to a non-existent meeting with the superintendent. Some things were better left in the past.

The rest of the day passed like volleys in a naval battle. Barrett never asked her to do things, he barked orders at her, as if firing missiles over her bow.

Early in the afternoon, the intercom bleated, "I need you in here for some transcription."

She took her laptop and set it up at the conference table, watching as he paced. She was already half-convinced he was just another rich prick riding on his family's fortune. If she didn't need the steadiness and income this job offered, she'd walk like everyone else.

Then he began to speak. Her fingers flew as he talked through the plan he had apparently wrestled with all day long. As he outlined his strategy to acquire several struggling Midwest publications, Tessa acknowledged what he had developed was brilliant. Even more important, the acquisitions he designed wouldn't cost jobs. She felt a new level of respect for the man, but didn't dare let that show in her face. He still had an arrogant and overbearing attitude toward his personnel that would never be tolerated in any company where he wasn't family.

At three, he abruptly stopped and stared hard at her.

"Go home," he growled as he tossed a Mountain Dew can in the basket next to his desk. When she arched one brow at him, he added, "Be back tomorrow morning at seven."

He had dismissed her, but not fired her. From what she heard, that meant she was a success. Tessa packed the laptop and headed for the door.

"Thanks, Teresa."

"Tessa," she corrected.

"Tessa."

As she left the building, she gave the surprised security guard a thumbs-up.

* * * *

By Friday, she began to think Barrett was an automaton programmed only to work and bent on driving her crazy. She could see why he had a reputation for chewing secretaries to bits and spitting them back out. His mind worked at light speed, so keeping up with him was a challenge, but Tessa had managed.

She never saw him smile. She wondered if he had no personality or if he just hated what he was doing. Neither option boded well for either long-term employment or pleasant working conditions. He was bound to lose his temper with her at some point.

A package arrived after lunch on Friday. Or rather, Tessa found it sitting on her desk right after lunch with Seth Barrett's name scrawled on it.

"I have a package for you, sir," she said over the intercom.

"How many times have I told you not to use that damn intercom? Bring it in."

Tessa grinned. He told her not to use it almost the same number of times he told her to stop barging in on him and use the intercom instead. She took the package and handed it to him. As she turned to go, he spoke.

"Take the rest of the day off. We're done."

Tessa stopped and stared. She supposed the amazement must have shown in her expression.

"Go!" he barked.

Tessa grinned as she tidied up her desk, locking drawers and file cabinets. She was always meticulous about her work area, probably a good thing with Mr. Psycho Clean on the other side of the door. A muffled sound from Barrett's office followed by a crash stopped her just as she was about to depart for the day. She hesitated for only a second before she pushed the door open and stepped back into his inner sanctum.

He sat unmoving in the chair behind his desk, staring out the window. His face was pale, and his jaw clenched and unclenched as if he were working hard to get his emotions under control. An expensive sculpture that had perched on his desk now lay on the floor in pieces.

"Mr. Barrett?" Tessa murmured. He must be furious at having smashed the artwork. He turned eyes on her that burned with such intense golden fire, she took a half step back, but she would not retreat. "Can I help you with anything else, sir?"

For a moment, she thought he might throw something at her, but she refused to be intimidated. He raked a hand through his thick, blond hair and blinked a couple times as if he were trying to fight his way through whatever disturbed him and focus on what she'd said.

"Check my calendar for this weekend."

She didn't need to check, she'd memorized it. "You have a Sigma Delta Chi dinner at which you are the keynote speaker this evening. The rest of the weekend is clear."

"Damn!" He stood up and paced his office, once again reminding her of a wild animal trapped in a cage not of his own choosing. He paused at the corner and looked back at her.

"Where's the jet?"

"Brandon Barrett has it, sir, in Puerto Rico."

"Then get me the first commercial flight you can after that damn dinner to Durham, North Carolina. First-class. There's never enough leg-room anywhere else."

Tessa had already logged off her computer. She gestured toward Seth's. "May I?"

"Yes." He waved her toward the oversized leather chair. She felt almost like a child sitting in it, her legs very nearly dangling without touching the floor.

It took a few minutes, and Barrett's gaze seemed to bore into her the entire time. The man was an expert at looming. It hadn't taken her long to figure out most of his attitude was not directed at her. The biting temper was who he was allowed to be. The arrogance, she was sure, was inbred at this point.

The controlled anger that bubbled up now and then was another matter, but not her problem. If Seth Barlow-Barrett was unhappy in what he did, that was too bad. There must be a lot that more than made up for it. Financial gain, for one thing. Right now, in her book, that was a pretty fair trade-off. With a couple more keystrokes, she turned to him.

"You leave National at five-fifteen a.m. and arrive at Raleigh-Durham at six AM Saturday morning," she said at last. "A rental car will be waiting for you. When would you like to return?"

"Sunday."

She punched a few more keys. "I can get you on a noon flight back."

"Book it. Use my travel account. The number's there next to the keyboard."

A couple more minutes and Tessa was pulling his ticket voucher off the computer printer.

"Done."

She crossed the room and handed him the voucher, and then Barrett did do something that caught her off-guard. He smiled. It transformed the lean features of his face and made him look years younger.

"Thank you, Tessa."

Now he'd rattled her. A smile and her correct name. She knew she was staring at him, probably with her mouth gaping, but she couldn't help it and could only nod in response.

"Go home. Enjoy your weekend."

She smiled back. "Thank you."

* * * *

Seth watched the door close behind her. Tessa Edwards. She'd made it through the first week, and that was an accomplishment in and of itself. It had taken him a few days to notice, but she was stunning in her own way. Hers was not a stand up and smack you in the face kind of pretty, but a harmonious blend of classic bone structure and subtle curves with the staying power pretty women seldom had. Not until she smiled at someone else had he seen the vivid personality to go with the flamboyant coloring. Fiery red hair, thick and straight, and the most unusual ice-blue eyes. Yes, he'd noticed Tessa Edwards, not just for her looks, but for the grit and unflappable serenity she'd demonstrated all week long.

He needed that right now, especially after the little nuclear bomb she'd unknowingly dropped in his lap with that package. Seth tapped his fingers on his desk.

He was not an easy man. He knew that. In fact, many of the people who had faced him across a negotiating table described him as a Class-A bastard who made his father look like a blessed saint. Seth knew what people thought, what some even voiced behind his back, but didn't care. He was what his father had molded him to be. He had taken over daily operations of Barrett Newspapers four years after college. When all was said and done, he was a Barlow-Barrett and couldn't drop that responsibility from his shoulders to pursue his own desires.

One soft spot remained in the armor he'd built around himself over the years. That was his sister Anna. He and Brandon were the only ones who called her that, yet that was the name she now chose to use in her professional life. Little Anna, the veterinarian. So different from the rest of them, yet she was the embodiment of what he longed to be. She was his heart, and he would do anything to protect her. He knew she viewed herself as the ugly duckling, but he saw her as the one Barlow-Barrett who had dared to be different, inside and out. When the rest of them had followed like sheep in the family footsteps, Anna had walked away. Phillip, his youngest brother, had taken a slight detour into law, but he was still right in the family fold. Anna was the rebel, and he admired her to no end.

His eyes lifted to the DVD player and the disc he still hadn't removed. Watching even a portion of it had made him almost sick. Then the anger had exploded, costing him a nose for. He wanted not only the blackmailers who'd sent the video, but the fucker on the disc with her.